The Cliff-Dwellers

Henry B. Fuller

Introduction by Paul Rosenblatt
The University of Arizona

Holt, Rinehart and Winston, Inc.
New York, Chicago, San Francisco, Atlanta,
Dallas, Montreal, Toronto,
London, Sydney

CONTENTS

INTRODUCTION

The publication of Henry Blake Fuller's *The Cliff-Dwellers* in
1893 marked a distinct stage in the development of literary
realism in America. With this Chicago novel, as Larzer Ziff
has observed in his study of the 1890s, "money fully enters
American fiction as motive and measure."

The reactions to
the novel at the time of its publication depended upon the
literary school to which the reader owed his allegiance.
While a realist like Hjalmar Hjorth Boyesen, a Norwegian-
American writer, was struck by the book's "sociological
bearing" and its depiction "without any moralizing of the
vital connection between the city and the type it produces,"
Charles Eliot Norton, a spokesman for the genteel tradition,
wrote to Fuller, "Your disgust [for the Chicago Fuller
described] seems to me to have carried you too far in your
book for its aesthetic perfection." The reviewer for the
London Times was dismayed at the "reek" of "squalor,
sordidness, and tragedies" in the pages of *The Cliff-Dwellers*, but William Dean Howells, the leading critic of the day,

praised the novel warmly for its realism and its epical qualities, and welcomed Fuller to the "cause" of realism. In a note to the author, he expressed a sympathetic foreboding: "I hope you may not have to 'suffer in the cause' quite so much as I have suffered." Years later, Howells was to write to Fuller, "Can't you see it your duty to write, hereafter, my novels for me?"

Fuller was born in Chicago on January 9, 1857, the last male descendant of a New England family. Henry Fuller, his grandfather, first arrived in Chicago in 1840, only seven years after the federal government had signed a treaty with the seventy-seven chiefs of the Chippewa, Ottawa, and Pottawattomie tribes to move the Indians west of the Mississippi, and only five years after the final war dance of the Pottawattomies at the site upon which Chicago's City Hall was soon to be built. The Fullers, however, after a short stay, moved on to St. Joseph, Michigan, where Henry Fuller within a few years became the county judge. Judge Fuller returned to Chicago during the gold rush of 1849. Easterners were coming through Chicago on their way to more glittering prospects, but the Judge established his fortune on the tangible realities of real estate, railways, and water lines in the growing city.

Henry Blake, the son of George Wood Fuller, was a delicate boy, perhaps more delicate than one would have expected the grandson of a strong-willed, prosperous "old settler" to be. He did not participate in the common games of childhood, and seemed more intent on gentle and cultured pursuits than his companions. "You know," one of Fuller's childhood neighbors remarked years later, "Harry was not really one of the boys. Often while we were frolicking, he preferred to knit or to play a sonata." Similiarly, Harriet Monroe, founding editor of *Poetry: A Magazine of Verse*, spoke of him as a "strange retiring boy who didn't fit in with the rather boisterous group that laughed and danced and rode horseback up and down Michigan Avenue. . . ."

Perhaps in part because of his intense consciousness of his New England past, Henry, from his earliest school days, showed a passion for self-culture. As he tells us, however, in an unpublished short story, markedly autobiographical, "Edmund Dalrymple," he worried that his passion for study—for a civilized pen, for literature and languages, for music and architecture—might prove too exclusive, might make him thin and pale, might in the end turn out to be a damnable, fateful thing for a young male in "a rough-and-tumble democracy."

Moreover, the landscape of the old Chicago of Fuller's boyhood literally disappeared in 1871 when the great fire destroyed the city. In the rebuilding of the new Chicago, the old ideals of a resident gentry in whom the values of the East in moral, political, and religious matters maintained a traditional influence, were being rapidly eroded by the influx of a flamboyant and heterogeneous population. As we learn in *The Cliff-Dwellers*, industrial growth and real estate speculation were leading to pollution and urban sprawl.

In its rise from the ashes, Chicago became the center of a school of functional architecture that has been unsurpassed in America, a school whose names include Sullivan, Jenney, Adler, Root, Burnham, and into the modern era, Frank Lloyd Wright and Mies van der Rohe. Fuller considered becoming an architect, but was reluctant to deal with such mundane matters as plumbing. His thinking about architecture was further stimulated by his reading of the English writer, John Ruskin, who was probably the first critic to define for him the idea that architecture reflected individual and national integrity and morality. Thus one begins to understand why Fuller chose an eighteen-story office building as the organizing device and symbolic center for *The Cliff-Dwellers*.

In 1874, one year short of graduation from high school, Fuller went to work in a department store. The following year he returned to school to complete his degree, and returned to Ovington's store upon graduation. In 1877 he worked as a messenger at the Bank of Illinois for several months and then joined the Home National Bank where his father was a vice-president. Evidently Fuller's family wanted the young man to get as early a start as possible in "the business of life," the making of money. He detested his work, but he was gaining valuable insight into how money is made and by whom. When he came to write *The Cliff-Dwellers*, he was well-experienced in economic realities and process.

The background of the times provides the reason why, in spite of his scholarly abilities and interests and his aversion to the business world, Fuller was not sent to college. His fate was doubtless a common one for young men in Chicago and for thousands upon thousands of young men in America. In "The Gilded Age" (Mark Twain's term) with the end of the Civil War, an older, agrarian America began to give way to an America urban in outlook, to an industrial capitalism, and a fierce scramble for wealth. It was the time of the rise of the great financiers, "Robber Barons," as they were called by some, entrepreneurs who controlled the destinies of millions of people. "The public be damned," William H. Vanderbilt had said. Wealth had become the basis of all value. Liberal education, ethics, the arts, culture were fine for women, but a man's worth was determined in the marketplace.

In 1879 Fuller realized a boyhood dream and sailed for Europe. This voyage to the Old World was the first of six he was to make in his lifetime. Above all other countries, Italy captured his imagination. Italy was beautiful. Italy was a romance, an affair of the heart, and offered him a new sense of freedom. "If absolute freedom is not to be found in the Romagna Campagna, where *is* it to be found?" he wrote in his European "Journal." He found in Italy, as a legion of American artists and writers had before him, the last refuge from a world of increasing materialism. The two poles of his life and writing had now become established. As Van Wyck Brooks has said, Fuller became "a divided soul, hovering, like many another, between America and Europe, drawn in one direction by birth and habit, by culture and aspiration in another." Although he was to spend his life in Chicago, his heart's dwelling was Florence.

Upon the death of his father in 1885, Henry was forced to manage for the family as best he could their business interests, chiefly in real estate. Clearly, he had to be a Chicagoan rather than a Florentine. Circumstances had bound him to the city. In this year, however, he completed an important essay, "Howells or James?," in which he committed himself to the cause of realism in literature and specifically to Howellsian realism: "the truthful treatment of material." How Fuller defined realism is evident from a reading of his essay on Howells and James.

Darrel Abel, editor of "Howells or James?," points out that the essay had its genesis in Howells' acknowledgment that Henry James was "to be the leader of a new American school of realistic novelists." Howells called realism "almost the only literary movement of our time that has vitality in it," and praised James as the leader of the new movement in the United States. The essay originated in Fuller's personal conflict between America and Italy. The discussion of antithetical values of Europe and America had become central to much of James's work. James felt that American life was not "rich" or "dense" enough to provide the necessary materials a novelist needs for his work. James had become an expatriate and Fuller had thought for a while that his own salvation as man and artist lay in expatriation.

The central problem of "Howells or James?," as Fuller states it, is to determine "which of these two representative writers is to be pronounced most instrumental in the shaping of American fiction. . . ." Fuller calls Howells a realist and

James an idealist, and he develops the idea that realism is coincident with modern democracy. In a democracy, Fuller tells us, we "take a very frank and undisguised interest in ourselves; we are a good deal concerned with our own day and generation—in our art as well as elsewhere." The realist deals with the normal earning of money at home, rather than "with the exceptional and priviliged spending of money abroad." The realist has "a healthy liking for the honest clay and gravel of the great middle stratum." James, on the other hand, prefers "weather-stained stucco to freshly-painted clapboarding," and "a pair of sabots strikes in him a responsive chord that a pair of plain cowhide boots quite fails to affect." Whereas Howells is sympathetic toward life and gives to us a cross-section of it, Fuller argues James is satisfied with surveying life and cultivating the "mere top dressing" of society. Fuller declares that the monopoly of literature by fortune, beauty, splendor, and general heroics is now at an end. Literature "has at length descended to the common level of general humanity, and has consented to take an interest in plain everyday people and plain everyday happiness."

In spite of his commitment to Howellsian realism, Fuller began writing in 1886 an Italian romance, *The Chevalier of Pensieri-Vani*. Published in 1890 at Fuller's expense under the pseudonym Stanton Page, the book came to the attention of Charles Eliot Norton. With James Russell Lowell, Norton championed Fuller's romance about decayed European nobility living an idyllic life in Italian sunshine. The charm of Fuller's descriptions of the post-roads and cities of an idealized and feudal Tuscany, the urbanity of his style, the gentleness of his satire, the lingering nostalgia in his pages, appealed strongly to readers of refined esthetic sensibilities. Thus Fuller comes into American literature under the mantle halophiles of an earlier generation.

He was known. *The Chevalier of Pensieri-Vani* was followed by *The Chatelaine of La Trinite* in

1892. In this book the setting is the Swiss Alps. The characters in *The Chatelaine*, like the characters in *The Chevalier*, are highly stylized. This second romance, however, has more plot and organization than *The Chevalier*, and Fuller has become more objective in his treatment of character and his description of scenery. John Pilkington, Jr., has observed, *The Chatelaine* "represents a movement away from the 'idealism' of Henry James toward the realism of William Dean Howells."

In writing these two books, Fuller relied heavily upon the journals he had kept to record his European travels. Indeed, he transcribed passages almost word for word from his European journals. Although he had produced two romances, his working method had been based partially on a transcription from the commonplace of daily experience.

Fuller had fondly relived his European travels in *The Chevalier* and *The Chatelaine*, but the reality of his life was a day by day life in Chicago. He continued to chafe at and resent the circumstances that had tied him to business, to the care of rental properties, and the mending of plumbing. In January and February 1893 he wrote down his protest, his case against Chicago. Published on the eve, as it were, of the opening of the Chicago World's Fair that spring, *The Cliff-Dwellers* more than fulfilled Fuller's commitment in 1885 to Howellsian realism: The realism of Howells had been one of faith in the cultural growth and social progress of urban life and of the American middleclass, the burden of *A Hazard of New Fortunes*, but in *The Cliff-Dwellers* Fuller does not share this faith, finds no evidence for it even though in the moment of the book's writing Chicago has become a center of the nation. Proud of the Greek, Romanesque, and Renaissance buildings which had been created on the shores of Lake Michigan for the Fair commemorating the discovery of America, the loyal Chicagoan believed with fervor that his city had arrived culturally, materially. To him the possibilities and prospects for growth were unlimited and The Columbian Exposition testified to the city's progress, to its aspirations for the beautiful.

Pervading *The Cliff-Dwellers*, then, is a fundamental irony: While Chicago is getting ready to lead the country forward, Fuller is depicting the city and its people as primitive, as savage, as backward. "Does it seem unreasonable," the banker Fairchild says, "that the State which produced the two greatest figures of the greatest epoch in our history, and which has done most in the last ten years to check alien excesses and un-American ideals, should also be the State to give the country the final blend of the American character and its ultimate metropolis?" And to Fairchild's wife, to the Chicagoan, "the name of the town, in its formal, ceremonial use, has a power that no other word in the language quite possesses. It is a shibboleth, as regards its pronunciation; it is a trumpet-call, as regards its effect. It has all the electrifying and unifying power of a college yell." But the events of the novel betray Fairchild's hope for Chicago and the college yell becomes a version of boosterism.

The theme and controlling form of the novel are innately related. In the first sentence of his brilliant Introduction, Fuller intimates the theme: "Between the former site of old Fort Dearborn and the present site of our newest Board of Trade there lies a restricted yet tumultuous territory through which, during the course of the last fifty years, the rushing streams of commerce have worn many a deep and rugged chasm." The effect of these streams of commerce is an erosive one, the depths creating heights, towering cliffs, the skyscrapers. The Clifton provides a symbolic center for the novel from which the story is to proceed. "In a word," Fuller writes, "the Clifton aims to be complete within itself, and it will be unnecessary for us to go afield either far or frequently during the present simple succession of brief episodes in the lives of the Cliff-dwellers." As Edmund Wilson has said, *The Cliff-Dwellers* "dramatizes the organism of an eighteen-story office building."

Within the Clifton itself there is a hierarchy of occupation, from errand boys and scrubwomen and elevator hands to lawyers, bankers, and wealthy entrepreneurs. Of the four thousand people who work in the Clifton, there are valuable specimens of nearly all the strata of Chicago life. The novel is a working out of the broad metaphor which the Introduction provides.

The theme of *The Cliff-Dwellers* emerges from the force of "the rushing streams of commerce" whose eroding effect has created the Clifton. During this period of American life, wealth had become the basis of value and a man's worth was determined in the marketplace: *The Cliff-Dwellers* examines the moral implications of a society that gives respectability to the worship of money.

The point of view of *The Cliff-Dwellers* is established by George Ogden. When we meet Ogden at the beginning of the novel, a Bostonian newly arrived in Chicago, he is eager for success in a city where young men are making early fortunes. He has come from an older and denser society, where the social and cultural orders have been settled and formulated, into a society that is on the make, almost anarchic in its get up and go, in the rawness of its energy. On a visit to his brother-in-law, an unscrupulous realtor, Ogden sees in Eugene McDowell "the spokesman of a community where prosperity has drugged patriotism into unconsciousness, and where the bare scaffoldings of materialism felt themselves quite independent of the graces and draperies of culture." Viewed in the light of George's innocence and simplicity, an innocence and simplicity that hearkens back to a pre-Civil War America, Ogden's education is one of painful discovery that money is considered the father of life. But money is, as Lionel Trilling has said in writing of *Huckleberry Finn*, "the father of ultimate illusions and lies."

The progeny of money, illusions, and lies provide the moral focus of *The Cliff-Dwellers.*

Looking back upon *The Cliff-Dwellers* about a quarter of a century after its publication, Fuller averred that the theme of *The Cliff-Dwellers* is the marriage question: "Is it better for a young man to marry a girl who has pleasant, well-disposed family connections, yet who is rather flimsy and deficient herself, or for him to marry a girl who is finer and stronger in herself, yet who has a disadvantageous and disreputable set of relatives?" But the marriage question is not a major theme so much as it is a controlling device which Fuller utilizes to bring into conjunction the social and business forces of Chicago. In marrying Jessie Bradley, "who is rather flimsy and deficient herself," Ogden reacts with a New Englander's sense of decorum and logic in choosing the proper family. To have married Abbie Brainard would have infected him, he believes, with the taint of ill-gotten wealth surrounding Erastus Brainard. Ogden fails to perceive until too late that Jessie is living in a world of dream and fantasy that only money can make "real."

The weavers of the spell by which money ensnares are Arthur J. Ingles and his wife, Cecilia. Arthur owns the Clifton. Arthur makes the money and Cecilia spends it. Because Arthur has more money than almost anyone else, Cecilia spends more money than anyone else. Since the ideals and values of the society are formulated on a dollar-to-dollar basis, Arthur and Cecilia stand at the head of the social procession. To a climbing go-getter husband, familiar entrance to the office of Arthur Ingles spells success. To the socially aspiring wife, Cecilia's smile is a benediction. Jessie's adulation of Cecilia and George Ogden's innocence and lack of understanding that Jessie's social ambitions have placed him in absurd competition with the Ingleses, brings about the doom of their family.

Fuller is brilliant in suggesting the illusory

quality of Cecilia. There is a magic about her; but we do not see her until the final pages of the novel when she appears at the opera "a radiant, magnificent young creature, splendid, like all her mates, with the new and eager splendor of a long-awaited opportunity." Until this moment, her presence has been only hinted at. When Cornelia McNabb, the socially aspiring waitress, tells George of her dreams of rivalry with Cecilia, George says, "She isn't real; she's only a beautiful myth." And when George's wife, Jessie, comes hurrying up to him after a reception, her cheeks flushed, her large eyes burning, to tell him he has just missed meeting Cecilia Ingles, George responds by teasing her with his disbelief. "There is such a person, then?" he says. At the opera, "in the vast hall that was luminous in ivory and gold," George's heart is "constricted by the sight of her. It is for such a woman that one man builds a Clifton and that a hundred others are martyred in it." Thus, the closing sentence of the novel contains the final revelation of its theme, the awful reality behind the "beautiful myth."

The illusion is that money, if we can get enough of it no matter how it is earned, will somehow transform us into knights and ladies, princes and princesses. This theme anticipates what was to become a familiar one in American literature, most notable in F. Scott Fitzgerald's *The Great Gatsby*. As the Ingleses represent the fairy-tale side of this transformation, Erastus Brainard represents the dark underside of power without romance.

Fuller very cleverly shrouds Brainard in mysterious origins telling us that he "had come from the southern part of the state—from 'Egypt' as it is called. A darkness truly Egyptian brooded over his early history. . . .The first definite point in his career is this: that as a youngish man he was connected in some capacity with a cross-country railroad on the far side of Centralia." Brainard comes into certain existence for us then in the context of a commercial fact. Brainard is "merely a financial appliance." He is incapable of ordinary social intercourse. His family life is barely existent. He has not even an "apparent consciousness of the physical basis of existence—for him diet, rest, hygiene were mere nothings." He has accumulated a vast capital through often ruthless means. He has no sympathy for the defenseless whom he exploits without conscience. In brief, the community is the oyster and he holds the knife.

The tale of opportunism in The Gilded Age is often a lurid and bizarre one. Opportunism, by violating human values and the rightness of communal relations, exposes us to an extravagant, unreasoning world. With the sensational and violent fate that overtakes Brainard when his son, Marcus—outraged because his desires for a world of art and culture have been thwarted at every turn by his father—insanely plunges a paper cutter into his father's neck, melodrama is made plausible and acceptable without offending the realistic treatment Fuller has given to his novel.

Moreover, Fuller has foreshadowed the catastrophe thus preparing us for its probability: George Ogden, victimized by his brother-in-law, in a desperate moment lets fall "away from him all the fetters that shackle the super-civilized man who is habitually conscious of his civilization." Smashing McDowell over the head with a chair, George leaves him "crushed and bleeding on the floor." This action has been preceded by Fuller's own reflection on insanity, suicide, and murder in a society whose "fine-spun meshes bind us and strangle us. Indignation ferments without vent; injury awaits with a varying impatience the slow and formal infliction of a corporate punishment; self-consciousness paralyzes the quick and free action that is the surest and sometimes the only relief."

Throughout the novel one event may anticipate and stand as metaphor for what occurs later, or a later event is made probable with the reverberations accompanying it from the reader's recognition of its earlier prefiguration. For example, Jessie Bradley's bold and reckless buggy ride in Hinsdale with George as the acquiescent and timid passenger holding on to the side of the buggy with one hand and ready to grab the reins—he never does—with the other, suggests what will be the inevitable course of their marriage. Or, when the Ogden baby dies and a salesman tries to sell George a lot in the fashionable section of the cemetery, just across from the monument put up by Arthur J. Ingles, we are chilled recalling the other monument of Ingles, the seven columns he had given as a gift to the hotel where he had spent a week of his happy honeymoon, the Seven Bridegrooms as they are called. At this hotel, George and Jessie spend their somewhat dismal, one day honeymoon, as Fuller notes, "along with the Seven Bridegrooms."

So while there is a largeness to *The Cliff-Dwellers*—a wide variety of social life and social types, a host of secondary characters, a succession of glimpses and insights into emerging institutional forms of modern city life, a multiplicity of marriage plots (George and Jessie, Cornelia McNabb and Burt Brainard, Mary Brainard and Russell Vipert, Kittie Ogden and Eugene McDowell)—there is also a closeness and thickness of texture because of the interlacing of events as event reacts upon event. The individual seems to have little room for free play as we witness the process by which society's "fine-spun meshes bind us and strangle us."

In another sense, however, we are also made to see in the Clifton not human relationships but a series of exchanges in locked cubicles that make human relationships impossible, or a series of elevator rides up and down under the command of a man with a gold band and gilt buttons.

Yet *The Cliff-Dwellers* does not depress us because it is finally a triumph of style. In "Edmund Dalrymple," Fuller asserted that form and style are the elements that make a work of art pleasing, that form and style may be "superior" to subject matter, that "the cultivated ear always welcomes the accents of refinement, and for the cultivated mind the graces of technique possess an abiding charm." Fuller often spoke of the redemptive power of style: "A nation's art centres on a nation's life. If that life, in some of its aspects is raw and repellent, the challenge is all the greater. Manner may redeem matter—as with certain fiction which paradoxically offers an absorbing, compelling interest in persons and conditions that, in real life, would repel and disgust in no time." Style is "of the man." It "follows immediately on a continued and confirmed mode of feeling." In one light, Fuller's concern over society may be viewed as a concern over manner, over form, over style. In *The Cliff-Dwellers* the novelist as stylist and the novelist as social critic are inseparable because the precision and elegance of Fuller's narrative style poised against the crudities of the life he describes asserts a civilized voice, the permanence of social values. In redeeming subject-matter by manner, Fuller becomes a kind of "socioesthetician."

His rhythms and diction take their origins in the spoken language. One of the dominating characteristics of American fiction from the post-Civil War era to modern times has been the development of a prose style derived from popular speech. Of course a style cannot be separated from its context, as the critic, Richard Bridgman, has pointed out. The problems facing Mark Twain, as an instance, in establishing an authentic voice for Huck Finn, are of a kind different from the problems in establishing a stable idiom for the middle-class that Howells or Henry B. Fuller wrote about. For example, the problem of remaining true to the often banal conversation of a middle-class and yet investing the dialogue with vitality, of even capturing the dullness and making the dullness interesting is obviously a difficult one.

In many instances in *The Cliff-Dwellers* dialogue is so pared
to the bone that the page looks like a page of Ernest
Hemingway's. The design of the following dialogue may
appear contrived and there is a lack of dramatic rhythm, but
it nevertheless builds easily and directly upon conversational trivia to a meaningful and ironic conclusion. George's
roommate, Brower, has just returned from a trip:

> "Back are you?" said George. "When did you get in?"
> "About seven."
> "How's Missouri?"
> "Weather good; eating bad."
> "Reading all this time?"
> "Went to theatre."
> "What did you see?"
> "'Crackling of Thorns.'"
> "Any good?"
> "Not much; one pretty girl. Where have *you* been?"
> "West Side; Brainard's."
> "Anybody there?"
> "The old people. And some friends—Valentines."
> "Valentine? I used to know a Valentine—nice, quiet
> fellow, light complexion. His name was Alpheus—no,
> Adrian."
> "That's the one."
> "Poor fellow! He deserved a better fate."
> "What's the matter with him?"
> "His wife owns him."

Eschewing literary language but not a civilized literacy,
Fuller in *The Cliff-Dwellers* was moving the novel forward
with a prose style that we recognize at once as modern. In
the smooth and fluid blending of the vernacular of his
narrative prose with the simple, direct, and colloquial voice

of his dialogue, he achieved that rich "continual and confirmed mode of feeling" that lends to the various, disparate, multiple elements of the harsh world he was depicting a unified and reassuring sensibility.

Theodore Dreiser once wrote that Fuller was "the most brilliant" of the early realists, that it was he "who led the van of realism in America." The Cliff-Dwellers is a prime example of the novel in transition between realism and naturalism. Fuller had given circumstances, the "fine-spun meshes" which "bind and strangle us" a more powerful control over his characters than Howells had done, freedom more circumscribed. Moreover, Howells in telling American writers to treat what he called "the smiling aspects of American life" reflected an optimistic outlook that the writers of the nineties who were exploring various facets of city life—Fuller in Chicago, Frank Norris in San Francisco, Stephen Crane in New York—were inclined to reject. Although Fuller never accepted the naturalistic hypothesis, a kind of realism with a vengeance which depicts man in a scientifically determined universe as the victim of forces of heredity and environment which he can neither control nor understand, The Cliff-Dwellers takes an important step beyond Howells in that direction. As the country was shifting from an agrarian to an urban way of living and as the imagination of the people was becoming increasingly urban, Fuller opened up fictional possibilities for exploration of the forces behind the city, behind the emerging patterns of metropolitan life, which securely places him, along with Stephen Crane and Frank Norris, "in the van of realism."

Fuller's second novel about Chicago, With the Procession (1895), is a return to the more gentle kind of realism for which Howells was the spokesman. As The Cliff-Dwellers searched the indwelling actualities of life in Chicago on the eve of the Fair, so With the Procession is a picture of Chicago after the Fair, a picture that presents a break in historical continuity, a rupture between those values belonging to an older past, agrarian and mercantile, and the new values of an industrial society that was trying to spread over money the veneer of cultural respectability. Tending toward the novel of manners, *With the Procession* describes the progress of one of Chicago's "old settler" families, the Marshalls, in joining and keeping up "with the procession." *The Cliff-Dwellers* gives us a kind of crude ore, *With the Procession* the refining process of that ore.

Fuller was never again to equal the considerable achievement of these two Chicago novels. His novels and stories were to alternate between European and American settings. He was to continue to produce work of high quality, well worth the reading today. *Under the Skylights* (1901), a collection of three satires on art in America, is a fine work on American studio society. *On the Stairs* (1918), which Edmund Wilson considers "one of his best things," is both a novel and an experiment in the art of writing a novel. And in *Bertram Cope's Year* (1919) he returned to the boldness of his early career by writing a story of sublimated affection and thwarted idealism in the life of a small mid-western town. This splendid book was badly received, perhaps because of its homosexual theme.

As book review editor and as literary critic, as lecturer, as friend to young writers, as habitue of literary club life, as adviser and proofreader for seventeen years on *Poetry: A Magazine of Verse* (which printed many of the great names of modern poetry including Eliot, Pound, Stevens, and Williams), and as occasional short-story writer and novelist, Fuller continued to participate in the literary life of his time. He had become the welcome "Uncle Henry B." or "Uncle Harry" in many a family. But toward the end of his life, the charming and shy bachelor became almost a recluse living in rooming houses, his address unknown even to closest friends. The "strange retiring boy" whom Harriet

Monroe had spoken of, had become the strange retiring old man.

In fact, from about 1900, Fuller was already showing symptoms of withdrawals into himself and of an increasing pessimism concerning the future of his art and of the modern world. He felt himself slipping as a writer. By the turn of the century, the worst tendencies of opportunism and expansionism of the post-Civil War era took new directions—now that the frontier was closed—with an imperialistic adventure abroad, the Spanish-American War. The United States emerged from this hundred-day conflict, "this splendid little war," as the Secretary of State, John Hay, had called it, with possession of the Philippines, Puerto Rico, and virtual control of Cuba. In *The New Flag* (1899) Fuller vented his rage against the war and the corruption of wartime profiteering in the McKinley administration by writing some very bad, heavy-handed verse satires. *The New Flag* was an eruption of American idealism and righteous wrath: its technique was invective. Robert Lovett of the University of Chicago argued at the time of Fuller's death in 1929 that *The New Flag* had aroused the resentment of the community against Fuller, and that the effect of the mood wrought upon him as a result was destructive and consuming. Righteous wrath had burned Fuller out as a creative artist.

Doubtless the Spanish-American War did affect Fuller's career adversely. It may have reinforced his refusal to commit himself to the new Chicago and intensified his longings and nostalgia for the post-roads of Tuscany. Finally, perhaps he had cut himself off from the promise of growth because he had suffered enough "in the cause" of realism and, as he told Dreiser, "desisted" because he found himself facing "social as well as literary ostracism."

Fuller was to see in his life a pattern of failure, and his novels often deal with failure, the failure of men and women to make of society a civilization, to redeem the crude, raw matter of life by form, by style, by manner. His struggle to do so was a poignant and heroic one. He would not clamor with the growing tumult of his society, but rather rose above it to understand and depict the cliff-dwellers, who, themselves, were without understanding.

Paul Rosenblatt

Tucson, Arizona
November 1972

ACKNOWLEDGMENT

I wish to thank Diana Haskell, Modern Manuscripts Librarian, and the staff of the Newberry Library for permission to quote from Fuller's unpublished manuscripts, and for the many kindnesses they extended to me while I was working on the Fuller Collection. I also wish to thank Bernard Koloski, a graduate student in my seminar on American realism, for helpful ideas about *The Cliff-Dwellers*.

BIBLIOGRAPHICAL NOTE

The Cliff-Dwellers was serialized in *Harper's Weekly*, from June 3 to August 12, 1893. This present edition is reprinted from the first edition, 1893, published by Harper and Brothers. There are two books on Fuller: Constance Griffin's pioneering study, *Henry Blake Fuller* (University of Pennsylvania Press, 1939) and John Pilkington Jr.'s *Henry Blake*

Fuller (Twayne Publishers, 1970), the most complete and significant consideration to date. Of special and recent interest is Edmund Wilson's appraisal of Fuller and his work, "Henry B. Fuller: The Art of Making It Flat," in *The New Yorker* (May 23, 1970), 112–139. Bernard Duffey's major study of *The Chicago Renaissance in American Letters: A Critical History* (The Michigan State University Press, 1956) has an important chapter on Fuller. So does Larzer Ziff in *The American 1890s: Life and Times of a Lost Generation* (The Viking Press, 1966). Although Fuller has not been treated at length in periodicals, he has not been neglected. I have selected the following: Floyd Dell, "Chicago in Fiction," *The Bookman*, 38 (November 1913), 270–277 and Part II, 38 (December 1913), 375–379; John Farrar, "The Literary Spotlight," *The Bookman*, 58 (February 1924), 645–649; Elwood P. Lawrence, "Fuller of Chicago: A Study in Frustration," *American Quarterly*, 6 (Summer 1954), 137–146; Robert Morss Lovett, "Fuller of Chicago," *The New Republic*, 60 (August 21, 1929), 16–18; Donald M. Murray, "Henry B. Fuller, Friend of Howells," *South Atlantic Quarterly*, 52 (July 1953), 431–444; J. H. Oppenheim, "Autopsy on Chicago," *The American Mercury*, 40 (April 1937), 454–461; and Victor Schultz, "Henry Blake Fuller: Civilized Chicagoan," *The Bookman*, 70 (September 1929), 34–38.

In addition to the fifteen books Fuller published, there are volumes of published but uncollected writings, reviews, essays, and short stories, written for the leading newspapers and periodicals of his time. The chief repository for the uncollected and unpublished writings is the Newberry Library in Chicago. Darrel Abel has edited two essays from this collection: "Howells or James?" in *Modern Fiction*, 3 (Summer 1957), 159–164 and "The American School of Fiction" under Abel's general title, "Expatriation and Realism in American Fiction in the 1890s: Henry Blake Fuller," in *American Literary Realism*, 3 (Summer 1970), 248–257.

The Cliff-Dwellers
A Novel
by Henry B. Fuller

introduction

Between the former site of old Fort Dearborn and the present site of our newest Board of Trade there lies a restricted yet tumultuous territory through which, during the course of the last fifty years, the rushing streams of commerce have worn many a deep and rugged chasm. These great cañons—conduits, in fact, for the leaping volume of an ever-increasing prosperity—cross each other with a sort of systematic rectangularity, and in deference to the practical directness of local requirements they are in general called simply—streets. Each of these cañons is closed in by a long frontage of towering cliffs, and these soaring walls of brick and limestone and granite rise higher and higher with each succeeding year, according as the work of erosion at their bases goes onward—the work of that seething flood of carts, carriages, omnibuses, cabs, cars, messengers, shoppers, clerks, and capitalists, which surges with increasing violence for every passing day. This erosion, proceeding with a sort of fateful regularity, has come to be a matter of constant and growing interest. Means have been found to measure its progress—just as a scale has been arranged to measure the rising of the Nile or to gauge the draught of an ocean liner. In this case the unit of measurement is called the "story." Ten years ago the most rushing and irrepressible of the torrents which devastate Chicago had not worn its bed to a greater depth than that indicated by seven of these "stories." This depth has since increased to eight—to ten—to fourteen—to sixteen, until some of the leading avenues of activity promise soon to become little more than mere obscure trails half lost between the bases of perpendicular precipices.

High above this architectural upheaval rise yet other structures in crag-like isolation. El Capitan is duplicated time and again both in bulk and in stature, and around him the floating spray of the Bridal Veil is woven by the breezes of lake and prairie from the warp of soot-flakes and the woof of damp-drenched smoke.

The explorer who has climbed to the shoulder of one of these great captains and has found one of the thinnest folds in the veil may readily make out the nature of the surrounding country. The rugged and erratic plateau of the Bad Lands lies before him in all its hideousness and impracticability. It is a wild tract full of sudden falls, unexpected rises, precipitous dislocations. The high and the low are met together. The big and the little alternate in a rapid and illogical succession. Its perilous trails are followed successfully by but few—by a lineman, perhaps, who is balanced on a cornice, by a roofer astride some dizzy gable, by a youth here and there whose early apprehension of the main chance and the multiplication table has stood him in good stead. This country is a treeless country—if we overlook the "forest of chimneys" comprised in a bird's-eye view of any great city, and if we are unable to detect any botanical analogies in the lofty articulated iron funnels whose ramifying cables reach out

4

wherever they can, to fasten wherever they may. It is a shrubless country—if we give no heed to the gnarled carpentry of the awkward frame-works which carry the telegraph, and which are set askew on such dizzy corners as the course of the wires may compel. It is an arid country—if we overlook the numberless tanks that squat on the high angles of alley walls, or if we fail to see the little pools of tar and gravel that ooze and shimmer in the summer sun on the roofs of old-fashioned buildings of the humbler sort. It is an airless country—if by air we mean the mere combination of oxygen and nitrogen which is commonly indicated by that name. For here the medium of sight, sound, light, and life becomes largely carbonaceous, and the remoter peaks of this mighty yet unprepossessing landscape loom up grandly, but vaguely, through swathing mists of coal-smoke.

From such conditions as these—along with the Tacoma, the Monadnock, and a great host of other modern monsters— towers the Clifton. From the beer-hall in its basement to the barber-shop just under its roof the Clifton stands full eighteen stories tall. Its hundreds of windows glitter with multitudinous letterings in gold and in silver, and on summer afternoons its awnings flutter score on score in the tepid breezes that sometimes come up from Indiana. Four ladder-like constructions which rise skyward stage by stage promote the agility of the clambering hordes that swarm within it, and ten elevators—devices unknown to the real, aboriginal inhabitants—ameliorate the daily cliff-climbing for the frail of physique and the pressed for time.

The tribe inhabiting the Clifton is large and rather heterogeneous. All told, it numbers about four thousand souls. It includes bankers, capitalists, lawyers, "promoters"; brokers in bonds, stocks, pork, oil, mortgages; real-estate people and railroad people and insurance people—life, fire, marine, accident; a host of principals, agents, middlemen, clerks, cashiers, stenographers, and errand-boys; and the neces-

5

sary force of engineers, janitors, scrub-women, and elevator-hands.

All these thousands gather daily around their own great camp-fire. This fire heats the four big boilers under the pavement of the court which lies just behind, and it sends aloft a vast plume of smoke to mingle with those of other like communities that are settled round about. These same thousands may also gather—in instalments—at their tribal feast, for the Clifton has its own lunch-counter just off one corner of the grand court, as well as a restaurant several floors higher up. The members of the tribe may also smoke the pipe of peace among themselves whenever so minded, for the Clifton has its own cigar-stand just within the principal entrance. Newspapers and periodicals, too, are sold at the same place. The warriors may also communicate their messages, hostile or friendly, to chiefs more or less remote; for there is a telegraph office in the corridor and a squad of messenger-boys in wait close by.

In a word, the Clifton aims to be complete within itself, and it will be unnecessary for us to go afield either far or frequently during the present simple succession of brief episodes in the lives of the Cliff-dwellers.

I

On the tenth floor of the Clifton is the office of the Massachusetts Brass Company.

Those whose minds are attuned to an appreciation of upholstery and kindred matters pronounce this little suite the gem of the whole establishment. Even many who are not adepts in the matter of house-furnishing, and who are much too rushed and preoccupied to become such, have been known to pause in their course through the Clifton's long corridors, on occasions when the ribbed glass door of the Brass Company happened to be standing ajar, and to say to themselves, with certain home offices in mind,

"Now, why can't our people do as much for *us?*"

Indeed, there is cause enough for envy in that small square of velvety Axminster, in the harmonious tinting of the walls, in the padded leather backs of the swivel chairs, in the polished brightness of the cherry desk-tops, in the fresh blotting-pads and the immaculate inkstands. To sit in this pleasant little apartment for half an hour is to receive quite a new impression of the possible luxury of business, the ultimate elegance of trade. This may be managed as easily as not if you happen to have any dealings with "D. Walworth Floyd, Agt."—according to the legend on the translucent pane of the door—who is quite unlikely to hurry you out before you have finished.

"Don't be in such a drive," he will perhaps say to you; "stay and smoke a cigar."

For business is not too exacting a consideration with the western branch of the Massachusetts Brass Company. It is less a hive of industry than a social exchange. The hours are easy, and the habitués are as frequently callers as customers. They are often Jacks or Toms, whose fathers are social pillars in Boston and large land-owners in Wyoming and Dakota, and Jack and Tom—birds of passage in Scotch cheviots and billycock hats—are given to alighting for a brief breathing-spell on this lofty perch, where they reproach the slipshod dress and careless speech of their friend's small office force by the trim neatness of their own clothes and conversation.

It may be guessed that this snug haven of refuge has been established and maintained less to extend the Company's trade than to provide a place for the Company's Walworth. I say *Company's* Walworth, for in this case "company" and "family" are interchangeable terms. The Massachusetts Brass Company is the Floyd family, and the Floyd family is the Massachusetts Brass Company. The Company pays no dividends, but it is very generous in its salaries. It is liberal with Hosea G. Floyd, who is its president, and with Winthrop C. Floyd, who is its treasurer, and with H. Lovell Floyd, who is its New York agent, and with Cadwallader P. Floyd, who looks after the Philadelphia interests; nor does it quite forget D. Walworth Floyd, who holds up one end more or less effectively in the West. But

Walworth is the last and the youngest of the Floyds; his marriage was not to the complete satisfaction of his family, and his single independent venture before leaving home, in the direction of coffee and spices, compelled his brothers to put their hands into their pockets rather deeply. So, while the rest of the Floyds think that, all considered, they have rather done the fair thing by Walworth, yet Walworth, on the other hand, regards his assignment to the West as a mild form of punishment and exile.

"It *does* give me a little elbow-room, though."

This is the silent acknowledgment that Walworth sometimes makes to himself—but grudgingly.

Walworth Floyd is a sleek, well-fed, prosperous-looking fellow of thirty. His figure is a trifle too short and dumpy to be pronounced absolutely good; but is always strikingly well-dressed—for he has lived in the West hardly a year as yet. His face is not handsome, but it is gentlemanly quite. One might, indeed, complain of the retreating lines of his forehead, and regret, too, that his chin, once perfect, now shows leanings towards the duplex; but, on the other hand, his well-bridged nose, you are sure, has been figuring in family portraits for the last hundred years, and his plump hands, by reason of the fine texture of the skin and the shapeliness of the nails, form a point that is distinctly aristocratic. Yet penmanship, under his manipulations, becomes a very crabbed and laborious affair, and this light species of manual labor is usually performed, so far as he is concerned, by other hands. He has a sort of general clerk, and he shares the services of a stenographer with two or three of his neighbors. He employs, too, an office-boy, who would idle away a good deal of time if Walworth were not in the habit of sending frequent communications to the steward of his club. Walworth, garmented in his plump placidity, has been accustomed to fare sumptuously every day, and to worry his head about as few things as possible.

His dining he does for himself; his thinking he has somebody else do for him. His book-keeping and auditing and so on are done in the East, and a friend of his—he has no enemies—once said that his stomach was in Chicago, while his brains were in Boston.

Walworth, considering his family training and traditions, is inexplicably expansive. Even more than his limited capabilities for business, even more than the exactions of a wife whose pinched girlhood has helped her to a full appreciation of her present membership in a wealthy family, has his own open-hearted bonhomie "kept him back." He is just the man to whom one writes a letter of introduction without any sense of imposing a burden, or to whom one may present it without experiencing any great sense of embarrassment. And it is a letter of introduction, in point of fact, which is now lying half folded on the extended elbow-rest of his desk, and has been lying there for a quarter of an hour.

Most of us know something about letters of introduction—promised so thoughtlessly, written so glibly, presented so reluctantly, received so grudgingly. But when the letter is merely a trifling and insignificant line—a line which has no great importance for the bearer and can cause no great annoyance to the recipient—and when its presentation here and its accounting for there may be considered as but a minute item in the general system of social book-keeping, then we have an episode that passes quickly and lightly for all concerned. Such appears to be the situation in the office of the Massachusetts Brass Company.

Walworth is tilted back comfortably in one of his handsome chairs and sends out a casual glance through the nearest window. The sun is struggling with a half-luminous haze, and through this haze a hundred streaks of smoke are driving headlong towards the lake. A tall clock-tower looms up three or four streets away, and one of its faces—on the looker's own level—gives the hour as half-past ten.

"Well, we are living up on Pine Street, Mr. Ogden," he is saying; "just this side of the Water Works—the place where the 'wheels go round,' you know. You beat me here by a few minutes this morning, but I think I can promise to be the first on the ground when you call on us there."

He is running his fingers over the edges of several little sheets of brass. A few bunches of these, together with a set or two of brass rings of varying diameters and thicknesses, are the only intimations of merchandise that the office yields. Sometimes even these are bundled away into a drawer, and then commerce is refined completely beyond the ken of the senses.

"However, don't go. I am a little late in getting around this morning, but the mail is light. Ferguson will look after it. Sit down again."

The visitor, thus urged, sank back into the chair from which he had just risen. He was a slender young man, of good height, and his age was perhaps twenty-four. His complexion was of the colorless kind that good health alone keeps from sallowness. His hair was a light brown and fine and thick, and it fell across his temples in the two smooth wings that were made by an accurate parting in the middle. He had the beginnings of a shadowy little moustache, and a pair of good eyes which expressed a fair amount of self-reliance and any amount of hope.

"And how are you finding the West Side?" Walworth pursued. "I don't know much about it myself. This is a big town and awfully cut up. A man has to pick out his own quarter and stick to it. If you move from one side of the river to another, you bid good-by to all your old friends; you never see them again. You said you were somewhere near Union Park, I believe?"

11

"Yes," George Ogden answered, "I have landed in a pretty good place, and I want to stay there if I can. They're a sort of farming people—or were, to start with. They came from New York State, I believe, and haven't been here but a year or two. Is there anybody in this town who hasn't come from somewhere else, or who has been here more than a year or two?"

Walworth laughed. "*I* haven't. But you go around some, and you may find a few that have."

"The mother cooks, the father markets, the daughter helps to wait on table. Nice, friendly people; make me think of those at home." He smiled a little wistfully. "About the only people so far that do."

"Well, I have heard that there are some pretty good streets over there," is Walworth's vague response.

"Ours is. We have trees—all of one sort and planted regularly, I mean. And ornamental lamp-posts. And I'm only a block from the Park. Everything seems all right enough."

"I dare say; but don't you find it rather far away from—?" queried Floyd, with a sort of insinuating intentness.

However, I have no idea of reproducing Walworth's remarks on the local topography. They were voluminous, but he would be found prejudiced and but partly informed. Besides, his little tirade was presently thrown out of joint by a dislocating interruption.

Walworth always experienced a mental dislocation, slight or serious, whenever his wife called at the office. Nor were matters much helped when his wife was accompanied by her sister. It was the latter of these who now opened the door with an assured hand and who shut it after the two of them with a confirmatory slam.

12

"Yes, here we are," she seemed to imply.

In Mrs. Walworth Floyd our young man met a lean and anxious little body, who appeared strenuous and exacting and of the kind who, as the expression goes, are hard to get along with. She had a sharp little nose and a pair of inquisitorial eyes. She was dressed richly, but as simply as a sword in its scabbard. If Walworth spent an evening abroad it was a fair assumption that his wife knew where he was and all about it. Otherwise the sword was drawn.

"We have been almost three quarters of an hour getting here," she said in a tense way. "Something was the matter with the cable and they kept us in the tunnel nearly twenty minutes. As I tell Ann, you can always count on that sort of thing when you've got anything of real importance on hand and not much time for it. And yet we talk about the jams and delays in Tremont Street!"

She drew down her mouth and blinked her eyes indignantly. She felt all the shortcomings of her new home very keenly; she made every one of them a personal affront.

"Ann thought it was amusing. Perhaps it won't seem so after it has happened to her three or four times more."

Walworth glanced apprehensively in the direction of his sister-in-law's chair. She was understood to be in his house on a brief visit. He trusted that she was not to be exposed a second time to so annoying an accident.

Ann Wilde was a stout woman who was nearing forty. Her appearance indicated that, while she had not escaped the buffets of the world, yet her past experiences had only seasoned and toughened her for her future ones. In this earthly turmoil of give and take she seemed to have played a full inning on each side. She had begun as a poetess, she had gone on as a boarding-house keeper, and she was now ready to take her first step as an investor. To turn from literature to lodgings indicates talent; to do so well in lodgings as to have funds for the purchase of property indicates genius. Miss Wilde, at fourteen, was a plain child whose straggling hair was drawn back from her forehead by an india-rubber comb that passed over the top of her head from ear to ear, and she was called Annie. At seventeen, conscious of the first flutterings of sentiment and prompted by indications of increasing comeliness, she re-named herself Annette. At twenty, somewhat disappointed in the promise of beauty, yet consoled in some degree by a spreading reputation as a versifier, she changed her name to Anne. At twenty-six, as the result of a disappointment in an affair of the heart and of a growing appreciation of the modesty of her social role, she resignedly styled herself Anna. And at thirty-five, fully convinced of her own hopeless plainness, of the completely practical cast of things generally, and of the uselessness of flying the flag of idealism any longer, she bobbed off at the same time both her hair and her name; she presented a short-cut poll of frizzled gray and she signed herself Ann. What's in a name? Sometimes nothing; sometimes a whole biography.

"I have been telling Mr. Ogden," said Walworth, "that he ought to be in our part of town—he ought to be one of our little circle." His wife looked up rather coldly; her little circle was not open to any new candidate that the uncalculating good-nature of her husband might propose. "That house around on Rush Street could take him in, I imagine. And all the people he will want to know are right around there. Why, you have been in Worcester, Frances; you know the Parkers. Well, Mrs. Parker is Mr. Ogden's aunt—aunt, I think you said?—yes, aunt; so you see about how it is. Always glad to welcome one more Eastern pilgrim to our little what-you-may-call-it—oasis, you know."

"Why didn't

you say Mr. Ogden was from the East, Walworth?" asked his wife, taxingly, and looked at the young man for the first time.

Her gaze was critical, but not forbidding.

"Yes, most of us are on the North Side," she observed.

"Ogden is as good as a neighbor already," Walworth went on, perseveringly; "a business neighbor. He is going into the Underground National. Letters and all that, you know. Pretty good for three weeks, I call it. If most of our fellows who come out here did as well in three months it would be money in Mrs. Floyd's pocket. To think of the fives and tens and twenties that have gone to old schoolmates of Win's and to fellows who knew Lovell when he was on the road!"

Ogden flushed a little and took the first step towards a frown. It is not pleasant to contemplate your possible inclusion in the reprehensible class of the strapped and the stranded, nor to feel that only a lucky letter of recommendation has saved a friend's wife from being crossed in some caprice or balked in some whim. But Floyd, although cordial and liberal, was not invariably fine.

"They stop me on the street, and they buttonhole me in the hotels, and you can't think how many of them come right here. Of course, I always do what I can. But how do they find me out? And why is it that when I am going up home late over the viaduct and somebody is hanging about to strike some man for a quarter, I am always the man to be struck? One or two of them have actually paid me back, but—"

"Who?" asked his sister-in-law. She had a loud, rasping voice. "The men on the viaduct?"

"The others," Walworth indicated briefly.

"You are too generous," said Ogden. What a position for a man who was *not* to enter upon an engagement to-morrow! And what might three months be, if judged by the hopes and fears and expectations and disappointments of his three weeks!

"The Underground?" repeated Mrs. Floyd, turning towards her husband. "Isn't that Mayme Brainard's father's bank?" she asked in a general way.

"Mr. Brainard is the president," assented Ogden, with a severe smile. "I addressed myself to the cashier," he added shortly.

"I was sure I had heard of it," she rejoined, with a glacial graciousness.

"Well, if you have heard of it, my dear," her husband joked, "how widely known it must be! You ought to have heard of it; you've had enough checks on it, I'm sure!"

But Mrs. Floyd did not pursue the subject. She looked at her sister with that prim seriousness which means something on the mind—or on two minds—and her sister returned the look in kind; and they both looked in the same fashion back and forth between Walworth and his caller. Ann Wilde snapped the catch of her hand-bag once or twice, and glanced between times at some loose papers inside it. Ferguson, in the other room, thought he perceived the approach of a domestic crisis—a disputed dress-maker's bill, perhaps. Yet there might be other reasons. He knew that the cook was sometimes impertinent, and that the market-man now and then forgot to send the white-fish. He himself was a mere boarding bachelor, yet he had come to learn something of the relief which follows the shifting of a housekeeper's cares to the shoulders of the housekeeper's husband. Ferguson had relieved the tedium of many a half-hour by short-handing bits of dialogue that accompanied connubial spats between his employer and his employer's wife.

These signs and tokens were not lost on Ogden; he rose again to go.

Nor were they lost on Floyd himself, whose apprehension of a bad quarter of an hour was heightened by the absence, as yet, of any exact data. He had no wish to hold the field alone, and he begged Ogden not to hurry his departure.

"Where are the girls?" he asked his wife. "I thought you said they came along with you."

"They did. They are in the building. They will be up in a few minutes. That child! —somebody ought to look after her."

"Then why not wait a little while?" Floyd suggested to Ogden. "My wife's affair won't take long. Ferguson, won't you just clear off that chair out there and find the paper? And now, what is it?" he asked the two women when they were left together.

II

"Well, Ann has heard from those Minneapolis people again. And she isn't any nearer making up her mind than before."

"Here's what they say," added his sister-in-law. She took a letter out of her bag and handed it to him.

"Oh!" said Walworth. He felt half relieved, half vexed.

His wife stood by the window, rubbing her forefinger along the edges of its silver lettering.

"I don't see whatever put Minneapolis into Ann's head. There seems to be a plenty of buildings right here."

She looked at the rough brick back of a towering structure a few hundred feet away, and at the huddle of lower roofs between. From a skylight on one of these a sunbeam came reflected, and compelled her to move.

"And

18

plenty of dirt, too, if she is after real estate; plenty to be sold, and plenty of people to sell it. I never saw a town where it was more plentiful."

She glanced downwards at the wagons and cars that were splashing through the streets after a rainy September night. "Why shouldn't there be more people to shovel it, too? You see their signs stuck up everywhere—the dealers, I mean."

"Ann can get to Minneapolis in thirteen hours," suggested Walworth, passing the end of his thumb along one of his eyebrows. "What's that, after the trip West? And then she can see for herself. You take the cars here late in the afternoon, and you get there in time for breakfast."

"I believe I'd just let it drop," said Miss Wilde, "if I happened to know positively of any good thing here. They write a nice enough letter, but I can't tell what state the building is in unless I see it. And I'm merely taking their word that the ground is worth a hundred and fifty. There's forty feet. I wonder if 'all improvements in' means that the street is paved."

"Drop it, anyway," said her sister, as if she were disembarrassing herself of some loathsome parcel. "Look around in Chicago itself. You can see what you are buying, then. Even if you do invest here, you are not compelled to live here." She became almost rigid in her disdain.

"Ah—um!" murmured Walworth, in a non-committal way.

The door opened suddenly, and two young girls entered in a brisk fashion. The first one had a slight figure, a little above the average height. To-day people called her slender; six or eight years later they would be likely to call her lean. She had long, thin arms, and delicate, transparent hands. She had large eyes of a deep blue, and the veins were plainly outlined on her pale temples. She had a bright face and a lively manner, and seemed to be one who drew largely on her nervous force without making deposits to keep up her account. Her costume was such as to give one the idea that dress was an important matter with her.

"Well, Frankie!" she called to Mrs. Floyd, "you found your way here all right, did you? You're a clever little body! Or did Miss Wilde help you?"

Mrs. Floyd passed back the Minneapolis letter to her sister and bestowed a lady-like frown on the new-comers. She disliked to be called "Frankie," but what is to be done between cousins?

"Jessie!" she expostulated softly, indicating Ogden in the adjoining room.

"You can't think," the girl went on, to Ogden *redux*, "how proud my cousin is of her ignorance of Chicago. She knows where to buy her steaks, and she has mastered the shortest way down town, and that's about all. Frankie, dear, where is the City Hall?"

"How should *I* know?" returned Frances Floyd, with a weary disdain.

"Why, there's a corner of it," cried Jessie Bradley, at the window, "not two blocks off. It's big enough to see!"

"And she's been here a whole year, too!" cried her husband, proudly and fondly.

Mrs. Floyd drew Jessie Bradley aside. "I know I'm very ignorant," she said, speaking in a low tone, "but there is one thing you can tell me about, if you want to. Why have you been so long in getting up to the office? You said Mayme—Mayme; I suppose that means Mary—you said that she was going to stop in the bank for just two or three minutes."

Jessie looked towards her young friend, who was seated near Ogden on one of the wide window-sills. Then she turned back to her questioner, with eyes that were steady and perhaps a bit defiant.

"Well, we stopped for a minute in that insurance office on the way up. We came part way by the stairs. Mayme said she had just got to see him. I don't see how she can meet him anywhere else. They won't let him come to the house. I can't see that her brother has treated him so very well."

Mrs. Floyd's regard travelled from the culprit before her to the greater culprit on the window-sill. Mary Brainard was a pretty little thing of eighteen, with a plump, dimpled face. She had wide eyes of baby-blue under a fluffy flaxen bang. The brim of her hat threw a shadow over her pink cheeks, and she was nibbling the finger-ends of her gloves between her firm white teeth.

Mrs. Floyd considered this picture with grave disapproval, and turned back to her young cousin a face full of severe reproach.

"Jessie, I don't like this. It wasn't a nice thing for you to do at all, and I'm sure your mother would agree with me. Don't mix in any such matter. Let her own people attend to it."

Mary Brainard noticed this whispered passage, and suspected herself under comment. Her face, rather weakly pretty generally, was quite flushed and brilliant now, and she looked out from under her wide hat with the forced audacity that a lightly esteemed nature may sometimes assume, and afterwards, to everybody's surprise, may justify. She began to chat brightly with Ogden. Her gayety, however, was evidently but the spending momentum of some recent impact, and the bright defiance with which she glanced around the group was not more a surprise to them than to herself.

Jessie Bradley crossed over to the window and found a third place on its wide sill.

Walworth gathered the two ladies behind the shelter of his big desk, and the Minneapolis matter was resumed.

"No," said Jessie, as she settled down, "Mrs. D. Walworth Floyd doesn't know where the City Hall is." She was in a slightly nervous state, and she caught hold of the first piece of conversational driftwood that came her way. "I ought to have asked her something easier—where La Salle Street was, for instance. I wonder if she knows she's on it now."

"Well, Mr. Ogden is going to have a chance to learn all about La Salle Street!" cried Mayme Brainard, with the air of one who dreads the slightest pause in the talk. "He's going into the Bank, he tells me."

"That will do very well for six days in the week," declared the other. "How about the seventh?" she asked with a twinkling directness. "Are you an Episcopalian, or what?"

"What, I fancy. Why, in Rome, I suppose, I shall do as the Romans do. For the forenoon there are the newspapers, of course. Then for the afternoon—the races, perhaps. In the evening—well, the theatre, I should say. That's about the plan at my house."

"Well, I've never been to the theatre Sunday evening, nor any of my people. And I don't believe that many nice people do go, either. Perhaps you think that there are not any nice people in Chicago—I've heard the remark made. Well, there are, I can tell you—just as nice as anywhere. I suppose you've noticed the way the papers here have of collecting all the mean, hateful things that the whole country says about us, and making a column out of them. I dare say they think it's funny. I don't know but what it is. There's my own father, now. He reads those things right after the market-reports, and time and time again I've seen him laugh till he cried. Yet he isn't any fonder of a joke than anybody else. He says it's better to be abused and

22

made fun of than not to be noticed at all. How does it strike you?"

She made a little *moue*, as she recalled one or two of these national love-taps.

"And I must say it's awful, too—the sort of news that is sent out from here—excursions and alarums, and nothing else. During the anarchist time folks down East were a good deal more scared than we were. And I remember, when I was at school, I read in the Philadelphia papers that typhoid fever was raging in Chicago. They gave the death-rate and everything. I came home as fast as I could. I expected to find the whole family dying. But *they* didn't know anything about it. And they took my pocket-money to pay the return fare. They were alive enough."

Ogden smiled. He saw that he was face to face with a true daughter of the West; she had never seen him before, and she might never see him again, yet she was talking to him with perfect friendliness and confidence. Equally, he was sure, was she a true daughter of Chicago; she had the one infallible local trait—she would rather talk to a stranger about her own town than about any other subject.

"I think we shall have to reform you," she went on presently, "in advance. I believe the proper place for you next Sunday would be St. Asaph's. But it's high, you understand. Come over; my cousin has room in her pew. There is a vested choir, and when you have heard Vibert's singing—"

She stopped, as if to appreciate her own daring—like a child lighting a match. Mary Brainard gave a little start and put her hand on her friend's arm, yet at the same time she blushed slightly—less, perhaps, in panic than in pride.

"—you will learn what it is that brings Mayme Brainard all the way over from Union Park twice every Sunday," were the words with which this sentence was mentally concluded. "It's like an angel," she continued aloud. "A certain kind of angel," she added to herself. "Do you sing?"

"Yes, a little."

"Then of course you play. But that doesn't count. Do you write? But everybody does that, too. I do. Or did. I carried off a prize once. It kept me in flowers for a week. Well, what is it—dialect or psychological?"

"Business letters," answered Ogden, with a balking sobriety.

"Pshaw! Well, then, can you sketch, or can you do anything in water-colors? I did a lovely head of Desdemona once—in crayon. That was at Ogontz."

"Kodak," Ogden confessed briefly. "Views along the wharves in Boston; some pretty bits from around Stockbridge."

"My own story was in Stockbridge! Our artist on the spot!" She clapped her hands together joyfully. "What else? Can you—cook?"

"No."

"Neither can I!"

"Can you keep books?" he asked in turn.

"Not a bit."

"Well, I can."

"You take the odd trick. Wait a minute, though. How about private theatricals?" she asked.

"I have acted in them once or twice."

She looked aslant at Mary Brainard. The girl seemed glad that St. Asaph's had been dropped, but she was hoping, fearfully, that it might be taken up again.

"Well, Father Tisdale has everything just about perfect. He's from St. John the Evangelist—Boston, you know. And you ought to hear little Mike Besser. He's our butcher's boy—only eleven. Sometimes he and Russell Vibert"—the other girl vibrated at this first audacious mention of the full name—"sing duets together, and then—"

Her eyes rolled around the room in a mock ecstasy and rested on the group of elders, whose three heads just showed above the top of the desk. Walworth's face made quite a picture of discomfort and distress, as he rose from his chair with the effect of trying to shake himself loose from the complications that his wife and Sister Ann were weaving about him.

"The whole building is full of them," he said, rather pettishly; "there are half a dozen on every floor. But *I* don't know anything about any of them."

He looked inquiringly towards the window seat.

"Ogden might."

"How is that?" inquired the young fellow, rising.

"Some real-estate man. Mrs. Floyd's sister here has about concluded to cast in her lot with us. She wants an adviser. Perhaps you happen to know of—"

He took on the ingenuous air of one who is earnestly searching for information—in the least likely quarter.

Ogden laughed self-consciously.

"Well, now, as a matter of fact, I do. His name is McDowell. He is on the second floor above. I have a sort of personal interest in him. He will be my brother-in-law within a month or six weeks."

A slight flutter among the women—the mention of matrimony.

"Do you want to try that, Ann?" asked Floyd.

"We became acquainted with him down East, last year," Ogden went on, proud to show his newness wearing off. "He was working up a syndicate. He calls himself a hustler. He tells me he has just opened a new subdivision out south somewhere—beyond Washington Park, I believe. I think you'll find him posted."

Older people than Ogden frequently go out of their way to run cheerfully the risk of advising others in business matters.

"I believe I'll see him, anyway," decided Miss Wilde. Like all women, she embraced the personal element in every affair. The people in Minneapolis became mere myths, now that she found herself so near to the future husband of the sister of the man who had just presented a letter of introduction to her own brother-in-law. The chain was long, to be sure, and some of its links were rather weak—but it served.

Mrs. Floyd arose, shaking out the folds of her dress and smoothing away the wrinkles that the last half-hour had accumulated on her forehead.

"I have asked Mr. Ogden to go to church with us Sunday," Jessie Bradley announced to her. "And he is going to bring some Stockbridge photographs."

"First-rate!" cried Walworth, relieved by any outcome whatever. "Stockbridge! Why, that's where I did my courting!"

Mrs. Floyd was caught in a melting mood.

"We shall be very happy to see Mr. Ogden," she pronounced primly.

III

In one of the first-floor corners of the Clifton is situated the Underground National Bank—Erastus M. Brainard, president.

The Underground is not so styled on account of the policy and methods of its head, oblique and subterranean though they may be; it is merely that the Clifton is almost entirely shut in by its tall neighbors, and that, so far as its lower floors are concerned, direct sunlight, except for a month or two in the early summer, is pretty nearly out of the question. We shall have to throw our own sunlight on the Underground and on the man who is its president and its principal stockholder.

The Underground is not one of the old banks, nor is it one of the large ones; if Brainard had no other irons in the fire he would not cut much of a figure in business circles. The Underground is simply one in a batch of banks that have sprung up in the last seven or eight years and that are almost unknown, even by name, to men who, in the clearing-house at that time, have since passed on to other and different affairs. It is spoken of as Brainard's bank, just as other banks are spoken of as Shayne's, or Cutter's, or Patterson's. Now Shayne, for example, began life with a fruit-stand—Jim Shayne they called him. The fruit-stand developed into a retail grocery, and Jim Shayne (about the time of the Fire) became J. H. Shayne. The retail grocery expanded into a wholesale grocery, and the sign read, "James H. Shayne & Co.," and the firm made money. But the day dawned when his wife began to figure at dances and receptions—her own and those of other people—as Mrs. James Horton Shayne, and when his daughter's wedding was not far away, with all the splendor that St. Asaph's could command. This was no juncture for laying undue stress on the wholesale grocery business; it seemed worth while to become identified a little less closely with mercantile circles and a little more closely with financial circles. Shayne & Co. went right on—both routine and profits; but the High-flyers' National was started, and James Horton Shayne was more likely to be found on La Salle Street than on River Street.

Cutter was in hardware. His daughter was a great beauty. One day he dropped hardware in favor of his sons, to become the head of a board of directors. Then people could say, "Ah! a fine girl that! Her father runs the Parental National."

Patterson's case was different. He had just invested half a million in a big business block, and his daughter had just invested her all in a husband. The best office in the new building remained tenantless at the end of six months, and the man of his daughter's choice continued practically without occupation during the same term. The office was worth ten thousand dollars, the son-in-law—in the present state of things—about ten thousand cents. So Patterson, in order to secure a tenant for his new building and a career for his new son, started a new financial institution—the Exigency Trust Co.

But no such considerations as these influenced Erastus Brainard when he founded the Underground. He was far aside from all social ambitions, and his domestic affairs took care of themselves. His business interests spread all over the city, the state, the West, even the Far West, and this vast web must have a centre. That centre was on the lower floor of the Clifton, where he ran a bank, true, but a good many other things besides.

Brainard had come up from the southern part of the state—from "Egypt," as it is called. A darkness truly Egyptian brooded over his early history, so that if it is a fact that he was an exhorter at Methodist camp-meetings in his early twenties, proof of that fact might be sought for in vain. The first definite point in his career is this: that as a youngish man he was connected in some capacity with a cross-country railroad on the far side of Centralia. How successful he was in transporting souls no one can say; that he has been successful in transporting bodies no one will deny. He is unrivalled in his mastery of the street-car question, and his operations have lain in many scattered fields.

To claim that Brainard has a national reputation would be going too far. However, his reputation might fairly be termed inter-state. If the man were to die to-morrow, sketches of his life would appear in the papers of Milwaukee, Indianapolis, and St. Louis; and the caustic and frankly abusive paragraphs would be copied appreciatively as far as the remoter counties of Nebraska. For Brainard's success is not without the elements of public scandal. His manipulation of city councils and of state legislatures has been freely charged. Old stories of his brief incarceration in prison, or of his narrow escape from it, sometimes arise and flutter; and there are those who think that if he never has been in jail, then this is all the more reason for his being there now. His demise would indeed set the clipping-bureaus to work; but the work would not be started by the direction of his surviving family. Such is the chief to whom young George Ogden has sworn allegiance.

"I shall marry him," said a voice quite firmly; "you may make up your mind to that."

Ogden started. These words came through a door which stood ajar in the partition that separated him from the president's room; the office was splendid with bevelled glass and oxidized iron-work, yet it was as compact as high rentals compel. They were words in striking contrast to most of the talk that his pen commanded. "Make it thirty days more"; "I'll take the rest in small bills, please"; It will be due day after to-morrow." And with these—"I shall marry him; make up your mind to that."

He knew the voice perfectly well; he had heard it a fortnight before in Floyd's office.

The door in the partition opened a foot or two wider; the bulky figure of Erastus Brainard appeared and his hard and determined face. He was a tall, broad-shouldered man with a close-clipped gray beard and a shaven upper lip. Two or three red veins showed prominently in his bulbous nose. He wore black broadcloth; his coat had a velvet collar, and on his shoulders there was a light fall of dandruff. He wore boots. On Sundays his boots had "tongues," and his trade was the mainstay of a German shoemaker who kept a shop behind his house, and whom, twice a year, he literally terrified into a fit.

But now his big figure clutched at the red-cherry door-jamb with a tremulous hesitancy, the hard, fierce eyes looked out appealingly from under their coarse and shaggy brows, and the proud and cruel lips opened themselves to address the young man with an order that was almost an entreaty.

"Ogden, won't you ask Mr. Fairchild to step this way?"

For a mouse had come into the place, and the elephant was in terror.

The Underground National Bank, with a surplus equal to a third of its capital, had not declared a dividend for several years. Brainard, along with his son and his brother, owned five eighths of the stock. Put these two facts together and surmise the rest. Understand, without the telling, how Brainard had bought back big blocks of stock from men who had invested on his own advice and representations, only to sell out at less than two thirds the price they had paid. Understand how widowed and unprotected women, with little realization of the remote possibilities of the science of banking and no realization at all of the way in which their five thousands had come to be worth so much less than five thousand, would come to his office to implore ingenuously with sobs and tears that he would give them back their money. Consider these and a dozen other phases of the pleasant pastime known as "freeze out," and then judge whether Brainard, by this time, were capable or no of braving, warding off, beating down, despising the threats, the imprecations, the pleadings, the attacks of the harmless domestic animal known as the investor. But now another domestic animal, the wilful daughter, had entered his lair, and with this new antagonist he felt himself unable to cope.

"Ogden, won't you ask Mr. Fairchild to step this way?"

Fairchild was only the cashier of the bank, while Brainard was its head; but Fairchild was a good deal of a man—and that was more than Brainard, with all his money and his brains and his consciencelessness, and all the added power of the three combined, could have claimed for himself. He was merely a financial appliance—one of the tools of the trade.

He had no friends—none even of the poor sort known as "business" friends. He had no social relations of any kind. He had no sense of any right relation to the community in which he lived. He had next to no family life. He had no apparent consciousness of the physical basis of existence—for him diet, rest, hygiene were mere nothings. But none of these considerations disturbed him very much. He could do without friends—having so good a friend in himself. He could dispense with social diversion—so long as the affairs of the Underground, and the Illuminating Company, and those Western mines continued to occupy his attention. He could rub along without the sympathy and respect of the community—while he and it held the relative positions of knife and oyster. He could do perfectly well without hygiene and proper regimen as long as dyspepsia and nerves and rheumatism were not too pressing in their attentions. And he could, of course, trust his family to run itself without any great amount of attention from its natural head.

His family *had* run itself for twenty odd years. It had gone on its scattered way rejoicing—after the good, new, Western fashion which finds the unit of society less in the family than in the individual; and now a very promising young filly, after having "run" herself for a good part of this twenty years, was on the point of taking the bit between her teeth and of running away altogether. The family carry-all, whose front seat he had left in order that he might irresponsibly dangle his legs out from behind, was in danger of a runaway and a smash-up, and he was forced to the humiliating expedient of installing a more competent driver than himself in his own place behind the dashboard.

Ogden slid rapidly along the narrow aisle which ran behind the row of coops that confined the tellers, and found Fairchild going over yesterday's balances with the general book-keeper. Here he was intercepted by the last of the messengers, who had had some delay in getting his batch of drafts and notes arranged properly into a route.

He was a boy of seventeen, with a pert nose and a pasty

complexion. He had put on his hat with a backward tilt that displayed his bang. He was the son of a millionnaire stockholder, and was on the threshold of his business career. He panted for consideration, and he had found, during an experience of six months, that most consideration was to be won from the newest men.

"What's up now, George?" he asked, familiarly. He twitched his narrow little shoulders as he teetered back and forth on his toes. "Old man on the rampage some more? He's had it pretty bad for the last three weeks."

"Oh, get out!" Ogden responded briefly.

Fairchild was a man well on in the fifties. He had a quiet, self-contained manner, a smooth forehead, a gray moustache. His general trust-worthiness was highly esteemed by Brainard, who generally treated him with civility and sometimes almost with consideration. He had his privileges. A member of the board of directors in the Brainard interest, he would be given the opportunity to resign whenever some especially dubious piece of business was looming up, with the certainty of re-election within the year. He was too old to tear himself up by the roots, and too valuable to be allowed, in any event, the radical boon of transplantation. Of course he paid for such a concession; he acted as a buffer between Brainard and the more pathetic of the stockholders, and now, as we see, he was summoned to deal with a domestic crisis.

"My dear girl," Ogden presently heard him saying in a dry, cautious, and yet somewhat parental tone, "you know what his position is. Not in the church; no, I don't mean that. He is only a policy clerk in that insurance office, at ten dollars a week, probably—hardly enough for him to live on decently, alone. Yes, I know he gets more from the choir, but even that—"

Ogden stopped one ear by propping his elbow on his ledger and putting his hand to his head, and went on with his writing as well as he could. But he had left the Underground for St. Asaph's; he was busy no longer with notes for collection, but with the notes—the melting tenor notes—of the all-admired Vibert. His fellow-clerks noiselessly retired, and a long train of choristers slowly made their way through the long aisle the others had left vacant. Among them Vibert—tall, dark, hard, and cruel; an angel, possibly; but if so, surely one of the fallen. And a little girl of eighteen, whose blue eyes showed out from under her fluffy blond locks, and whose lips were parted in a radiant, reverent smile, steadied a trembling hand on the back of a pew and looked after him with a fond, open, and intense regard that was a perfect epitome of love.

Those same blue eyes were now on the other side of the partition, regarding her father's lieutenant with a look as bright and hard as was ever her father's own; and as she listened to the words of warning, those same full and pliant lips set themselves in a firm line that Brainard himself could not have made straighter or more unswerving.

"Nobody really knows," the cashier went on, "who his people are, or where he is from, or anything definite about him. He is one of thousands. Here is a town full to overflowing with single young men. They come from everywhere, for all reasons. They are taken on faith, largely, and are treated pretty well. Most of them are all right, no doubt; but others— Of course I know nothing about Mr.—about this one; but your own brother, now—"

"That's just what I tell her," broke in Brainard, with a distressful whimper. "Burt says, and he knows it's true, that—"

Ogden again stopped his ears. If by any possibility there was aught good under that chaste surplice, he would not wilfully deprive himself of any chance for belief. If that full neck and heavy jaw and sinister eye and world-worn cheek and elaborate assumption of

34

professional sanctity offered the slightest prospect of decent manliness and of happy home life, he would not allow one mere solitary phrase to shut that prospect out. But he could not shut out a disgust that gradually crept in upon him—a disgust for the man who would arrange the most sacred and confidential affairs of his family circle in the same general fashion that he would use for dealing with the concerns of an ordinary business acquaintance; a disgust for the family life in which such a state of things was possible. Had the girl no mother? She had, indeed; but that mother was an invalid—one who, with the advancing years, had come to know more and more of tonics and cordials, and less and less of her daughters' needs. Had she no brother? But what can a brother do?—order the intruder from the premises and intimidate him from returning, which Burt had done. Were there no friends or relations to see how matters were going and to speak out their minds boldly? But whenever has such a course availed? The friends cease to be friends, and the relatives are relatives at a greater remove only, and all goes on as before. No; there was only one way to settle this affair—the "business" way; and that way Brainard took—necessarily, instinctively.

He had never lived for anything but business. He had never eaten and drunk for anything but business—his family shared his farm-like fare and his primitive hours. He had never built for anything but business; though constantly investing in grounds and buildings, he had occupied his own home for fifteen years as a tenant merely, before he could bring himself to a grudging purchase. He never dressed for anything but business—he had never worn a dress-coat in his life. He wrote about nothing but business—his nearest relative was never more than "dear sir," and he himself was never otherwise than "yours truly"; and he wrote on business letter-heads even to his family. And now that the present domestic difficulty was to be adjusted, no other method was

35

available. But he had the satisfaction of feeling that his daughter was meeting him in his own spirit and on his own ground.

She eyed him with a cold and direct gaze like that of the sun which is setting in a clear winter sky. Not a single cloud-shred of affection showed itself in the wide expanse of crisp and tingling atmosphere which she seemed to have created about her; not a particle of floating vapor helped to diffuse a glow of sentiment over a situation which had much need of some such softening influence. Her fierce little glance tore down every scrap of reverence, of home love, of filial duty: life had never seemed to him quite so bald, so unfurnished, so bereft of unbusiness-like non-essentials.

"I shall marry Russell," she declared, "in spite of you and in spite of everything. You may say that he has no money, and that you don't know his family; and Burt may forbid him the house and go prying into his private affairs; and you may say that he has no friends and no abilities, and as much more as you please. I don't care; I shall be his wife. I won't believe any of these things, and nobody shall separate us."

She rose, flushed and frowning, and walked out firmly. Fairchild opened the opposite door and moved off quietly to his own place. Brainard brushed aside a pile of abstracts and mortgages that encumbered his desk, found an opening big enough for his elbow, and leaned over his blotting-pad with an air of utter dejection and defeat.

IV

On the twelfth floor of the Clifton—at the far end of a long corridor—is the office of Eugene H. McDowell, real estate.

Ogden, at the beginning of one of his brief noonings, took the elevator up to the quarters of his coming brother-in-law.

He found McDowell stretching himself violently in his swivel chair, which was tilted as far back as its mechanism would permit; his head was thrown back, too, as far as anatomical considerations would allow. His eyes would have seen the ceiling if they had not been so tight shut; his Adam's apple appeared prominently between the turned-down points of his collar. His desk was strewn with a litter of papers, and the tassels depending from his map-rack began a trembling at varying heights as Ogden closed the door behind him.

"Waugh—oo!" yawned

McDowell, with his mouth at its widest. Then he let his chair down, all at once. "Oh, it's you, George, is it?"

He used the careless and patronizing freedom of a man of thirty odd to another several years his junior—of a man in business for himself to a man in business for some one else—of a man who was presently to undertake the protection and support of the other's sister.

"Sit down." He motioned Ogden to a chair which stood close to the window—a window that looked out on the court and that commanded the multifarious panorama of daily business going on behind the ranks and rows of great glass sheets which formed the other three sides of the enclosure—the ends of over-crowded desks, the digital dumb-show of stenographers, the careful handling by shirt-sleeved clerks of the damp yellow sheets in copying-books, the shaking fingers and nodding heads that accompanied the persuasion and expostulation of personal interviews.

McDowell presented a physiognomy that seemed to have been stripped of all superfluities. He contrived to avoid the effect of absolute leanness, yet he was without a spare ounce of flesh. His cheek-bones did not obtrude themselves, nor were his finger-joints unduly prominent; yet his trousers seemed more satisfactory as trousers than his legs as legs, and his feet were in long, narrow, thin-soled shoes, through whose flexible leather one almost divined the articulations of his toes. His hair had shrunk back from his forehead and temples, but his moustache sprang out as boldly and decidedly as if constructed of steel wires. His nose was sharp; his eyes were like two gimlets. The effect of his presence was nervous, excitant, dry to aridity. He had a flattish chest and bony shoulders; his was an earthly tabernacle that give its tailor considerable cause for study.

"Your friends called again this morning," he began, folding up two or three documents and thrusting them into the pigeon-holes before him. "We have had quite a session. But they're fixed finally. Does that cousin of theirs live with them?"

"Cousin? Isn't she their sister—sister-in-law?"

"I mean the other one; Miss—Bradley, isn't it?"

"Oh! Well, no; she comes in and stays with them a week now and then. But her people live in Hinsdale."

"Hinsdale; nice country around there. Seems as if you just had to get outside of Cook County to find anything hilly or even rolling. I'd like to take it up first rate. The minute you are over the county line you get clean out of all that flat land and everything's up and down—like around Worcester. But I don't believe they save much on taxes."

He tore some pencilled memoranda off the top of a pad and threw them into the waste-basket.

"Yes, the sister-in-law was here, all right enough. She's a pretty smart woman, too; got a good deal more head than any of the rest of them. She's striking out a little late, but she may make something of herself yet.

"But she wants to get that poetical streak out of her," he went on. "What was it she said, now? Oh, yes; all this down-town racket came to her like the music of a battle-hymn. Our hustling, it seems, resembles a hand-to-hand combat from street to street—she lugged in mediaeval Florence. And to finish up with, she told me I was like a gladiator stripped for the fray." He ran his hand down the stripes of his handsome trousers. "What did she mean by that? Was it some of her Boston literary business?"

He lifted his hand and thoughtfully twirled the scanty locks over one of his ears.

"Here's a letter I got this morning from Kittie."

He drew out a small folded sheet from the bottom of a pile of correspondence. "She has about come around to my way of thinking. There don't seem any very good reason for my travelling away down there again, especially when your father and mother are going to move out here anyway. I'm awful busy. She'll have her own family at the wedding, then, and she'll give me a show to scare up some of mine. Things are just too rushing—that's the amount of it."

"I'm glad to have it settled one way or another," George said. "And how about that other affair—have you made any report to father?"

"Yes. That's as good as settled. The deeds are all made out; they've only got to be signed." He reached into one of his pigeon-holes and brought out a bulk of bluish paper whose fractious folds were held in some shape by a wide rubber strap. "Here's one of the abstracts—just come in. The other is a good deal longer and the copy isn't finished. I suppose they'll put that one on a board."

He snapped the band once or twice and put the abstract back again.

"I'm glad," he said, "that your father has finally decided to pull up altogether and to transfer everything to the West. That old block of his was wanting repairs all the time; I don't believe it paid him four per cent. It takes more than soldiers' monuments and musical festivals to make a town move."

George felt his heart give an indignant throb. He seemed to see before him the spokesman of a community where prosperity had drugged patriotism into unconsciousness, and where the bare scaffoldings of materialism felt themselves quite independent of the graces and draperies of culture. It seemed hardly possible that one short month could make his native New England appear so small, so provincial, so left-behind.

"You've got to have

snap, go. You've got to have a big new country behind you. How much do you suppose people in Iowa and Kansas and Minnesota think about Down East? Not a great deal. It's Chicago they're looking to. This town looms up before them and shuts out Boston and New York and the whole seaboard from the sight and the thoughts of the West and the Northwest and the New Northwest and the Far West and all the other Wests yet to be invented. They read our papers, they come here to buy and to enjoy themselves." He turned his thumb towards the ceiling, and gave it an upward thrust that sent it through the six ceilings above it. "If you'd go up on our roof and hear them talking—"

"Oh, well," said George; "hadn't we better get something to eat?"

"And what kind of a town is it that's wanted," pursued McDowell, as he pulled down the cover of his desk, "to take up a big national enterprise and put it through with a rush? A big town, of course, but one that has grown big so fast that it hasn't had time to grow old. One with lots of youth and plenty of momentum. Young enough to be confident and enthusiastic, and to have no cliques and sets full of bickerings and jealousies. A town that will all pull one way. What's New York?" he asked, flourishing his towel from the corner where the wash-stand stood. "It ain't a city at all; it's like London—it's a province. Father Knickerbocker is too old, and too big and logy, and too all-fired selfish. We are the people, right here. Well, Johnny, you hold the fort," he called to a boy who was dividing an open-eyed attention between this oration and his own sandwich; "I've got to have a bite myself."

"How are you getting on downstairs?" he asked, as they tramped over the tiles of the long corridor towards the elevators. "I hear you were over at Brainard's house last night—he's a fine bird. And his son is like him. He's got another, hasn't he—a younger one? In the bank, isn't he? Used to be. Well, he might be without your

41

knowing it. Queer genius—his father don't know what to do with him. He's kind of in the background, as it were. How did you happen to go over there?"

"Papers to sign. Mr. Brainard was at home, sick. It was something that they could hardly give to any of the boys to manage. I met his other daughter."

"Other? Didn't know he had any. Got two, has he? And two sons. Well, he's a great old father, from all I hear, and I shouldn't—D—ow—n!"

But the elevator was too far past them to return.

"Here's another coming," said George, to whom the indicator showed that a cab had left the top story and was half way down to their level.

Ogden had now gone through a novitiate of five or six weeks. After his first wrench—from the East to the West—his second one—from the West Side to the North—seemed an unimportant matter. He had learned his new neighborhood, had made a few acquaintances there, had become familiar with his work at the bank; and the early coming of his own family, who had elected to swell the great westward movement by the contribution of themselves and all their worldly goods, helped him to the feeling of being tolerably well at home. From the vantage-ground of a secure present and a promising future he became an interested observer of the life that swept and swirled about him. He found that there might be an inner quiet under all this vast and apparently unregulated din: he recalled how, in a cotton factory or a copper foundry, the hands talked among themselves in tones lower than the average, rather than higher. The rumble of drays and the clang of street-car gongs became less disconcerting; the town's swarming hordes presently appeared less slovenly in their dress and less offensive in their manners than his startled sensibilities had found them at first; even their varied physiognomies began to take on a cast less comprehensively cosmopolitan. His walks through the streets and his journeyings in the public conveyances showed him a range of human types completely unknown to his past experience; yet it soon came to seem possible that all these different elements might be scheduled, classified, brought into a sort of *catalogue raisonné* which should give every feature its proper place—skulls, foreheads, gaits, odors, facial angles; ears, with their different shapes and sets; eyes, with their varying shapes and colors; hair, with its divergent shades and textures; noses, with their multiplied turns and outlines; dialects, brogues, patois, accents in all their palatal and labial varieties and according to all the differentiations in pharynx, larynx, and epiglottis.

He disposed as readily of the Germans, Irish, and Swedes as of the negroes and the Chinese. But how to tell the Poles from the Bohemians? How to distinguish the Sicilians from the Greeks? How to catalogue the various grades of Jews? How to tabulate the Medes, and the Elamites, and the Cappadocians, and the dwellers from Mesopotamia?

During the enforced leisure of his first weeks he had gone several times to the City Hall, and had ascended in the elevator to the reading-room of the public library. On one of these occasions a heavy and sudden down-pour had filled the room with readers and had closed all the windows. The down-pour without seemed but a trifle compared with the confused cataract of conflicting nationalities within, and the fumes of incense that the united throng caused to rise upon the altar of learning stunned him with a sudden and sickening surprise—the bogs of Kilkenny, the dung-heaps of the Black Forest, the miry ways of Transylvania and Little Russia had all contributed to it.

The universal brotherhood of man appeared before him, and it smelt of mortality—no partial, exclusive mortality, but a mortality comprehensive, universal, condensed and averaged up from the grand totality of items.

In a human maelstrom, of which such a scene was but a simple transitory eddy, it was grateful to regain one's bearings in some degree, and to get an opportunity for meeting one or two familiar drops. It had pleased him, therefore, to find that Brainard's house was in the neighborhood of Union Park and in the immediate vicinity of his own first lodgings; and when he went over there with his documents in his pocket he appreciated the privilege of ringing the bell of a door behind which were one or two faces that he might recognize.

The Brainards lived on a corner, and the house was so set as to allow a narrow strip of yard along the side street. It was built in the yellow limestone which used to come from quarries at Joliet, and the architect had shown his preference for the exaggerated keystones that had so great a vogue in the late sixties. The house had a basement, and above the elaborate wooden cornice there was a mansard with several windows that were set in a frame-work of clumsy and pretentious carpentry. Behind the house was a brick stable; it had been built of cheap material and covered with a cheaper red wash. The dampness of the lower walls had caused this wash to discolor and then to fall off altogether. Around the premises there ran an old-fashioned iron fence; it stood on a stone coping that was covered with perpendicular streaks of yellow rust. In the yard a meandering asphalt walk led past a few lilacs and syringas, which were looked down upon by a painful side porch that nobody ever used. The walk in front of the house was of stone; that at the side was of plank and showed three long lines of nail-heads.

The interior, so far as it came under Ogden's notice, was furnished with a horrible yet consistent simplicity. The large rooms were set sparely with chairs, tables, and sofas that represented the spoil of Centralia, and there were few modern additions to

44

introduce discords. An ideal sculptured head, placed on a marble pedestal swathed in a fringed scarf of saffron silk and set between the lace curtains so as to show from the street, would have ruined the effect both within and without. Perhaps the same might be said of any other house.

Brainard himself was not visible; he was only audible. His deep voice came in a sort of deadened growl through the closed door of a small side room; and mingled with it were the querulous tones of a woman's voice—an elderly woman, a woman in poor health, a woman whom some sudden and distressful stroke had brought to the verge of tears.

The house had been built in the primitive days when local architecture was still in such exact accord with local society that anything like graded receptions was undreamed of. Everybody who seemed too good to be kept waiting in the hall was shown into the front parlor. This room had a carpet whose design was in large baskets of bright flowers, and a ceiling that was frescoed in a manner derived from a former style of railroad decoration. This scheme of decoration centred around a massive and contorted chandelier with eight globes. Nobody had ever seen the whole eight "going" at one time. Lincoln and his family were on one side of the marble mantel-piece; Grant and his family on the other.

It was in this room that Ogden was received by the elder daughter of the house. She seemed a quiet, self-poised girl, four or five years the senior of her sister. She amply filled her gown of gray woollen; her hair was drawn back from her forehead and made a knot just above the nape of her neck. She had a pair of cool, steady gray eyes. She appeared wholesome, stable, capable of keeping herself well in hand.

"My father isn't able to see you," she said; "but if you will give me what you have brought I will take it to him."

There was a tremulousness in her voice, quite at variance with her manner and appearance. She put out her hand with a wavering motion; the flaring of the gas in her face seemed to strike her with a positive pain.

A door opened suddenly and her brother Burt came in. He was a stocky young man three or four years older than Ogden. He seemed stuffed with importance both present and future, both personal and parental—he was himself and his father rolled into one.

"Abbie," he said, in a sharp, curt way, "I wish you'd find father the copy of that report you made for him yesterday." He looked at Ogden in a fashion that changed the young man from a person to a thing. "We have been looking for you some time," he said. "I'll take those papers myself."

He spoke in a way that was abrupt and autocratic. Ogden recognized it as the utterance of a masterful nature, but he was unable to see that the masterful nature was moved by an emotion that must be controlled and concealed. His indignation made no allowance for this, and his subsequent ten minutes of solitary reflection left a bitterness that passed away but lingeringly. More and more, with every moment of this short wait, did he feel himself a gentleman turned into a lackey by his inferiors.

There was no salve for his wounded sensibilities save, perhaps, in the look of dumb expostulation which the girl cast upon her brother and in a few commonplace words which she addressed to their caller before she went out.

"Kindly wait a few moments, and the papers will be ready to take back. Perhaps you will find this other chair more comfortable."

It was after this fashion that he first met Abbie Brainard; met her—as he reported it to

46

McDowell—and hardly more. He followed his brother-in-law into the elevator and they dropped swiftly to the ground floor. At this level is situated the Acme Lunch Room.

V

McDowell took a cup of tea and an expeditious doughnut standing, and hurried away. Ogden, who had not overcome his habit of leisurely eating, lingered behind.

The Acme occupies a square, low-ceiled room in the hindermost corner of the Clifton: perhaps, with a lower ceiling and a situation on a level lower still, it would have been called the Zenith. It is fitted up with three or four oval counters, and a very close calculation of space allows room for an infinitesimal cashier's desk as well. Each oval encloses a high rack that is heaped with rolls, buns, and cakes, and close to each rack stands a brace of big, cylindrical, nickel-plated tanks that yield coffee and tea. Each oval is fringed with a row of stools—hard-wood tops on a cast-iron base; and in warm weather a pair of fans, which are moved by power supplied from the engine-room, revolve aloft and agitate the stifling atmosphere.

Ogden had spent the past week in

trying a succession of dairies, lunch-rooms, and restaurants, and had ended by returning to the Acme, which seemed as decent and convenient as any. He found a place in a quiet corner; ordered his coffee, wheat-muffins, and pie, which all came together; and fell to work with his eye soberly fixed on the shining expanse of the freshly-wiped counter. Was he consistent, he wondered, in claiming any great consideration until he could lunch at a higher figure than fifteen or twenty cents?

The girl who had waited on him turned away, but another one, who stood a little distance off, called her back.

"Here, Maggie, change that mince. This gentleman don't want a piece with a whole corner knocked off."

Ogden buttered his muffin without raising his eyes. The second girl herself placed the new cut of pie before him and stood looking down upon him. The hour was a little late, and but three or four customers held places around the counters. Presently she spoke.

"Well, Mister Ogden," she said, with a humorous tartness, "you don't seem to recognize your old friends."

Ogden threw up his head. "Why, Nealie, is this you!" he exclaimed. It was a girl who had helped wait on table at his West Side boarding-house.

She wore a dark dress with a plain white collar. Her brows made two fine straight lines over the yellowish green of her eyes. She had a strong, decided face, yet there was a certain lurking delicacy in the outlines of nose and chin.

"That's what," she replied. "I've made a change, you see. Been here pretty near a week. Come in often?"

"I'm in the building. What was the matter with your other place?"

The girl hitched up her shoulders.

"The fact of it is, I couldn't get used to it. Never tried anything like that before."

She looked about cautiously and then resumed in a confidential voice,

"To tell the truth, I was just forced into it. Pa and ma didn't want me to come to Chicago, but I couldn't make out that I was going to have any terrible great show there in Pewaukee. I didn't s'pose it was going to be so awful hard to find something to do in a big place like this. But I made up my mind, all the same, that I wasn't going to cave in and go back to Wisconsin—not straight off, anyway. Kept right on trotting about. Any port in a storm, says I. And when I met that good old soul in the intelligence office, that settled it. She only wanted a second girl; but I thought I could stand it."

"Couldn't you?"

"I didn't tell ma, though, that I was living out. I wrote to her that I was clerking—ten dollars a week. Ten dollars!—I'm looking for the girl that gets more than six. I don't know what the folks would have thought if they'd known of me a-being ordered around by a lot of young fellers—run and fetch and carry for a parcel of strangers. It don't come natural to me to be bossed, I can tell you."

"But Mrs. Gore used you well?"

"She did, for a fact. But it wasn't the sort of thing I wanted at all. So I told her I guessed I'd go. 'Well,' says she, sort of resigned like, 'if you've made up your mind to, you must, I s'pose'; she was sorry to lose me, I know. She walked to the basement door with me to say good-by—with her specs on top of her head. 'Be a good girl,' says she, 'and let us hear from you'— 'most exactly what ma said when I came away. Gray hair, just like ma's, too. 'Yes, ma'am,' says I. I didn't say 'ma'am' because I thought I was a servant—I wasn't; but because she was older and because I had a respect for her. And so I *shall* let her hear from me; when I get along a little further I'm going to call on her. And I'm going to get along, let me tell you; I haven't jumped on to this hobby-horse of a town just to stay still."

She nodded her head with great decision.

"It broke her all up when you went away," she resumed. "She kept a-wondering for two or three days what the matter was. Poor soul, she's a good deal too tender for this town. What was the matter?"

"Nothing. I had friends in a different part of the city."

"In a different paht of the city," she repeated. She spread her palms far apart on the inner edge of the counter and brought her face down almost to a level with his. "D'you know, I always liked the way you talked; it's real genteel. And you say 'cahn't,' too. And 'dinnuh' and 'suppuh.' Hardly anybody says 'cahn't' around here—except actors. Say, I went the other night. It cost fifty cents; but I was just wild to see a real out-and-out city show—couldn't hold in any longer. They all talked kind of artificial, except one man. He had a bad part—erring son, sort o'. He talked right out in plain, every-day style, and he was about the only one I really cared for. Of course, though, I don't like bad men better than good ones. But your way is nice, after all."

"Thanks."

"Well, I'm in a different par-r-t of the city myself." She gave a comprehensive glance over the sizzling coffee-urns. "Second in command." She tapped her breast-bone. "I don't think so everlasting much of Duggan here, but he recognizes talent. It didn't take him long to find out what I was and he raised me. I boss and help around when there's a rush, and now and then I take the cashier's place. It's all just like a store. Oh," she proceeded, after a shrewd look at him, "I know well enough what you've been thinking all this time. But here's your counter and there's your goods; and people just say what they want and get a check for it and pay at the door. No boarding-house in that, is there? They don't bulldoze *us* very much."

The door opened and a belated clerk came in.

"Here, Gretchen," she called to one of her force, "see what this man wants." The new-comer dropped mechanically on to one of the stools and submissively took the damaged pie that had been taken away from Ogden. He had ordered apple.

"Most of 'em are tractable enough," she commented.

"I've got ten girls here," were her next words, "and they're quite a fair lot. But that moon-eyed German girl over there—"

"Gretchen?"

"I *call* her Gretchen; she don't look as if she knew beans, does she? Well, she don't. She was going on in the pantry yesterday about the rights of man. I knew she was due to break a saucer pretty soon. Well, she did. And we've got a Swede girl here who would be the best all-around one of the lot if it wasn't for her temper. All of a sudden she gets mad and she stays mad, and you can't for the life of you find out what it was that made her mad. Those three Irish girls are pretty smart. H'm, yes; they were rigging up a strike Tuesday. They wanted fifty cents a week more. They found out their want at a quarter to twelve. 'All right, girls,' says I, 'you can go out if you want. Our regular people will kick and go somewhere else for a few days, perhaps; but the first rainy noon they'll all come in again, and they'll see that things are running all right with a new crew, and after that they'll stay.' Goodness me! I've heard more about rights and less about duties this last week than I ever did before in my life. My uncle says it's the same with him. He's the engineer here. He really got me this place. If you look down through that grating out there as you go along you may see him. It's talk and argue all the time—his men have more half-baked

52

notions than you can think of, and he's kept on the k'jump all the time looking after things. Do *I* kick? Do *I* squeal? Not much. And if I had come in from outside with a different language, maybe, and a different training and a different set of notions, and if I had been a real, dyed-in-the-wool, down-trodden peasant and all my folks the same for nobody knows how far back, perhaps I'd find some reason there for not keeping abreast with the tolerably smart lot of people that had let me in."

She cast a lofty eye over her various underlings. "Kind of a plain lot, ain't we? You know there's one place like this in town where they won't take a girl unless she's pretty. Their cashier is a regular bute. But I wouldn't work in such a place; no, indeed."

She paused. Ogden made no response. She eyed him with a sharp impatience.

"Not but what I could, though, if I had a mind," she remarked, with a vindictive little explosion.

"No, I couldn't, either," she added suddenly; "they're all brunettes this year."

And she laughed forgivingly.

"And you don't see me a-wearing rings and chains," she pursued; "I guess not. And I sha'n't, either, until I finish my course."

"Course"? Was she hinting at the close of her earthly career?

"Yep. Shorthand. But don't hurry away." He had dropped his feet to the floor. "Duggan went right off after the rush, and I guess I've been hard pushed enough to enjoy a little restful conversation. Shorthand and type-writing—that's what I'm steering for. I'll stand this for a while—until I can do eighty words. I've begun at the Athenaeum already. I don't see why anybody should want to take 'lessons' in typewriting; it's practice you want. Same with the other. Well, I'm practising hard enough. I-shall-be ready for b-usiness in-three-months," she traced with her finger on the counter, giving considerable pressure to the "b" in "business." "I'm ahead of the class now."

"I'm educated, too," she continued. "I taught school one term up in Waukesha County. I know how to spell—you ought to see how some of those girls write out their notes. And I can punctuate—semicolons just as easy as anything else. Say, do you know Mrs. Granger S. Bates?"

"I've seen her name in the papers," said Ogden, emptying his glass and feeling in his pocket for his handkerchief.

"Sorry we don't give napkins. Well, she was a school-teacher, and look at her now. I went by her house on Calumet Avenue last Sunday. She's got about everything. She is one of the patronesses of the Charity Ball. Still, I suppose she must be getting along in years—her husband has come to be the Lord High Muck-a-muck of Most Everything; I've read about him for years. Hope I haven't got to wait till I'm fifty to have a good time."

Ogden was shuffling his feet on the floor.

"Won't you have another piece of pie? No? Well, try a cream-puff, then; it'll be my treat. And do take time with it. Anything but fifty men eating away like a house afire."

Only one other customer remained. The Swede girl began to collect the cream-jugs.

"I don't care so extra much about Mrs. Bates, though. But there's Mrs. Arthur J. Ingles, three-hundred-and-something Ontario Street—do you know her? Now there's a woman that interests me. She's in the papers every day; she goes everywhere. She's 'way up, I guess; I'd be wild if she wasn't. She was at a dance last Tuesday, and she gave a reception the day before, and her sister is going to be married next month. It's easy to follow folks since the papers began to print their names all bunched up the way they do, and Mrs. Arthur J. is one that I've followed pretty close. She must be young—I never see his name except with hers. I guess he's just a society dude. Well, dudes are all right; you've got to have 'em in a big town. You wouldn't have the whole million and a half of us be grubbers?"

"I suppose not."

"She gave a dinner last week. Covers were laid for ten—what does that mean?"

"Probably that she and her husband had eight people."

"She wore heliotrope satin. Ornaments, diamonds. Great, wasn't it? One of our girls brought down a book this morning about Lady Guinevere. Guinevere—your grandmother! What are we to Lady Guinevere, or what is Lady Guinevere to us? But when it comes to people living in your own town, why, that's getting down to business."

"Yes, let us talk about realities—Balzac."

"I should say so," she assented, missing the allusion. "Now then, why shouldn't *I* be wearing heliotrope satin to dinner some time?—if not under the name of Cornelia McNabb, then under some other as good or better. Anyway, I'm going to keep my hands as nice as I can; a girl never knows what she may have a chance to become. I don't imagine it will disfigure me much to run a typewriter. Dear me," she sighed, "how much time I've lost! If I hadn't been such a darned goose, I might have begun Pitman at home a year ago."

She reached down under the counter and pulled a newspaper up out of a dark corner.

"Some lunch-rooms have papers around—as many as a dozen, sometimes; but Duggan says this place is too cramped for him to give people any inducement to dilly-dally. It's eat and run. So I have to buy my own. This is the first chance I've had to look at it. I wonder what she's been up to now."

She opened the paper and ran down its columns with an expert eye.

"Yes, here she is, first pop. *Mr. and Mrs.*—Cluett, Parker, Ingles. My sakes, how I envy that woman! Course I don't want that she should come down here and wash my dishes, but wouldn't I like to go up there and eat off of hers! What did she wear?—it don't tell. Where was it?—at Mrs. Walworth Floyd's—a small dinner. Don't know them. How about the *Misses?*—Jameson, Parker, Wentworth—she's a great goer, too. And here are a few *Messrs.*—Johnson, J. L. Cluett, George Ogden—"

She stopped abruptly.

"You?"

There was a world of reproach in her voice.

"Yes."

"And you sit there and never let on! You're as mean as you can be. What is she like? Tell me, do. Ain't she young, now? What did she wear?"

"I didn't go. I had a trip to the West Side."

"Your name's here."

"The reporters get the names in advance. Sometimes they copy them from cards or regrets."

"And you wasn't there?"

"No."

"Too bad! But you've seen her?"

"Never."

"How hateful! But you was really invited?"

"Yes."

"H'm!" she said deliberately; "I see now why you moved. I don't blame you. I'm trying to get along, too. We're both in the same boat."

Ogden rose.

"What else is there?" she asked herself, looking over other columns. "Here's a marriage; it's in Milwaukee. Don't know whether it's a society item or not. Who are they?—J. Russell Vibert is the man, and Mary Adelaide Brainard is the woman. Both of Chicago—know 'em?"

Ogden sat down suddenly.

She eyed him curiously.

"That's the first sign I've seen that you was willing to stay a single minute longer than you had to. You can go now, whenever you want. We've got to clean up. So long!"

VI

Ogden had been balked in his first social advance by the inconsiderate and unwarranted demands of the Brainards. He failed on Proposition No. I., but its attendant corollary he disposed of after the proper interval. He had missed the dinner, but he accomplished the dinner call.

He was moving around his room in his shirt-sleeves; he had the leisurely air of one whose social orbit was so small as to involve no relations with the courses of cabs and of street-cars. To set himself right with the Floyds he had but to step around the corner.

His room was rather small and cramped, but he had preferred indifferent accommodations in a good house to good accommodations in an indifferent house—just as he would have chosen an indifferent house in a good neighborhood to a better house in a poorer one. His quarters, however, were well enough for a single young man of moderate pretensions. He had space for a three-quarter bed, a bureau, a wash-stand which displayed a set of pink-flowered crockery and two towels, a cane-seated chair, and a pair of book-shelves on the wall. And by means of a good deal of dexterous manoeuvring he contrived to extract some comfort from an undersized rocker. His decorations were principally photographs, which showed to the extent common under the circumstances. Some of these were grouped in twos and threes, in frames faced with Chinese silk; they helped to achieve the disordered and over-crowded effect that the present taste in house-furnishing aims at, and can always accomplish in a back hall bedroom.

The photographs stood in the position in which he had first placed them a month and a half ago, although the recent arrival of several of the originals had given their shadows an altered importance. Everybody knows of the inertia that overtakes decorative detail, even when portable. There were the pictures of his father and his mother, arranged in a pair. His father offered a placid, gray-bearded face; it seemed rather forceless, though that effect may have been due to retouching; yet, independent of any practical processes, it was the face of a man who obviously could not have risen in advance to any adequate conception of the Western metropolis.

The face of his mother was serious, strenuous. She had in some degree the semi-countrified aspect of one who has run a quiet course in a quiet quarter of a minor town.

His sister's picture had been taken in the East just before her starting for her new home. It was now in the hands of Ogden's next-door neighbor, who had come in carrying a choice of white ties, and who now wove around it a contemplative cloud of tobacco-smoke from his briarwood pipe. He was a young man with a high forehead and a pair of shrewd but kindly brown eyes.

"A mighty pretty girl," Brower said, heartily.

"Get the right kind of a New England face, and you can't do much better. I must haul out my own photographs and fix them up some time."

Brower kept his collection in his trunk, along with his shirts and underwear generally. He used his bureau drawers for collars and cuffs, and for a growing accumulation of newspapers, magazines, and novels. He had been in the house two years, yet his trunk had never been unpacked and put away. He was an adjuster for an insurance company, and was subject to sudden calls to remote localities, in accordance with the doings of the busy monster that the press knows as the "fire fiend." If Isaac Sobrinski, off in Des Moines, had the misfortune to be burned out, at the close of a dull season or in the face of brisk and successful competition, then Des Moines was the place to which Brower immediately posted. He estimated the damage on the building, figured the salvage on socks and ulsters, and endeavored to decide, so far as lay in his powers, whether the catastrophe had been inflicted by Providence or had been precipitated by Sobrinski's own match-box. However, he never carried anything except his valise on such excursions; the general state of his trunk is to be accepted simply as the mental index of a constant and hurried traveller.

"Yes, she's a mighty pretty girl," he repeated, thoughtfully. "Where have they gone?"

"Oh, not far. There's been a good deal of travelling done already. They just went up to Milwaukee; Eugene had something to see about there. They'll be back to-morrow, I expect."

"Milwaukee, eh? That's come to be quite the fashion, hasn't it? Some folks go there after they're married, and some of them to *be* married. We had one in our office a week or two ago; Vibert—have you met him?"

"It's in your office he is, then, is

it? No, I've never met him. I've seen him and heard about him. Is he much thought of?"

"Well, the office doesn't have a great deal to say to a man as long as he keeps hours and attends to his work—when the position isn't responsible, I mean. What are you looking for—whisk-broom? Here; I'm sitting on it, I guess."

"I suppose he does attend to his work?"

"Oh, so-so; but a little break like that doesn't help a man any. He struck high, didn't he?"

"Yes."

"Wonder what he's got to keep her on. Great question—all that; ain't it? She's a rich girl, I hear. Subject for debate: is it safer to marry a rich girl or a poor girl—for a young man in moderate circumstances, I mean?"

"Oh, dear," said Ogden, sitting down on the edge of the bed, helplessly; "if you're going back to *that* chestnut!"

"Well, it's timely," rejoined Brower, knocking the ashes of his pipe into the cover of the soap-dish; "and always will be. Pro: if the girl's rich, she'll have had things, and got used to them, and perhaps tired of them. If the girl's poor, she'll be ravenous after her long starve-out, and will expect her husband to feed her with everything."

"Lay on."

"Con: if the girl's rich, she'll expect all the comforts and luxuries she has been used to at home. If she's poor, she'll have had some sense ground into her; she'll know how to manage and contrive. So there it is. What's your idea?"

"No general rule. Depends on circumstances."

"What does?"

"The girl. To begin with."

"The girl depends on circumstances. And after?"

"After? Oh, then circumstances depend on the girl."

"H'm! Can't lay down any general law—same as with little Johnny. Pshaw! You go to the foot."

But they both agreed on one point, as young men always do when they discuss this standard subject: they stood together on the assumption that such a venture concerned only the two people primarily involved.

Brower preceded Ogden into the hallway; he stood with the toe of one slipper on the heel of the other. "Well, remember me to the swells."

"Oh, shucks!" said George, turning back and laughing.

He walked down and out rather sedately, and picked his way over the muddy sidewalks with his thoughts fixed on the two recent marriages. That in his own family had just occurred under such disadvantages as must prevail in a disorganized household, and with the infliction of such discomforts as will sometimes be undergone by people who, while not in society, still feel impelled to have such a function proceed after the fashion that society prescribes. Kittie Ogden was duly married, then, with a certain regard to cards, carriages, caterers, and the rest; and the feast was graced by a number of McDowell's family and friends—people of a fairish sort, who called for little comment in either way. At least, little comment was bestowed by Ogden, whose principal thought was that his sister was now the wife of a fellow of some means and ability, and who felt that it would not come amiss to have a good business man in the family.

At the Floyds' he found the other wedding the subject of much comment, more or less discreet. On the other hand, the affair in his own family received but a mere civil mention; the Ogdens, he felt, must be only an insignificant little group, after all. Must they—must he—always remain so?

The Floyds occupied a snug little house which filled a chink between two bigger and finer ones, and commanded a view of the back yard of a third, which was bigger and finer still. Mrs. Floyd had lately begun to fill a chink in the social world as well, by having an "evening." She had approached the idea with a good deal of deliberation, and she had achieved something very small and quiet. She overcame her husband's weakness for knowing people and inviting them to the house; she was not after a deluge, but a drop; and if her tardy distillation did not equal the perfumes of the fragrant East, still it was the best result to be arrived at under the circumstances.

He found the Fairchilds there, and he came upon Fairchild and Floyd smoking, *sub rosa,* in a secluded corner of the library, which was furnished in a sombre and solid fashion. In the Floyd family the household divinity was the lace-curtain, whose susceptibility to offence from the fumes of tobacco is well known; her high-priestess was Mrs. Floyd, and her chief victim was Walworth. Associated with the two smokers was young Freddy Pratt, whose solicitude regarding Brainard's mental state on the occasion of his daughter's call at the bank has been already touched upon, and who was now puffing a cigarette with a learned and expert air. This attitude was displeasing to Ogden, who was perhaps over-disposed to feel official differences on social occasions; but no oppressive sense of his own subordinate rank troubled Freddy Pratt, who had but a feeble and intermittent realization of the orders of the business hierarchy, or indeed of anything else.

"It was a matter that concerned just her and him," Fairchild was saying as Ogden entered, with a contemplative regard fastened on the lengthening ash of his cigar. "It was nobody else's business."

He stopped. He had

spoken in a low, quiet voice, but he had conveyed unmistakably the presence of quotation-marks.

"I called on 'em the other night," volunteered Freddy Pratt, unabashedly. His perky little nose was tipped in the air, and his eyes were closed to the two fine slits that denote the complete enjoyment of the smoker. "I wasn't going to stand off. They're at the Northumberland—big name, but not much else. Ragged matting in the halls, and the janitor didn't look very slick. I guess they've rented ready furnished. Mayme was real glad to see me. But *he* was rather grumpy, I thought."

"Everybody ought always to be glad to see *you*, Freddy," smiled Walworth, with a caressing irony.

"I suppose," resumed Fairchild, thoughtfully, "that the human family will always go on considering a wedding as a joyous occasion. It always has; it always must—hope springs eternal."

Ogden wondered what other view there might be to take. Everybody had seemed lively and happy enough when Kittie was married.

"But there's the other side—the side that turns to view with a consideration of the complicated relations of a good many new and diverse elements—new people coming in. We had a case in our own family some years ago, when my young cousin married. Poor Lizzie; she is dead now. Her father died six months before her and left a good deal to be divided up. Her husband was trustee for the boy after she herself went, and he made us a good deal of trouble. He had his eye on the estate from the start, and more than his share in the handling of it. There were a good many meetings in lawyers' offices—more trying that the courts themselves. There was a good deal of money lost, and there is a good deal of feeling that will never be got over. He traded on his wife's memory all through. Yet the family welcomed him very cordially and trustfully; we thought the poor girl was going to be so happy. She was; she never knew."

Ogden sighed; this was dismal matter.

"Oh, well," continued Fairchild, resuming his cigar, with an air of passing to lighter topics, "this can't apply here. All of us are happily married or are going to be—"

Freddy Pratt nonchalantly blew an ineffable smoke-ring across the room; Walworth slipped around the table to close the last inch of crack in the door.

"Oh, dear, yes!" he exclaimed.

"—and none of us are being troubled through relations by marriage."

The door was shut, but the penetrating voice of Ann Wilde came through it clearly, and Walworth winced.

"Oh, dear, no!" he protested.

"I should say not," chimed in Freddy Pratt, with his self-satisfied little ba-a.

The cigars were ending. "Come, let us go out to the others," said Floyd.

In the drawing-room Ogden presently encountered Jessie Bradley and her parents. The girl herself appeared as dressed as the occasion could warrant, but her father and mother wore the every-day habiliments in which he had first seen them, a fortnight before, on the occasion of a call at Hinsdale. They had an easy-going aspect, as if they hardly cared to put themselves out greatly. They were present in the triple capacity of relatives of the hostess, of suburbanites, and of body-guard to escort their daughter back home after another of her frequent visits in town, and their effect was quite provisional and transitory.

Mrs. Bradley was a pleasant woman whose face was full of the fine lines of experience and whose hair had thinned greatly without changing its dry, sandy brown. She wore an old-fashioned tortoise-shell comb. She met Ogden here precisely as she had met him in her own house. He noticed presently that she treated everybody else in exactly the same fashion, and he learned subsequently that she had, practically, one invariable manner for all times, places, and people. It was a manner that he found very quiet, simple, straightforward, and friendly. It showed that she valued herself, and was also disposed to accord a good value to anybody else. It seemed to say, as plainly as words: "The Lord is the maker of us all; so let's have no more fuss about it." It was the good American manner in full bloom.

Her husband had a jovial eye, a grizzled moustache, a rotund, polished forehead, and cheeks that hung downward fatly into his big, round, short neck. He appeared to have valued his peace of mind sufficiently to preserve it and to be satisfied with the moderate success that comes from moderate effort. He wore a short-waisted, double-breasted frock coat, and there were no wrinkles in it, either front or back: he would have found it impossible to thrust his plump hand in between any two of the buttons.

He was given in the directory as "Bradley, Danl. H., secty. and treas. Darrell & Bradley P't'g & Lith'g Co." He had been one of the organizers of the corporation, but had since yielded the lead to others of more push and means. He had a moderate salary and a small block of the stock. Since he was assisting the business as an officer, rather than directing it as an individual, he had little personal annoyance from typographical unions and from the paper manufacturers' trusts. As for "pi" and proofreaders' errors, matters which have a power to make some men agonize, he merely laughed at them. The concern, besides its central establishment, had a few retail branches placed here and there through the business district; one of them, on the ground floor of the Clifton, supplied the La Salle

Street banks and insurance offices with ledgers, ink, and blotting-pads.

He had an acre of ground and a two-story frame house at Hinsdale, and Ogden remembered the small green-house where he fed his craze for chrysanthemums.

"We have come to take our girl back home," he said to Ogden as he laid his plump hand lightly on his daughter's shoulder. "That is, if she can make up her mind to go with us."

"Just us two all alone in the house," added her mother, with a humorous pathos. "No chick nor child."

Jessie laughed and shook out a bit of her frivolous finery. Her face had a tired look, but motion seemed more restful to her than rest itself.

Ogden canvassed the three. Whence could this girl have got her supple leanness, her light, gay, rapid, incisive air, her aspen-like quiverings of nervous force? Not from her parents. From the March winds, perhaps, that sweep down from Mackinaw, over the limy and choppy expanse of Lake Michigan; from the varied breezes, hot and cold, that scour the prairies on their way from scorched-up Texas or from the snow-fields beyond Manitoba.

"Not even a relative," pursued her father; "not one in all the country round—except Frances. All our people are down East," he continued, addressing Ogden more directly. "They write every so often to learn if we are millionnaires yet. We always have to say 'no,' and that discourages them. They stay where they are."

"But Jessie goes around to look after them," contributed her mother, with combined complacency and reproach. "She goes to Pittsfield and Nantucket and everywhere. People are beginning, now, to ask her up to Wisconsin, summers. And sometimes Florida."

The girl shrugged her shoulders in a fidgety fashion.

"Oh, well, mamma," she said, "I have to circulate. Let's circulate some now," she suggested, turning to Ogden. "I'll be ready to go when you are," she called back to her father.

VII

"We have been expecting to see you out at the house again," she said to the young man, as they settled on the stairs. They were seated just below the landing. Her dress, trimmed with silver braid and little groups of flaunting bows, grazed his knees; he could number every stone in the rings that crowded her long, thin fingers. "We didn't suppose a matter of eighteen miles would scare you."

"It doesn't. But you're never home."

"Oh, yes, I am—once in a while. When you do favor us again, get a time-table for the next time after. I never heard of the 'Q.' charging anything for them."

"I will."

"Awfully sudden about Mayme, wasn't it?" she said, with a suddenness of her own. "I didn't suppose it was going to end like that—at least, not right away. I dare say you have been noticing how Cousin Frances looks at me, every now and then. You might think I was the one to blame. She's been talking to mother about it to-night—and me. I guess I'm going home all right enough."

"Don't you want to?"

"Oh, I don't mind. But what's the dif.—far as Mayme is concerned, I mean? She was bound to have him; she wouldn't have anybody else. It was their affair, wasn't it? Well, then, why not let them manage it?"

"I suppose so," assented George, dubiously.

"Her father won't see her, I hear. I'd like such a father. Her sister can't do anything with him."

"Her sister?"

"Yes; she's got about as much influence as anybody. Have you seen her?"

"Yes. Are you very well acquainted with her?" he asked.

"Not very. She belongs to the next older generation."

"How much older? Two or three years?"

"Twenty or thirty. She's about the same age as her mother. But more useful. Mayme thinks everything of her. She's a good, steady, plodding stay-at-home. She ought to have been let out and given a show—she's buried there. He makes her do lots of work."

"Her father?"

"Yes. She writes and figures a good deal of the time. She keeps the grocer's and butcher's books, for one thing. Mayme says she knows how to telegraph—they've got their own wire right to the house. When she wants dissipation she goes to her 'Friendly.' And she belongs to a club over there where they read papers and discuss. She was a good deal upset."

"Um," said Ogden,

abstractedly. He recalled the girl's appearance and her little ordeal of having to face a complete stranger at so distressful a juncture. Yet she had borne herself with dignity and composure; nor was he able to deny that she had been as perfectly courteous as her brief appearance permitted. Now that he understood, he had less cause for complaint against her brother, and none at all against her.

He dwelt lingeringly on the idea of "a complete stranger." He did not feel that it would have been infinitely more trying to face a curious neighbor. He had begun to idealize the ordeal and the victim of it.

"A penny for your thoughts," he presently heard his companion saying. He came out of his study and looked through the stair-rail at the little throng below. Two gentlemen had just come out of the dining-room.

"I was wondering who they were," he replied, at a venture.

"Who?"

"Those two."

The pair was followed by Walworth, whose pleasure it was to pour libations whenever the gathering of two or three together gave a pretext for that ceremony. One of the two sucked in his upper lip with due caution, and both united in a pretence—decent, but slight and futile—that the ladies knew nothing of these hospitable doings.

"The tall, brown one is Mr. Ingles. Haven't you met him here before?"

She indicated a man of forty, whose face was shaven except for a small pair of snuff-colored whiskers, and whose mouth made a firm, straight, thin line.

"Ingles? Arthur J.?"

"I don't know; I guess so. He owns the building—the Clifton."

71

"He's no dude," murmured Ogden to himself.

"Eh? Who said he was?"

"Oh, nobody. Who is the other?"

"That's Mr. Atwater—Mr. Ingles's architect. They're chums; were in college together. Isn't he the most fascinating-looking man you ever saw?"

"By Jove, he *is* distinguished, for a fact! Was he born—here?"

"Don't you think it's lovely for a man of his age to have gray hair—gray that's almost white? I shall do all I can to make *my* husband gray-haired before he is middle-aged!"

She laughed at her own audacity. He turned about and stared at her, and she laughed more heartily yet.

"And don't you like the twirl of his moustache? Or would you have preferred him with whiskers?—cut in a straight line right across his cheeks, with the corners near his mouth rounded off—but not too formally. And do you notice the bridge of his nose and the air it gives him? And his eyes—wait till he turns around; there, did you ever see such a hazel? He seems to have everything—youth, experience, style, family;—why did you ask if he was born here?" she demanded suddenly.

"Did I? I must have meant—is he going to die here?"

"Why not? You don't suppose that men of talent are going to leave Chicago after this?"

"Do you expect to provide them with careers?"

"I don't see why we shouldn't. We're on the crest of the wave, and we're going higher yet. From now on anybody who leaves us is likely to be sorry for it."

Ogden looked back

at Ingles; he stood in a doorway, between Fairchild and Jessie's father.

"Is his wife here?"

"Oh, he isn't married, I don't believe."

"Not married?—Ingles, I mean."

"Oh! Yes, he's married."

"Is his wife here?"

"Dear, no; you have to speak weeks ahead to get her."

"He's the one, then," Ogden assured himself.

"Which one?"

"Her husband. Do you know her?"

"I've met her here." She leaned over the railing. "What are they all laughing about, down there?"

"Do you want to go and see?"

Mrs. Floyd and her sister had appeared in the doorway. Between them was a little girl of five; she had one hand in her mother's, and with the other she clutched a dilapidated doll. The child wore a guimpe and a prim little frock with puffed sleeves; she had long, smooth brown hair that turned thickly at her shoulders, and a pair of big, round, wondering brown eyes.

"It's Claudia," said Jessie Bradley. "Yes, let's go down."

Atwater had placed himself before the child, half crouching, half kneeling. He had the persuasive and ingratiating manner proper to a fashionable architect whose clients were largely women and wealthy ones, and he seemed willing enough to bring his batteries to bear on the tiny woman before him.

"Isn't it pretty late for dolly?

73

Oughtn't she to be put to bed in her own little house?"

The child looked at him soberly. "She hasn't got any house."

"Hasn't got any house?" He glanced at her father. " 'Oh, it is pitiful—in a whole cityful.' But if I were to say that I would make you one?" he went on; "one with four rooms. And windows in each room."

The child pondered, fixing a bashful look on his handsome face.

"Would there be stairs?"

"Yes."

"And closets? Mamma says we never have enough closet-room."

"That's right, Claudia," said Ingles, commendingly; "score the profession."

"Yes, closets, if you insist."

"And glass in the windows?"

"Yes. Dear me, they get more exacting with us every year!"

"And—and—" she rolled her eyes around the group, as if wondering whether any important detail had been overlooked—"gas-fixtures? Would there be one in every room, with four globes on it?"

"Perhaps."

"But don't charge the poor child a full commission on them," said Ingles, grimly.

"Ah!" murmured Atwater, with a world of meaning. "And if I were to promise to put a nice little red chimney on the roof—what would you say?"

The child clasped her doll firmly and looked down at the carpet. "I shouldn't know whether to belave you," she said, shyly.

74

There was a burst of laughter. "You dear little tot!" cried Mrs. Fairchild, gathering her up, on no very definite grounds, for a kiss. Her father laughed loudest of all, but her mother contracted her eyebrows in distress.-

"That dreadful Norah!" whimpered the poor woman. "She must go."

"Don't dismiss your *bonne*," laughed Atwater, thankful for the diversion; "she'll produce a beautiful accent in time."

"Well, after that," said her father, "I think our little McGintums had better retire. Say good-night, Claudia."

"Not yet," said Ingles. "Not before she has learned that she may have her doubts about a contractor, perhaps, but about an architect—never. Remember that great truth. Good-night, my child. Won't you kiss me?"

He lowered his face, but Claudia drew back. "I don't like whishky," she said, solemnly.

"For Heaven's sake, my pet," cried Floyd, "are you trying to start a panic? There's Norah; go—go."

"Good-night, Claudia," called Atwater; "we won't forget your house. Upon my word, Ingles," he went on rapidly, and with a face still slightly flushed, "I believe I shall have to reconsider that determination of mine I spoke to you about the other day."

"What's that?" asked Walworth.

"To give up sky-scrapers and to do nothing but colonial houses for the nobility and gentry. Sky-scraping is bad enough, but the demands of the modern house-builder are worse. Ingles, you're not as evil as I said you were; I'm sorry I ever called you a Philistine."

"Why did you do that?" asked Fairchild, amused.

"Because," answered Ingles, "I took two weeks to consider whether I could afford to let the Clifton have four good street-fronts."

"Didn't you say," demanded Atwater, "that you wanted to put up an architectural monument that would be a credit to the town? Would an eighteen-story flank of bare brick have been a pleasant object? Or, rather, is it?—for you see that sort of business all over the city. Heavens!" he went on, "we're doing some horrible things here, but we are not the ones who are altogether to blame."

"Who says you haven't done well with the Clifton?" demanded Ann Wilde. Most of the ladies had retired from these masculine topics, and huddled in a gossipy little group at the foot of the stairs; Ann had remained behind, as an owner of real property. "That system of elevators is the most magnificent thing I ever saw."

Atwater groaned. "That's all a building is nowadays—one mass of pipes, pulleys, wires, tubes, shafts, chutes, and what not, running through an iron cage of from fourteen to twenty stages. Then the artist comes along and is asked to apply the architecture by festooning on a lot of tile, brick, and terra-cotta. And over the whole thing hovers incessantly the demon of Nine-per-cent."

"A slap at me," said Ingles.

"It's enough to make you wonder whether Pericles ever lived. I doubt if he did," concluded Atwater.

"Are you the only sufferer?" asked his client. "How many of our sub-contractors failed?"

"Two."

"How many times were we set on fire by salamanders?"

"Three."

"How many drunken night-watchmen were discharged?"

"Four or five."

"How much of the tin-work did you condemn?"

"Lots."

"How many of the contractors suffered a penalty for over-time?"

"Too many."

"How many times did carpenters wreck plaster-work?"

"Fifty."

"How many times did plasterers ruin wood-work?"

"A hundred."

"How many men were killed or injured?"

"Thirteen."

"Thirteen!" cried Ann Wilde; "how horrible!"

"Then you don't encourage building," commented Bradley; "and Mr. Atwater wouldn't encourage young men to go into architecture."

"As engineers, not as architects," replied Atwater. "Or shall I say—as constructionists?"

"Good word," murmured Ingles.

"Thanks. I've got fifteen draughtsmen up under the roof of the Clifton. When a new one comes, I say, 'My dear boy, go in for mining or dredging, or build bridges, or put up railway sheds, if you must; but don't go on believing that architecture nowadays has any great place for the artist. There won't be another Fair until long after you are dead and gone.' "

"I think I've had one of your young men with me lately," Bradley said. "He told us that he had been designing labels out at the Stock Yards, but had been in your office before that. Art may cover a wide range, you see," he said, laughing.

"Yes? What is his name?"

"Brainard, I think. He was a dark young fellow. He looked a little dissipated, it seemed to me."

"That's the one," said Atwater. "Now there's a case. That boy's father has treated him shamefully. He might have been made something of. He had a decided taste for drawing, and hardly any other. I won't say he had any great ability, but that wouldn't have mattered so much with training. However, he had no training to speak of, and we couldn't use him. He hasn't got the slightest faculty for business; they wouldn't have made a teller out of him in twenty years. But that was what they tried to do, and when it failed—"

Fairchild gave a delicate little cough.

"You don't have to listen, Fairchild," said Atwater. "Neither does Mr. Pratt, unless he chooses."

Fairchild withdrew a little from the group and stood with his hands behind his back, while the toe of his boot moved the corner of a rug to and fro over the polished floor. Freddy Pratt held his place, but moderated his show of interest. Ogden followed this new recital with a curious concern.

"His father lost all patience with him," Atwater went on. "Naturally, such a father would with such a son. He's altogether out of the family now. Is he with you yet?" he asked Bradley.

"We had him for a while, but he was pretty irregular and unreliable—I never knew why until now. He was pretty shabby, too. I guess he was about grazing bottom most of the time. I never knew what Brainard he was."

"Anyway, he seems to have made a good try," said Ingles. "I suppose he'll live on post-obits, now, and go to the dogs as fast as possible."

78

"If he's let go his hold lately," declared Atwater, "it's on account of his brother. Everything's done for him; he is just run right ahead. Do you know," he continued, dropping his voice and glancing aside towards Fairchild, "that Brainard has just pushed that Burt of his into the vice-presidency? Right over everybody. I don't see how Fairchild can stand it. And what could be better calculated to infuriate the other one—what is his name?—Marcus. I'd take to drink myself."

Ogden listened to all this, and was swayed accordingly. His brief, fluttering attempt to idealize Abbie Brainard ended, and he saw her only in the cold, garish light of crass reality that was beating down so fiercely on the rest of the family. He had been meditating on calling upon her at her father's house, moved by the kind of sympathy that anticipates an invitation, or does without one; this project he now determined to abandon.

VIII

McDowell had not quartered himself on the twelfth floor of the Clifton—as distinguished from the eleventh or the thirteenth or any other—by a mere chance. He had not been influenced by any finicky consideration of light, prospect, ventilation, or nearness to the elevators. His sole reason for selecting room number 1262 was that room number 1263 was occupied by Arthur J. Ingles, the owner of the building.

Ingles occupied a very small room, upon whose door was his name—his name and nothing more—in very small letters. The next door beyond was lettered "Office of the Building," and this second room had communication with the first by a door between. None of these three doors, however, had as much interest for McDowell as the one between his own office and the private office of Ingles. This door was closed, but it was McDowell's dream and ambition to see it open. In his thoughts he constantly saw it standing ajar in an intimate and friendly fashion, while he and Ingles and other magnates of Ingles's ilk circulated through it freely and all did business together.

Up to the present time this door had never been opened, nor had McDowell ever had access to the other suite except by the farther door, through which tenants passed to request repairs or to pay their monthly rent.

Ingles was enough of a lawyer to be a real-estate man, and enough of a real-estate man to need to be a lawyer. He supervised the drawing of his own deeds and leases, and seldom took counsel in matters between landlord and tenant. As a landlord, he had found it advantageous to divest himself of his soul by making the Clifton into a stock company; he himself held all the shares but five. He had an extraordinary faculty for keeping himself out of the papers; but this did not prevent McDowell from knowing that he was constantly engaged in enterprises of the first magnitude, and he felt that association with this great capitalist would be immensely to his own advantage.

But he had accomplished only one step that might be reckoned an advance: he had undertaken the financial arrangements connected with St. Asaph's choir. This was a large, well-trained body, and was provided with all the expensive paraphernalia of a "high" service. It included four or five tenors and basses who commanded rather good salaries, as well as an expert organist and an experienced choir-master who commanded larger ones. The management had been by committee, and several of the pillars of the church, Ingles among them, had learned the difficulty of mediating between music, money, and ritualism. A member of a previous committee had delighted in translating and adapting Latin hymns for Christmas and Easter, and in putting his hands into his pockets now and then to make good a small deficit in the budget. Ingles and his compeers were ready enough to put their hands into their pockets, but they were glad, one and all, to escape the details of administration.

It was here that McDowell stepped forward; he cynically acknowledged that religion must be made to play into the hands of business, and he justified himself to himself by many good arguments. The details of the new dispensation were arranged in a down-town office. McDowell had tried to contrive that that office should be Ingles's own, but the meeting was held, after all, in another tall tower a block or two down the street, and Ingles himself was not present more than ten minutes. McDowell regretted this; he felt very well disposed towards Ingles. He would have done almost anything for him—for a commission.

But McDowell did not push this choir matter to the neglect of his own proper business. He was engaged at about this time with a new subdivision out beyond the South Parks. He had bought up a ten-acre tract, which he himself acknowledged to be rather low-lying, and which his rivals, with an unusual disregard of the courtesies of the profession, did not hesitate to call an out-and-out swamp. He had mended matters somewhat by means of a dam and a sluice, which drained off a part of his moisture on to grounds lying lower still—other men's grounds; and on the driest and most accessible corner of his domain he had placed a portable one-story frame shanty which had already done duty on other subdivisions, and alongside of it stood a tall flagpole which flaunted a banner with his own name and number on it. This tract, by the way, had absorbed some moderate portion of Ann Wilde's hoarded savings.

A week of rainy weather now and then would lay a complete embargo on McDowell's operations in this quarter. His plank walks would float off in sections; the trees along his avenues would sag deeply into the slush and would sway sidewise, in spite of their networks of rusty wire; and the cellars of the three or four unfinished houses that he had artfully scattered through this promising tract would show odds and ends of carpenters' refuse floating around in muddy water a foot deep. It was an appalling spectacle to one who realized the narrow margins upon which many of these operations were conducted, or who failed to keep in mind the depths that human folly and credulity may sound.

"Oh, it's all right enough," McDowell would say. "It's going to dry up before long."

Occasionally it did dry up and stay so for several weeks. Then, on bright Sunday afternoons, folly and credulity, in the shape of young married couples who knew nothing about real estate, but who vaguely understood that it was a "good investment," would come out and would go over the ground—or try to. They were welcomed with a cynical effrontery by the young fellow whom McDowell paid fifty dollars a month to hold the office there. He had an insinuating manner, and frequently sold a lot with the open effect of perpetrating a good joke.

McDowell sometimes joked about his customers, but never about his lands. He shed upon them the transfiguring light of the imagination, which is so useful and necessary in the environs of Chicago. Land generally—that is, subdivided and recorded land—he regarded as a serious thing, if not indeed as a high and holy thing, and his view of his own landed possessions—mortgaged though they might be, and so partly unpaid for—was not only serious but idealistic. He was able to ignore the pools whose rising and falling befouled the supports of his sidewalks with a green slime; and the tufts of reeds and rushes which appeared here and there spread themselves out before his gaze in the similitude of a turfy lawn. He was a poet—as every real-estate man should be.

We of Chicago are sometimes made to bear the reproach that the conditions of our local life draw us towards the sordid and the materialistic. Now, the most vital and typical of our human products is the real-estate agent: is he commonly found tied down by earth-bound prose?

"You fellows," said Floyd to McDowell, during one of Sister Ann's sessions, "are the greatest lot I ever struck." He spoke in a half-quizzical, half-admiring way, and showed some effort to handle the language with the Western ease and freedom of those to the manner born. "Do you know, when I had been here three or four months some fellows took me with them to the banquet of the Real Estate Board. Well, it was an eye-opener; I never saw anything like it. It was Chicago—all Chicago. Heavens! how the town was hymned and celebrated! It was personified—"

"That's right," said McDowell.

"And glorified—"

"Of course."

"And deified—"

"Why not?"

"Why not, indeed?" cried Ann Wilde. "I haven't been around much yet, but you strike me as the most imaginative lot of people I ever saw."

"Whenever Chicago is involved," amended Walworth.

"Sure."

"How you idealize it!" cried Ann, enthusiastically. "How you—"

"It needs to be idealized—and badly," said her sister.

But McDowell's interests in the southern suburbs as well as at St. Asaph's were soon set aside by another matter; domestic interests claimed his attention.

His father-in-law had now passed some two or three months in Chicago. He had entered the city without any conception of its magnitude, and he had remained in it without rising to any conception of its metropolitan complexities. He had made a change that was too great and too late. He made but an ineffectual attempt to connect and identify himself with the great rush of life going on all about him. He came down town almost every day to spend an hour or more in McDowell's office, where he took a certain satisfaction in following out the intricacies of the local topography by passing a thin, blue-veined hand over McDowell's maps and his canvas-bound books of plats. McDowell treated him with considerable patience and with as much respect as was due to a man who had no great experience in real estate and little aptitude for learning. One day old Mr. Ogden, who apprehended the lake winds little better than the local "lay of the land," took a slight cold in returning home from the office; two days after pneumonia developed, and within a week he died.

George undertook the charge of such arrangements as recognized the old New-Englander as a dead man merely, and McDowell subsequently took charge of those which recognized him as a dead property-owner. First, the funeral; afterwards, the Probate Court.

A funeral is more disagreeable than a wedding, chiefly because its multifarious details make their demands with but a scanty notice in advance. All of these details George was now called upon to face and to dispose of.

He squared his jaw, set his eyes, put a cold, heavy paving-stone in place of his heart, and met these details one by one. It was a man's privilege.

Brower went with him to the undertaker's, and mediated between grief and rapacity.

"Be careful here," Brower said to him in an undertone. They were in a room where sample caskets stood on end against opposite walls and were let down one by one for the inspection of purchasers.

"They always show the most expensive ones first. Don't look at these. You don't need to pay a hundred and fifty dollars. You can select a suitable one for eighty or ninety—perfectly good and no loss of respect."

"How about the outside box?" asked the man in due course. He was in his shirt-sleeves and wore a high silk hat.

"Here," whispered Brower, "you'll have to take the most expensive. It's chestnut—fifteen dollars. Nothing else but plain pine for a dollar fifty. Shameful, isn't it?"

Brower arranged for the handles and the plates. He also met the family at the railway-station next day, and saw the casket put on board the east-bound express.

He and George were walking slowly up and down the platform alongside the train when a man in blue overalls leaned out of the door of the baggage-car and called to them. He held a paper in his hand.

"This ain't quite regular," he said. "Our road is pretty strict. The air-tight casket is all right for inter-state travel, but the doctor hasn't signed this certificate."

George turned on Brower with a look of anguish.

"Here!" cried Brower, stretching up his hand. "How forgetful of me! I'll sign it now. Go along, Ogden."

The man hesitated. "Not contagious?"

"Certainly not. Hand it down. Got a pencil? There! Here's a two. Take extra care."

The dead man's son paid for the music and flowers, his wife and daughter folded away his clothes, and his son-in-law undertook to see his estate through the courts.

"I don't believe you'd better pay the doctors and undertaker yet," he counselled. "Let them file their claims with the Probate people. It doesn't cost but a dollar, and if you pay without, you might be liable over again—you are on other claims. I'll keep a general eye on matters, of course, but questions will be coming up all the time. I don't know but what we'd better have a lawyer first as last. The Probate arrangements are different now from what they used to be—more expensive, for one thing. Now there's Freeze & Freeze—they're as good as any, and they're right there in the Clifton, George, only five floors above you."

"Have we got to go into this thing right away?" asked George, as if in physical pain.

"Oh, no. Wait a few weeks—wait a month, if you like."

"Yes, we'll wait," he sighed.

McDowell made no opposition to his wife's suggestion that her mother now come and live with them. He had not anticipated his mother-in-law as a member of his own household; but he liked her well enough, and he generally treated her with a dry and sapless sort of kindness. Besides, he looked on domestic arrangements as a mere incident in business life, anyway. George, who for some time had been anticipating a home with his parents, could not find an equivalent in a home with the McDowells, and he remained with Brower on Rush Street.

There was no will; the recasting and consolidation of the small estate had required too much time and attention to leave much for any thought of its redistribution. Mrs. Ogden went into court at the proper time and qualified as administratrix. She was a figure-head, of course. She signed various documents at George's instance; George himself was guided by McDowell, principally; and McDowell got a point, now and then, from the attorneys. However, the legal labors of Freeze & Freeze on the Ogden estate were chiefly clerical; this did not prevent them from charging like chancellors and chief-justices.

These charges and others were paid by McDowell, who began informally by giving checks on his own private account. He came to receive, too, most of the rents and other payments, which were more conveniently made to him in his own office than to George in the office of the bank. And since he paid the estate charges out of his own private account, it seemed natural enough that his own account (which was with the Underground) should receive the sums coming in. This arrangement came about gradually, without receiving any formal acquiescence; but George appeared satisfied with the business capacity of his sister's husband; while his mother was an inmate of her son-in-law's house, where inquiry and explanation were easily enough made.

These details, once in hand, appeared to give little hinderance to the course of McDowell's regular business. His acquaintances in his own line noticed its increasing spread, and agreed among themselves that he was flying a little high for a man of his limited resources. He had more work for the surveyors and sign-painters, and he presently added a clerk or so to his office force.

Various small claims were filed in the Probate Court and were allowed. "I think," said George to McDowell, "that we'll use Kastner's rent for them. To-day is the third; he has been in, I suppose?"

"He'll have to be punched up," replied McDowell. "It doesn't do to give them any leeway."

"He has always been prompt on the first," said George, somewhat annoyed.

The next morning

he entered the paying-teller's pen for a moment, as occasionally happened. His eye chanced to alight on the balance sheet that ran from L to Z.

McAvoy, Louis M. 81.93
McCloud, Peters & Co. 1187.25
McDowell, E. H. 0

"How's this, Jo?" asked Ogden. "What's the matter with McDowell?"

       "Pulled out yesterday," responded the payer, briefly.

IX

McDowell's defection from the Underground was presently followed by an addition to its working force. One morning, a month or so later, Ogden, in an interval of leisure, glanced across to the window before which Burton Brainard had railed in his desk, and saw a young woman within the enclosure. She sat there alone, before a desk of the peculiar kind that has been contrived for the typewriter, and her effect at the moment was that of leisure finally and elegantly achieved.

He was at once struck by her peculiar facial expression; she had one eye open and the other shut. All at once she effected an instantaneous change which closed the open eye and opened the closed one. Then she opened both and gave out a smile of recognition, surprise, and pleasure, which he now perceived to be the work of the features of Cornelia McNabb.

"Here we are!" she seemed to say.

She had followed Burt's elevation to the vice-presidency, along with the new desk and the handsome rail-work enclosing it. Burt's concerns, despite his rise in rank, were now, as heretofore, largely outside the bank proper; he did something in stocks now and then, and he kept the run of things on the Board of Trade. But he was like his father in looking upon the bank as a personal and family matter—a point of view which the action of the body of stockholders somewhat justified: as a general thing they made up a chorus that huddled in the wings—several of them declining to come "on" even for the election that advanced Brainard, Jr., to the second place. So he saw no very good reason why the bank generally should not foot the bill for his own clerk-hire.

"Why can't you use the man we've got here already?" his father had asked him, however. "Ain't one enough?"

"No. Somebody else has always got him. If I could have one for myself just for an hour or so, it would be a great help."

"Why don't you get one of those girls that circulate around upstairs? I hear there's one or two of 'em."

"I believe I will." And thus Cornelia McNabb came in for a brief daily attachment to the Underground.

She sat in her place quite unoccupied for an hour or so, looking about inquiringly, fidgeting a little, and watching the clock. Ogden glanced over in her direction once or twice. He saw that she had contrived to express her rise by several subtle alterations in her dress, and that she had succeeded in enveloping herself in a promising atmosphere of gentility. She, in her turn, kept an eye on him and contrived to time her own luncheon along with his. She thrust her hat-pin into place just as he buttoned on his cuffs, and she drew a black-dotted veil across the tip of her nose just as he was reaching up for his hat.

They sauntered out separately, but came together in the hallway.

"Do I look nice, or don't I?" she asked him, as she passed one of her gloves over the smooth surface of the massive marble balustrade. "You needn't think the Pewaukee girls are jays; they're too near Lakeside and Waukesha for that."

"You do, indeed. But where are the chains and rings?"

"Fiddle! I hope I know better than that, now."

The elevators were sliding up and down behind their gilded *grilles* with great rapidity, and hundreds of hungry helpers were stepping out of them in search of brief refreshment. Some of these stopped in the basement vestibule, and our young people, looking over the balustrade, saw them buying packages of cigarettes or the noon papers. There came to them, too, the voice of the man who stood at the foot of the elevator shafts and who regulated the movements of the various cabs by calling out their numbers with a laconic yawp. He wore a blue uniform with gilt buttons and he had a gold band on his cap. He was as important as Ingles himself—perhaps more so.

"I believe I'll go up to the restaurant to-day," said Cornelia, with a precious little intonation. Her mincing tone intimated a variety of things—altered conditions among them.

"I go up there occasionally myself," said Ogden. "You have entertained me several times downstairs, and you ought to give me my chance now, don't you think?"

"Quite happy, I'm sure," she murmured demurely.

"Up!" called Ogden, and up they went.

"Well," said Cornelia, a few minutes later, taking off her gloves with a self-conscious grace, and pushing aside her tumbler so as to find a place to lay them, "I can't say I've been overworked *this* morning. I haven't seen my new man at all."

"He's out a good deal."

"But the old one was on deck."

"In what way?"

"Oh, he put me through a regular drill. Made quite a number of remarks. I shouldn't care to take *him* down. May have to, though, if he gets too bossy. Eh?—oh, well, I don't know that I care for so very much, thank you. What are *you* going to have? Chicken-soup?—all right. Yes, chicken-soup, John."

She leaned back in her chair with a genteel grace, and looked out of the window down on the snow-piled roofs below.

"Do you know, I used to think I was a pretty smart girl, but I begin to believe I'm a good deal of a dummy, after all. That man has been in the building all this time, and I have just found it out."

Ogden's eye involuntarily followed the waiter.

"Not that black man—nix. But how could I be expected to spot his name among all the 'steen hundred on that bulletin by the door? I did see it there this morning, though—just by accident."

"Whose?"

"Oh, Ingles's. Arthur J. Ingles. Think of his being in this very building all this time!" She put the rim of her tumbler up under the edge of her veil.

"In it?" repeated Ogden. "He owns it."

"He does? Great Scott!" she choked and spluttered, setting her glass down suddenly. "Well, I'll be switched!"

She gave another

gulp. "I suppose his father willed it to him."

"No; he put it up for himself; I heard him say so."

"And you know him?" A new light shone in her brimming eyes.

"Yes."

"Well," she declared with emphasis, "now I see my way. He's got to have me do shorthand for him, and then I shall see—her."

"Ah!"

"Yes. Can't you tell Mr. High-and-mighty that you know a respectable girl who is trying to make her own living?" She ran her fingers over the edge of one of her cuffs, which was slightly frayed. "You see how poor I am."

George laughed. "The laundries *are* pretty rough, for a fact."

"How mean of you!" she exclaimed, and laughed too.

She thrust back her soup.

"I don't want it. I don't want anything. I can't eat a mouthful. Then I was wrong about his being a society dude?"

"Completely."

"And how is she? S'posing I've made a mistake about her, too?"

"I don't know, I'm sure. I've never seen her."

"You're telling me a fib."

"No, truly, I never have. I don't believe there's any such person. I think she's somebody that the papers have just made up. How many people have you found to work for?"

"Oh, three or four. But time for more. Rhyme, ain't it? I'm trying for the

Massachusetts Brass, but I'd rather get Ingles. She gave a dance at Kinsley's night before last."

"How many words can you do?"

"About ninety—enough for business; of course I couldn't manage courts or banquets or sermons. I expect she comes down to his office for a check every now and then. Why don't she ever have her picture in the Sunday papers?"

"O Lord! I hope they're above *that!*"

"What's the objection? I'd have mine there quicker 'n scat if I could. I will some time—bet you. And not in any office togs either."

"But don't dream of rivalry. She isn't real; she's only a beautiful myth. What will you take next—roast beef?"

"I don't mind; yes. When I'm alone I usually skip right from soup to pie—or pudding. But I guess I will take something a little solider this time; nothing makes me tireder than sitting still and fidgeting." She tapped her toes on the mosaic pavement, and gave a hitch and a pat to the dimity curtain alongside her. "I squirmed around for an hour, with a whole bookful of other people's notes that I might have been writing out. What sort of a young fellow is he?"

"He has his own way."

"Only child, I suppose?"

N—no."

"Only son?"

"No — yes — I don't know. How do you like your work?"

"Middling. I'm terrible enterprising, but I guess I was never meant for a drudge. Say what does a patroness really do?"

"Oh, nothing much; she just has her name on the list. Sometimes they don't even go."

"I notice that your Mrs. Floyd is beginning to be one; I've seen her in the papers two or three times."

"She doesn't like it, though; sometimes names get put on just to fill up. 'My dear Mrs. Floyd, we thought you wouldn't mind; you don't, do you?' they say. 'But my name in the papers,' she objects. 'You are too sensitive,' they reply. 'You've had your name in the papers at home,' her husband reminds her. 'Yes,' she answers, 'but—here!' She hates the town."

"Well, if I was a patroness I guess I'd have some say—no figure-head for me. I wouldn't be put on either; I'd put the others on."

"I see you were cut out for a 'society' career."

"I guess you've about struck it. I went to a dance a week ago to-night—Periclean Pleasure Party."

"Like it?"

" 'Twa'n't much. And I was invited to a fireman's ball—such impudence!"

"Right—don't cheapen yourself."

"I guess I understand that."

Meanwhile a nooning of a different character was going on in the director's room of the Underground. This is not to be taken as indicating that the green-baize plane of the long centre-table was littered with reports and memoranda, and that the high-backed, leather-seated chairs were filled with the solid figures of a dozen solid men. No; the aspect of the room was that of Sunday-like disoccupation, and the only people in it were an appealing young woman and a stubborn old man.

"Let her come in, father; please do."

"Take care, Abbie. You know what I think of you, but you make a mistake when you try this."

Abbie Brainard passed her handkerchief across her tearful face. Her father stood before her with his legs spread wide and his feet firmly planted; he had his hands thrust deeply into his trousers pockets. His jaw was set, and his shaggy brows were drawn down over eyes that glared fiercely at nothing.

"Then meet her out in the hall somewhere, just for a minute." She laid her hand tremblingly upon the old man's arm. He moved, as if to shake it off.

"Then just walk by outside; she can see you from the cab."

He turned his eyes upon her, half in expostulation and half in threat. "Abbie!"

"Then, father, just step here to the window; she'll see you and know it's all right. Come." She caught hold of a fold of his sleeve. "You won't keep her waiting out there such a cold day as this?"

Brainard moved his feet, but he turned his back on the window and fixed his eye on the fireplace. His daughter's light touch was quite powerless on his huge bulk.

"Father, you know Burt says—"

"Abbie," he interrupted sharply, "don't you say a word to set me against Burt. I won't hear it. Don't drag him in, or you'll be sorry for it."

"But, father, don't you understand? He *struck* her; there's a mark on her face now."

Brainard's great frame shook, but he made no other sign. This quiet she took as a favorable symptom. She would have done better in perceiving that he was between two contending forces so nearly equal as to hold him almost in equilibrium. The wretch had struck his daughter—a brutal, hateful thing as regarded his daughter or any daughter or any other woman; but his daughter had defied him, overridden him, and the man whom she had chosen for a master was now the instrument of her punishment. The accounts appeared to balance. However, figures do lie, and his own agitation indicated that the x of human emotion had not been completely eliminated from his problem.

He cleared his throat. "She has made her bed, Abbie," he said in a husky tone, "and now she must lie on it."

"No, father; you must hear what Burt says. He has had to go up there and—"

"Burt? Is that where he has been this morning? Has he turned against me too? Good God! what have I done to deserve such treatment as this? First it's Mark, with his drawing and his trying to play the fiddle; and then it's this pen-pusher that puts on those things Sundays and marches around singing songs; and now it's Burt, who's had every chance to make a good business-man of himself, and everything done for him. It's too bad; it's too almighty bad."

Abbie steadied herself against the corner of the table. Her breast heaved with fearfulness; she had never before openly protested to her father against himself.

"Why haven't you done anything for the others? Why didn't you give Mark an education?—the kind, I mean, that would have helped him, and the only kind. Why haven't you taken this Mr.—Mayme's hus—this man and made the best of it, and found something for him to do?—he can work in an office. Oh, father," she moaned, with a softening note of deprecation, "you have made it pretty hard for all of us."

"Abbie," he gasped, "are you turning against me too? Abbie, I've always thought so much of you, and I've done well by you. But I want you to go away—I won't see her. I won't. She must go away, and you too."

He caught her by the arm and tried to move her towards the door—gently, as if she might go of her own accord.

Ogden, on coming in from lunch, found himself intercepted by Freddy Pratt. This youth had a few moments' leisure, and he assailed Ogden between the wardrobe and the wash-stand.

"I went over to see the Viberts again; last night," he communicated. "Poor Mayme—I wasn't going back on her, if others did. She was sitting there all alone in the dark. I guess she had been crying. Anyway, when I lit the gas her eyes looked red. She wouldn't say much—"

"Good plan."

"And after he came in she wouldn't say hardly anything at all. Slow work talking to *him!* He wasn't drunk exactly, but he had been drinking; didn't need a light to tell that. I wasn't doing anything at all, and all of a sudden he blurted out, 'I say, you young fellow you, what do you mean by coming here and destroying the peace of a man's family?' You can bet I was taken back. Then he got up and came towards me—he looked big, too! 'You get out of here'—that's what he said."

"And did you?"

"Oh, yes, I got out," responded Freddy Pratt, with a meek complacency.

"You surprise me. You showed sense."

Freddy looked at him doubtfully. "I heard this morning that he had just lost his place with those insurance people," he resumed cautiously. "That was what was the matter, I guess."

"Possibly," said George, who had heard from Brower that something of the kind was likely to occur. The fellow's work had been done indifferently of late, and he was far from being worth the increased salary he had asked for.

As Ogden passed up to the other end of the office Brainard appeared in the doorway of the directors' room and beckoned to him. His face was pale and disturbed; the veins in the end of his nose showed redly; his eyes burned with an appealing fierceness.

"Ogden," he said, in a loud, hoarse whisper, "where is that type-writer girl? Tell her to bring some water here as quick as she can."

"She isn't here, sir; she has gone back upstairs."

"Then you get some yourself. Here; take this tumbler. Be quick, and don't make any fuss."

Ogden hastened to the wash-stand near which Freddy Pratt had detained him. Returning again, he saw through the half-open door that Abbie Brainard was lying back in one of the big chairs with her face pallid and her eyes closed.

Her father dipped two of his great clumsy fingers into the glass and made an awkward attempt to sprinkle her face. "My poor girl has fainted," he said.

The girl's eyes half opened; she seemed to see Ogden standing just outside.

She clutched both arms of the chair and raised herself half up. Her bosom heaved; her mouth was drawn tensely.

"Fainted?" she tried to say; "not at all!" She gasped once or twice and rose to her feet. "I never fainted in my life," she said grandly; "I never should think of doing such a thing!"

She reeled; her eyes closed. George rushed forward to catch her. Her hand dropped numb on his arm, and her head fell heavily on his shoulder.

X

Ogden and his mother were now beginning to have frequent conferences with regard to the management of the property and to McDowell's connection with the matter. Perhaps the word "conference" puts, however, too set and formal a stamp on the brief, hap-hazard interchanges of ideas that took place, as chance permitted, within McDowell's own house—a few words after a Sunday dinner or at the front door late at night. And besides being handicapped as to occasion, they were further hampered by McDowell's new relation to them and by their own presence under his roof. Besides, Mrs. Ogden, with a multitude of small experiences, had no ability for grasping things in a large and general way; while George, with a broader and more comprehensive outlook, was embarrassed by a lack of experience in the actual details of business transactions. Added to this, he was a new-comer, under all a new-comer's disadvantages; he hardly knew where to turn for the proper agents, legal or financial, that might have been employed;

while many of the agencies—courts, for instance—were different in procedure and even in name from anything he had known East.

"All the same, though," he said to his mother, "things ought to be in different shape for you. I'm bound hand and foot in that bank—no time or thought for anything outside. I don't know but what you'd better put everything with some good real-estate firm, and let them look after repairs and collections and taxes."

His mother fixed a pair of anxious eyes upon him, and the wrinkles of perplexity appeared on her forehead.

"Eugene is real-estate."

"Or those lawyers," he went on. "Anyway, you ought to have an account as administratrix with some bank. I believe I'll open one to-morrow. Something has got to be done to make things quicker and clearer."

He presently took upon himself the delicate task of intimating to McDowell that a simpler and more regular way of doing things was desired.

He went up to McDowell's office in the latter part of the afternoon. As he entered, a tall, dark man was standing in the middle of the room. There was a sinister look in his eyes and a contemptuously sarcastic smile on his heavy red lips. He gave a last fold to a small piece of paper that he held in his hands and thrust it into his vest pocket. It was Vibert.

"It's pretty near four now," he was saying to McDowell, "so I can't try again to-day; but I expect to find this all right after ten to-morrow morning."

He gave his hand a hardy flip across one side of his dark moustache and passed out. McDowell looked after him sourly. "Damn the brute!" he muttered.

As Vibert's words implied, he had been in McDowell's office once before on the same day. His salary at St. Asaph's now meant more to him than it had meant a month ago, and he had called with reference to it and to the delay in its payment. Hitherto, the financial arrangements of the church had gone on with the same precision as its anthems and its processionals. In the present condition of things delay to Vibert was more than a surprise, more than an embarrassment; it was an exasperation.

"I don't sing for glory," he had declared with an offensive brusqueness. "It's the here and not the hereafter that I'm busy with."

McDowell looked at him uneasily. "I'm going to fix up all the salaries next week in one batch. I don't see why any particular man should be favored."

"Favored!" repeated Vibert, with a loud insolence. "I should say not. I don't feel favored in running my legs off for money three weeks overdue. We can't live on air. We have bills to pay. We ain't singing for the pleasure of it."

McDowell contracted his eyes to a critical narrowness. "You may not be singing much longer for anything else, either."

"That's another matter; it isn't you that put the the choir together."

McDowell tapped his fingers on the yellow varnish of his desk. "I don't know about that. From what I hear, you're not making the sort of record for yourself that's useful in a church."

"My private life is nobody's business. I sing; I'm worth the money."

"That may work on the stage; it won't work quite so close to the pulpit. Come, now; I know a little something of your daily doings. Plenty of men sing who *don't* hang around race-tracks and loaf in pool-rooms. And, from what I hear, you're helping that young Brainard along at a good gait, too. You'd better wait—along with the others."

"Waiting be hanged! I'm here for money—money that's mine. If I can't work it with the man who pays out the loaves and fishes, I'll try one of the men that contribute them, in the first place." He tossed his head insultingly towards the door that led to Ingles's office.

McDowell's elbow rested on the edge of his desk (his thumb on the tip of his ear and his middle finger rubbing his farther eyebrow) as he looked out steadily on Vibert from under his hand. "Joseph," he called to his clerk, "bring me that check-book."

The man opened a lower drawer and brought out a book whose covers enclosed a number of stubs and three or four blank checks.

McDowell wrote and passed the check to Vibert, who went out with no further words on either side.

McDowell did some figuring and saw some people, and somewhat later Vibert returned. He threw his check on McDowell's desk contemptuously. "That's no good."

"How's that?"

"No account with 'em."

"No ac—oh, I see. We've changed banks, and I forgot to change the name in the check." He picked up a ruler and drew the red-ink bottle a little nearer. "I'll fix it. Sorry to have troubled you. We want to look out for this, Joseph."

Vibert withdrew, speaking the words that Ogden had heard on his entrance—words that would have been the reverse of assuring if he had fully understood them. "Bad egg," said McDowell to him, wagging his head in the direction of the just closed door.

George looked at him studiously. He appeared to be in a state of extreme nervous irritation. His wiry moustache moved up and down stiffly as he felt about with his teeth for the inner membrane of his lips. His long, lean fingers were interlaced, and a clicking sound came from his snapping his finger-nails together. It was clearly no occasion for more than a partial statement of Ogden's matter, and this was the most that he permitted himself.

But McDowell was in the sensitive state of mind when one word does the work of three, and in the irritable state of mind when talk is such a relief that three words evoke thirty in reply. He met George's brief and modest suggestions with a hitching of his shoulders, and answered them in a harsh and strident tone.

"The first thing in doing business," he said, "is to have an office to do it in." He looked about his own—his desks, his cashier's window, his letter-press. "And the second is to know how to do it." He looked out of the window in a wholly impersonal way, but his words had a more personal slant than he would have given them at almost any other time. "Gad knows I've got enough to do already, but Kittie's affairs are mine. She has equal interests with the others, and she seems to feel that I am able and willing to look after them."

He spoke with some show of reason, and George was obliged so to concede.

"There's taxes, for one thing. Or, take special assessments alone; they're almost a business by themselves. Say you've got ten acres or so just beyond the limits. Some fine day it's six hundred dollars or more for half a mile of sidewalk—a sidewalk that won't be walked on by seven people a week. What's the reason? Oh, some one of those township politicians or other has got a friend that's a carpenter. Now, who's going to tackle the boards and stave off such things?"

George looked at him silently.

"There's tax-sales— I guess you never went to one of them. You'd strike a bloodthirsty crew if you did. Supposing you've got a mortgage, and the mortgager don't come to time with his taxes? You've got to buy 'em up to protect yourself. And you've got to get there first. Last year I fought this point for a week with one of those tax-sharks. And so it goes. Real estate is no kindergarten business, I can tell you."

The truth of this view was becoming more and more apparent to Ogden. He withdrew, after some further parleyings, in a confused and inconclusive state of mind—well convinced, however, of McDowell's abilities and more fully conscious of McDowell's position as the husband of his father's daughter. Never did the town of his adoption seem less, indeed, like a kindergarten than when he took his way northward to dinner, or when, later in the early evening, he made his way over to the West Side to call at the Brainards. The thousands of acres of ramshackle that made up the bulk of the city, and the tens of thousands of raw and ugly and half-built prairie that composed its environs, seemed together to constitute a great checker-board over whose squares of "section" and "township" keenness and rapacity played their daring and wary game. And through the middle of the board ran a line, a hinge, a crack—the same line that loomed up in all those various deeds and abstracts of his with the portentousness and unescapability of the equator—the "line of the third principal meridian."

The Brainard house reared itself in the same frivolous ugliness that we have already viewed; but an excess of light came through the front parlor windows, and Ogden was prepared to find that at least four of the eight burners in the big chandelier were lighted. This turned out to be the case; it was as great a tribute as the family ordinarily paid to society. The family he found represented by Brainard, his wife, and his elder daughter; society was present in the shape of a young couple who were called Mr. and Mrs. Valentine.

The elder daughter received him with a quiet and simple cordiality. He could not help looking about furtively for the possible presence of the younger. He had not remained ignorant of her half-hour wait in a cab outside the bank; but he might have surmised the inflexibility of her father's will. The old man had refused to see her or to let her see him; the most that he would yield was a species of non-committal communication through Burt.

Mrs. Brainard presented herself to Ogden as a peculiarly faded and ineffective person; it was easy enough to grant her an abysmal incapacity. Her husband, in fact, had fallen upon her, crushed her, absorbed her—as a heavy blotting-pad falls on a page of light and delicate writing. Except for one thing she had no aim, no occupation, no diversion—beyond her ills and remedies. This was a penchant for chess. To those who object that chess is an intellectual game, one may simply put the question: have you ever seen it taken up by an elderly, invalided female who has rested content with a mere learning of the moves? It was thus with Mrs. Brainard; she played a good many games with herself every day, and they really soothed and rested her.

On the social board, however, she had hardly learned the first "opening," and the entertainment of the brilliant young couple now in her house fell almost altogether on Abbie; for the girl's mother sank back into a passive silence, while her father toured through the rooms occasionally, and threw out remarks, more or less a *propos,* in a gruff and abrupt fashion peculiar to himself.

His manner with young men had simply closed the house to them. To him it was an inexplicable and harassing thing that a young fellow of twenty-five should not possess the capacity, experience, and accumulations of a man of thirty-five or forty. He regarded every intruder in the light of a potential son-in-law, and no more potential than undesirable. Most of these callers would gulp down once, with such smile as they could master, the old man's abrupt ways and disconcerting comments; then they got out of the house in good order and never came back. However, at the present juncture he did not appear to resent Ogden's appearance—notwithstanding the young man's share in the episode at the bank; perhaps he looked upon him as a serviceable prop in another bad quarter of an hour.

"Yes, Mr. Brainard," Mrs. Valentine was saying, as George entered, "it's just as I have been telling Abbie; you ought to move over on the North Side, too."

Brainard happened to be passing through the room; it had occurred to him that he might turn down one of the side-burners in the back parlor.

"Um, no," he said, in an off-hand way; "too near the lake: fog; damp; rheumatism."

"And pneumonia too, perhaps," his wife suggested feebly.

"I'll risk it!" cried Mrs. Valentine, vivaciously. She had an expansive and affluent effect; she appeared mettlesome, decisive, confident. "It seemed to me that, so long as I was going to build, I might as well make a complete sweep—an out-and-out break. I've always had a fancy for that part of town. So I sent Adrian around to the different offices—"

She threw a look of passing reference towards her husband, who made a little bow in return.

"—and I had the good luck to get a lot on Bellevue Place—one of the last left, and only a block from the Lake Shore drive. Then I went to Mr. Atwater, and he has made my house a perfect little dream! I thought it best to have him to dinner once or twice, and I'm glad I did—he's been so interested all through. There hasn't been the least hitch to speak of, and I expect to get in within a fortnight. This," she went on, turning to Ogden with an undiminished vivacity, "is really my P.P.C."

Ogden glanced at the husband of the lady whose use of the first person singular was so frank and continuous. He was a young man with a pleasant and amiable face, and that face was set in a meek little smile, from whose forced lines the element of deception was most pitifully lacking.

"Yes, Abbie dear," Mrs. Valentine went on, "I'm afraid it's good-by—or nearly the same thing." She took the girl's hand within her own and gave it repeated pats in a rather careless and self-absorbed way. "I shall try to see you often, of course; but it will be so far. How nice it would be if you could only come up there and settle down right next door to me."

Ogden sighed unconsciously. He had fancied the first rays of social illumination as falling upon this benighted family; but it was only the last faint glow of a speeding twilight, after all.

Abbie withdrew her hand with a quiet dignity; she seemed to put but a moderate value on these protestations.

"I believe we are satisfied where we are, Fanny," she said in a low and even tone. "We have always lived here; we feel more at home in this house than we could anywhere else. All our—all our—friends are near us"—a desolate little blush came in here—"and then there's the church and everything. I've heard my sis—I'm told that the North Side is very pleasant on some accounts, but I don't think we are likely ever to change."

"Change!" called her father, suddenly. "I wouldn't live anywhere else if you paid me to. What's better than this?"

"So attached," murmured her mother, vaguely.

Mrs. Valentine continued for some time further to flutter her hands, her clothing, and her conversation, but she was very slow about getting up and fluttering away. She was a neighbor, and her return home was a matter of three minutes. Ogden's return was a matter of nearly an hour, and he left first. He carried away the discontented feeling of a young man whose aim in the direction of a young woman is frustrated by the presence of uncongenial elders and irrelevant outsiders. He had been quite certain of his ability to meet Abbie Brainard after the bank episode without any particular embarrassment or restraint; certainly he had come to view with more interest a girl whose hand had lain in his and whose head had rested on his shoulder. There had been no embarrassment in her greeting of him; her manner had been as straightforward and sensible as it always was. But never mind; he should try again; he was only too certain of soon finding her alone.

He took his hour through the clamor and the slime of the public ways. He escaped from these by his talismanic night-key, and stumbled up thoughtfully to his room.

There was a light burning in it, and the fireplace showed the faint red of dying coals. A valise, open and half unpacked, stood in the middle of the floor, and sitting up in bed was Brower, busy with the last volume of "Monte Cristo." They now occupied a large front room together, which Ogden had to himself a good half of the time.

"Back, are you?" said George. "When did you get in?"

"About seven."

"How's Missouri?"

"Weather good; eating bad."

"Reading all this time?"

"Went to theatre."

"What did you see?"

110

" 'Crackling of Thorns.' "

"Any good?"

"Not much; one pretty girl. Where have *you* been?"

"West Side; Brainard's."

"Anybody there?"

"The old people. And some friends—Valentines."

"Valentine? I used to know a Valentine—nice, quiet fellow, light complexion. His name was Alpheus—no, Adrian."

"That's the one."

"Poor fellow! he deserved a better fate."

"What's the matter with him?"

"His wife owns him."

George smiled. Brower hitched himself up on his pillow and put his finger into the book to keep the place. "He was a first-rate fellow—good all through and kind of capable; that is, he was worth a salary of eighteen hundred a year—or two thousand. He married a girl with two thousand a month. No head book-keeper, no cashier, no secretary could she let him be after that; no, Johnny must be his own master—except as regarded her. To-day he sort o' hangs on the outskirts of business, and picks up a little here and a little there—he has desk-room somewhere in the Clifton, I believe. He does the best he can to preserve his self-respect, but I don't see how he can pay the bills and the house-rent too."

"House-rent? They're building—I mean, *she* is."

"Yaugh!" cried Brower, with deep meaning.

"Atwater's doing the house for them—for her."

"Atwater?" Brower gave a second hitch to the pillow,

and threw the book to the foot of the bed. "He's another. He's had a trip in the same boat."

"Why, he isn't married."

"I guess he is—just about as hard as any man ever was. But he has fought through gallantly—I'll say that for him."

"What's *his* story?"

"Begins in the same way. She was rich, too, and a high-flyer. He had education and family and his profession—and no money. He struggled up for ten years, and now—now he stands on his own legs; his wife has her own money for her clothes and amusements. He saw he had got to strike society, and he struck it—hard; he costs like smoke. But he snatched victory from defeat. It was a great act. Speaking of acts—who do you think I saw there in a stage-box to-night?"

"Who?"

"Burt Brainard. Just kick that valise out of the way if you want to."

"All alone?"

"Nope. Girl with him. One of the Clifton type-writers—the one who used to be down in the lunch-room."

"Nealie McNabb?"

"U'm h'm."

XI

McDowell's second check to Vibert proved good on the opening of business next morning. It was paid in the usual mechanical and impersonal fashion that gives no possible clue to the amount of the balance remaining after; but paid it was, all the same, and Vibert's anticipated opportunity for further invective—an opportunity which he considered quite possible, and would have been by no means sorry to embrace—came to naught.

McDowell's friendly intimation that St. Asaph's might presently dispense with Vibert's services was soon found to have as solid a backing as his signature. Within less than a fortnight Vibert was dismissed, though on grounds not altogether the same as those that McDowell had figured upon.

If Vibert, after descending to the ground floor, had immediately crossed the great court of the Clifton instead of lingering there for a moment, the outcome might have been quite different. But he paused in the midst of its mosaicked expanse to pull out the check from his pocket and to take another look at it. He projected his vision so far into the future as the next forenoon, and saw the check again rejected—this time by the teller of the Highflyers'—by reason of "no account," or perhaps by reason of "no funds." He dramatized a precipitous visit to McDowell's office, and improvised the scene of denunciation and vigorous action that was to accompany it.

"It had better be good this time," he muttered, with his eyes on the pavement. "I'll strangle him if it ain't."

He tossed up his head and sent a fierce and frowning glance through one of the great plates of French glass that shut in the court. His eye darted forward on its own level, but it saw nothing save McDowell in his office, ten or twelve floors above.

Most of the panes that enclosed this central space were of great height and breadth, and were lettered with the silvered styles and titles of various railroad and mining companies; others, smaller, gave light and some ventilation to a few booth-like shops; a few others, immovable half-lights, admitted a little daylight and no air at all to certain closet-like crannies that had a squeezed and crowded role in the Clifton's general economy. One of these last looked out from under a kind of secondary stairway; it lighted the scullery of the Acme Lunch Room, and it commanded a view of that side of the court on which Vibert was standing.

Vibert's heel gave a vicious dig into the mosaic pavement and made a quick and rasping turn towards the exit; he crossed the court with a heavy yet rapid stride, and passed out into the street. He was quite unconscious of observation, but he had been seen.

Through the half-pane under the stairway a young woman had noted his presence and witnessed his departure. She was a thin, faded creature, in the forlorn garments of an undisguisable poverty. All but the

114

faintest traces of good looks seemed to have been taken from her by a long experience with illness and suffering. She stood close against the pane. Her thin fingers, red and chapped, showed, as they pressed against the glass, the crinkled puffiness that comes from long immersion in hot water, and she stared through with a look of mingled fear, entreaty, and agony. At the glance which Vibert's indignation over McDowell's trickery sent in her direction, she started and cowered like one who had encountered that glance before; and when he turned to go she recovered her self, and flung her bosom and her hands against the pane as if bent upon breaking through and following him.

A moment later she appeared in the court; she had put on a shabby hat and a flimsy, faded shawl. She crossed over hastily, and approached the head of the elevator squad.

"The tall, dark man who just went out—you saw him?" she inquired hurriedly. She spoke in two quick expulsions of the breath, and seemed left without a third.

"Um?" The man opposed his gold band and gilt buttons to her forlorn and bedraggled shabbiness. His brief inquiry, made without opening his lips, had the true official indifference; but it caused his questioner to feel some of the disadvantage that comes to a young woman from a public and impulsive inquiry after a young man.

"You saw him standing over there; he had a paper in his hand. Tell me, does he work in this building?" She was panting and all a-tremble, but she found breath for these words and will to use it.

"Yes, I saw him," the man answered, with the slow reluctance of his kind to be interested in individuals as individuals. "Used to work here, I believe. Haven't seen much of him lately."

"Where can I find him?"

The man turned towards the elevators; one had

115

just that minute come down. "Chicago!" its youthful conductor had called with an airy drawl.

"Pete," said his superior; "a tall, dark man who's been standing around here." He threw his thumb over towards the girl, to indicate that the inquiry was hers. "Had on a soft brown hat."

"Yes, I seen him," said the boy. "Used to be in one of them insurance offices, didn't he? Vibert—was that his name?"

"Vi—?"

"Vibert," said the man, impatiently. "Come, come, don't block the way—sev-en!" he cried, in his professional tone, and the boy at once slammed his door to and started roofwards.

The man retired into himself with a resumption of his air of idle dignity. The girl, at a short remove, stood looking at him with an anxious face. She made a timid attempt to approach him again and presently stole away.

Vibert was followed down from McDowell's office, in the course of half an hour, by Ogden. McDowell's dissertation on tax matters, with its pointed presentation of extreme cases, had left him, as we have seen, in a state more or less stirred up; and it had occurred to him that if he were to stop on the way down he might find some legal sedative in the office of Freeze & Freeze. But the hour was now rather late; Freeze & Freeze were being locked up by the last of their junior clerks; and Ogden was left to ramble through the corridors in a confused and disconsolate state.

He was presently accosted by a young woman, who appeared to be roaming through the building in a state even more dazed and forlorn than his own. She approached him with appeal so plainly written on her features that his hand went instinctively to his pocket for the ready dime. He was used to addresses of this sort; Brower had told him many times that he was a "soft mark." He soon ascertained, however, that what she wanted was not alms, but information—an appeal which is more familiar still in the great down-town buildings; it comes frequently enough from simple, inexperienced creatures who know what they want, but not at all how to get it.

The girl thrust back a straggling lock and gave him a glance both wild and timid.

"Please, sir," she said, "do you know any one in this building named Vibert—in an insurance office?" She pronounced the name with an effort of overcoming its strangeness.

There was a certain primitiveness in her speech; it was provincial, rustic—a fine ear might have called it uncouth.

Ogden was struck with her plaintive "please, sir." He had never before heard that literary form of speech in actual use.

"Well," he said, with the unceremonious kindness proper to the occasion and person, "I think you can learn something about him in the office of the Vesuvian—next floor below."

"Oh, thank you, sir!" She made a movement suggestive of an abbreviated courtesy; it was as much in the way of acknowledgment as her sense of strangeness and confusion of mind appeared to permit.

"Not that way," called Ogden after her, adding a benevolent postscript. "Here; come along down these stairs with me; I'll show you where it is."

She stumbled after him down the marble steps with a heavy-footed clatter that could hardly have been expected from her slightness, and with a timorous hold on the bronze of the hand-rail.

"There," indicated Ogden; "the sixth door along, on the right. 'Vesuvian Fire Insurance Co.'

117

it says." And he himself continued an abstracted descent by the stairway.

His nearest way home lay through the court and out of the door that led into the asphalted alley. Just within the archway of this door two men stood. The one was Vibert and the other was a dark young fellow of twenty or more whom Ogden, by a brief glimmer of fancy, made to be Brainard's younger son. Vibert was in the act of receiving a roll of bills from him.

The youth had a pinched and slender aspect; there was a furtive tremulousness in his hands; his eyes were reddish and the pupils swam half hazily in a lucent humor.

"I didn't know, Mark, but what you'd gone back on me, too," Vibert was saying to him. "If you'd managed to get around a little sooner you'd have saved a certain party from the grand razoo." He smiled grimly. "It's pretty close sailing—thirty, forty, forty-five"—he ran over the bills, rolled them up, and thrust them into his pocket.

The boy looked at him with some doubt and with a shade of fear. He seemed to have been fascinated and then dominated by the bigness and the hardihood of the other.

"It's all right, Mark," Vibert presently went on with a dogged vagueness; "I'm his son, too. Why wouldn't he give me any show? Why wouldn't he let me have a chance to show him what I am? Why did he go and shut down on me at the very start?"

"You!" cried the boy. "What can you expect, after the way he's treated me—his own son? They're up there now, I dare say"—with a bitter glance towards the corner of the Underground—"but they can never make things right with me. If it hadn't been for Abbie—she's about the only one that's turned a hand for me."

"Haven't I done well by you, too?—don't forget that. Well, you don't—'sh! I say you don't. Let the executors settle, and give 'em plenty to settle, too; they'll get enough for doing it." Vibert glanced up at the Underground windows. "He can't live forever." He brought his eyes back to the boy. "You've got to live yourself, though, and so have I. You've got some rights, haven't you?"

The boy did not accept this cue; perhaps he had already followed it more than once. He studied Vibert with eyes that seemed to indicate a change of thought.

"Say, Russ," he hinted, deprecatingly, "you're going to be a little more patient with Mayme?"

Vibert scowled. "Come, now, Marcus, that's all right; only don't let's have any preaching. What I like is a cheerful house—and an orderly one. Less sniffling and better meals. I guess you won't deny that, for a housekeeper, your sister is a good deal of a fizzle. She doesn't have to wash her own dishes, does she? And that girl I got her does the scrubbing and takes up the ashes, doesn't she? And we always take our dinners out, don't we? Well, then! I don't see what else we can do but go out altogether."

He drubbed his foot impatiently on the pavement.

"Well, so long!" he said carelessly to his companion. "Better not take anything more this afternoon. Do I see you on the track to-morrow?"

Ogden, of course, heard next to nothing of this talk, and his own preoccupations left him no opportunity to scandalize over the relations between Vibert and the young woman of the corridors, even if his inclinations had run that way. But it need not be denied that so close a grouping of these various persons turned his thoughts in the direction of the Brainard household, and his feet later in the direction of the Brainard house. He had lately been cultivating a more sympathetic apprehension of Abbie Brainard's position; it seemed possible that an hour's talk would offer opportunity for the delicate insinuation of his friendly interest. He rehearsed a number of suitable phrases; they took felicitous advantage of remarks on her side—remarks which he himself constructed—and left her, as she thought them over, in no doubt of his feeling sense of her position and of his desire to make his sympathies known and operative. That all these pretty paces would have been gone through in the absence of the Valentines is by no means certain; but their presence excluded the least attempt to try them, and it was with lagging feet indeed that he made his late return home to Brower and "Monte Cristo."

XII

Cornelia McNabb's campaign against the tenants of the Clifton proceeded apace. Such as pleased her fancy or promised advantage to her future she attacked one by one; she made quite a succession of engagements, dropping here and picking up there, until she reached the point where, for as many hours of the day as she chose, her time was occupied, and occupied to her taste. We have already seen her in the office of the Underground National, and we may now see her in the office of the Massachusetts Brass Company. She did good work within the limits she had set for herself; she was accurate and fairly rapid, and therefore was in considerable request.

"I'd a good deal rather work around like this," she expounded to Ogden, one day, "than put in all my time in one place. Lots more variety, to begin with, and lots more pay. 'Most every one gives me half as much as I could get in any single office; and then I can skip around and have more of a show. You can talk about your rolling stone; that's all bosh."

Cornelia was now doing a daily stint of an hour or so in the office of the Brass Company. This hour came in the middle of the forenoon, and the work was oftener performed under the severe eye of Mrs. Floyd than our young amanuensis could have wished. Mrs. Floyd's presence in the office had always been rather frequent, and her prejudice against female stenographers did not operate to make it any the less so. She bestowed considerable scrutiny on Cornelia, and Cornelia returned the interest in kind. She recognized in Mrs. Floyd one of the minor lights of "Society," and she became more deeply indebted to her for points in costume, speech, and behavior than either perhaps realized.

Mrs. Floyd was generally accompanied by Miss Wilde. This provided Cornelia with a double course of instruction: she learned what to do and what to avoid.

Miss Wilde was generally accompanied by her hand-bag, and that receptacle was capable of an endless yield of documents calculated to irritate and perplex her brother-in-law. Mrs. Floyd encouraged this. Who, indeed, should take an interest in the affairs of her own sister if not her own husband?

One morning Ann produced a memorandum that stunned him. As he studied it she stood above him like the spirit of Bankruptcy.

"For Heaven's sake, Walworth, tell me what it means. Am I a ruined woman, or what?"

Floyd glanced at the sum total; the figures mounted high. "They *have* struck you pretty hard, that's a fact."

It was a bill for special assessments levied on the possessions of Ann E. Wilde, in one of McDowell's subdivisions. Paving, so much; sewers and water-mains, so much; stone sidewalk, so much.

"And

eighteen dollars and a half for a quarter of a lamp-post," wailed Ann. "Why, Walworth, I haven't got the money on hand for all this; I never anticipated such a thing."

"What's a quarter of a lamp-post good for?" asked her sister.

"I suppose the cost is levied on four property-owners," said her husband.

"And who's going to see by it when it's up?" asked the disconsolate investor. "Nobody ever goes past."

"Not this year, perhaps; but there'll be plenty next year. You've no idea how the town is spreading about. Why don't you step upstairs and see McDowell?"

"Who starts these things going?" asked Ann. "Who fixes the amounts?"

"I guess it's done sometimes on the petition of other owners about—according to the frontage."

"And who's the principal owner all about there?" demanded Ann. "Ain't it McDowell himself?"

"Well, I don't suppose he's sold off very much yet."

"And so he's taxing me to make his own property more valuable. I like that. I'm glad I went to him. And your young Ogden—I suppose I can thank him for this."

"Good gracious, Ann; McDowell is taxed, too. The town's growing, and all outlying property is subject to such things. And don't blame poor Ogden."

"What more can you expect, Ann, in such a half-baked place as this?" queried her sister.

"Go up and see McDowell," repeated Walworth. "He can tell you all about it—when it's payable, and how, and whether there's a rebate or anything." He passed the papers back to Ann with the definitive air that closes a matter. "Jessie didn't come with you, then?" he inquired, turning towards his wife.

"No, poor thing; she is away down this morning. Why, what do you think, Walworth? They've been asking her if she can't testify."

"Testify fiddlesticks! What could she say? They don't need her; they've got a clear enough case as it is."

"But think of her in court."

"Don't think of her in court. She may be a thousand miles away by the time the thing comes up. Has anything more been seen or heard of that interesting vocalist?"

"Nothing. He left the poor child all alone in that big place, with not three days' supplies and the—"

She looked sharply over towards Cornelia. The girl's hour was ended, but she had engaged in a pretence of tidying up the desk.

Ann creased her papers thoughtfully between her fingers. "I had no idea that curb-stones cost so much," she sighed. "If I had only sold out on that offer last month!"

Cornelia was now engaged in complicating her apron-strings. Her interest in the Underground people, while becoming no less professional, had become a good deal more personal. She would have given anything for a decent pretext to remain. It was hard indeed to tear herself away from this discussion of the affairs of Burton Brainard's sister.

"—and the gas turned off," Mrs. Floyd finished, as the door closed on the reluctant girl. "And that's the state Jessie found her in—everything just about as bad as it could be."

"Well, no," Floyd dissented, thoughtfully. "There's one important consolation—this suit could be brought."

"Oh, yes," answered his wife, quickly. "This Canadian woman doesn't claim to be his wife—only that she ought to be, and that he promised to make her so."

"Interesting family," murmured Walworth. "Should like to be related to 'em."

"She knew him in Toronto. She found him here before she had been in town a week."

"Small world," remarked Walworth, negligently. He played with his penholders.

Mrs. Floyd became silent. Gossip seemed out of the question with an indifferent husband and a preoccupied sister.

Vibert's detection by the girl he had betrayed and discarded, and his desertion of his young wife, were immediately followed by the proper steps on the part of Brainard's attorneys. The old man had received the intelligence of Vibert's double misdeed with a tremendous outburst of wrath and vituperation. His indignation revived in him all the crude violence of his youth; he drew out from the disused corners of his memory such a vocabulary and such turns of phrase as are possible only to one whose boyhood has been spent on the crass and barbaric frontier. He towered and swayed like a rank plant that has sprung rapidly from the earth and has brought up the slime and mould on its sheath and stalk. His prodigal and picturesque indecencies were heard but half understandingly by his son, and were lost, as to everything save their animus, on his advisers.

The equilibrium of the scales (whose mathematical poise he had once proven to his own satisfaction) was now destroyed; this outrage on his daughter and himself and all his belongings put another and a different face on the matter. The girl was received back into her father's house. It was the understanding that she was to remain there until the legal undoing of all this mischief had been accomplished, and that, afterwards, she must prepare herself for an indefinite exile among certain of her father's relatives still resident in Centralia.

During this interval Brainard allowed himself only the minimum of communication with his daughter; her mother's fluttering sympathies were too tenuous and too faded to furnish anything very definite or vivid in the way of consolation; her brother did not readily abandon himself to the softer feelings—particularly when work of so much sterner character was before them; and but for her sister this crushed and unfortunate child would have received but slender support and comfort. Abbie was not only sister, but mother and family circle too; she found a use for all the pent-up tenderness and domesticity of her nature.

The bill in the case of Vibert *vs.* Vibert was filed without receiving any undue attention from the press. Some exertions were taken, some influence was used, and the matter merely made a cold, official, numerical appearance in the legal columns of such of the dailies as affect complete court reports. The relations between Vibert and Jane Doane, however, made too good a "story" to be ignored in every quarter; some brief mention of it appeared in a new and struggling one-cent evening paper. The friends and well-wishers of the Brainards were surprised by the extent of that paper's circulation—a good many people appeared to have seen it.

The case of Vibert *vs.* Vibert had its place near the head of a short docket and was reached with much less than the usual delay. It was tried quietly and privately rather late one afternoon at a sitting which might have been termed either a prolongation of the regular session or a supplement to it. Perhaps only a legal mind could have distinguished; probably the legal mind that dominated the occasion did not attempt the distinction.

The matter was adjusted in a small and compact court-room high up in a certain vast and pillared pile—a room which differed little in size and not greatly in furnishings from an ordinary office. The court reporters and the crowd of court loungers had withdrawn; nobody remained behind save the clerk and a bailiff or two. Yet the spectre of publicity seemed hovering there; it hurled a flood of glaring light in through the high and curtainless windows, it shimmered on the staring yellow oak furnishings of bench and bar, and it searched out the darkest corner of the yawning jury-box. Abbie Brainard, standing beside her sister, peopled all this void with jargoning lawyers and callous constables and malicious witnesses and indifferent jurymen and sharp-witted reporters and trivial, time-killing spectators; and then she set her unveiled sister in that revolving witness-chair and brought to bear upon her the searching glare from the lofty windows and the more pitiless glare of the thousand-eyed crowd. She shuddered, and thanked Heaven—without going too deeply beneath the surface of things—that present conditions were so favorable.

For they involved none of the ordinary phenomena of a "trial." There was no wrangling, no eloquence, no auditory; there was no humiliation—beyond that which was inevitable. It was hardly more than a conference. The judge, with a quiet gravity, took a simple conversational tone—a keynote to which the indignation of Burt, the mortification of his sister, the sorrow of Jane Doane, and the juvenility of Freddy Pratt all came to be attuned. There was a simple recital of uncombated facts, the separation was decreed, and Mary Vibert was presently at liberty to resume her maiden name. It was considered best that she be known henceforth as Mrs. Mary Brainard. There was no report in the next day's papers, nor the next; on the third day things took a different turn.

One or two of the newspapers had sacrificed the Vibert-Doane story with considerable reluctance. They felt a certain degree of martyrdom, too, in withholding their hand from Brainard, who had been a standard subject of attack throughout the careers of all the younger writers. Nor were they at all sure that their position as guardians of the public morals justified any such suppression of the truth. They learned of the clandestine trial of the Vibert case, and that decided them. Their virtue was strengthened; the whole affair was reopened and thoroughly ventilated. The encroachments of wealth and privilege were held up before the alarmed eyes of the public; the entire episode, with everything leading up to it, was minutely rehearsed. A good many people were interviewed—a few who knew something of the circumstances, a good many who did not. Reportorial requisitions were also made on the bank and the house. Some persons contributed facts relating to the matter in hand; others, facts relating to matters whose connection was not so close; still others volunteered opinions on the method of procedure that made the trial noteworthy. "Vox Populi" and "Ruat Coelum" wrote letters "to the editor." Rough cuts from sketches and photographs made their appearance. The whole career of Brainard was reviewed with merciless detail, and the issue of one edition of a particular publication was attended with the shouting of his name through the streets. Certain sheets whose existence is unknown to the majority of reputable people and whose circulation is in accordance therewith, gave their clients a scare-head full of exclamation-points; and one pink publication, whose single connection with respectability is through the barber-shops, devoted its whole front page to the illustration of the case: the wronged girl claimed her surpliced betrayer at the altar-rail, while the equally wronged wife swooned in a front pew. There was an appropriate Gothic background, while one corner of the foreground—piquant touch of innocence—was filled in by an open-eyed choir-boy.

All these manifestations of public interest caused Ogden a keen personal distress that surprised him. He heard the names of

Brainard and Vibert bawled in the streets. He became familiar, for the first time, with the salient points in Brainard's career. He heard himself referred to once or twice as a clerk in Brainard's bank. As he handled that pink sheet in the Clifton barber-shop while awaiting his turn, he half expected some acquaintance to brand him as a caller at Brainard's house. As he lay, lathered and defenceless, in his chair, he almost dreaded lest some pitiless friend might happen in and stamp him as a suitor for the hand of Brainard's daughter. . . . He paused and blushed under the barber's eye; he saw now the reason for his personal distress over these odious domestic entanglements. His surprise passed away, but it left behind it a distress greater still.

XIII

The appearance and deportment of young Frederick Pratt as a witness in the Vibert case offered several delicate shades whose noting and whose accounting for may justify a paragraph or two. His general effect, then, was in the highest degree sobered, chastened, depressed. To what was this to be attributed?

To his consciousness of the overshadowing majesty of the law? No; for the law had turned its softest and most silken side outward; the little party had taken up its informal grouping at the judge's elbow and had replied conversationally to the interrogations of the judge himself or to the prompting inquiries of Brainard's attorney. Justicia had appeared in her most sympathetic and domestic aspect.

Was the youth disappointed as to his performance of a *beau rôle?* There is no doubt that he had anticipated with some relish his first appearance in the witness-box. He would have been obliged, it is true, to confess himself a minor, and he might have been exposed to the humiliating necessity of declaring that he understood the nature of an oath; but after that all would have been smooth sailing. Only to be for full fifteen minutes the observed of all observers, to be able to lift up his voice and tell—all —he—knew! Yet to be balked in this called for exasperation rather than deep dejection, and deep dejection, after all, was what he chiefly showed.

Was this dejection the sign of sympathetic sorrow for the woes of his former friend and playmate? Not quite. His sympathy, while real enough, was largely the sprightly product of novelty, curiosity, and conscious self-importance; unentangled with other considerations, it would have shown itself in a nervous and volatile loquacity.

But Freddy in court was not loquacious; he gave his testimony after a benumbed and backward fashion that indicated other and deeper troubles. The boy, in fact, was under a cloud. An issue of some importance had arisen between the Underground National Bank and its youngest messenger; it involved no less a question than that of *meum* and *tuum*. Freddy Pratt, as messenger, had been in the habit of making two or three daily trips through the business district, during which the notes and acceptances that filled his big official wallet came to be exchanged for checks and greenbacks that represented corresponding values. One or two discrepancies had developed that called for attention.

The boy's father came down to the Underground to contribute his share of this attention. He was a grave, repressive, saturnine person, who might have been set down as possessed of far greater means to meet the requirements of a growing boy in the midst of a circle of well-to-do urban acquaintances than of inclination to study those requirements. He was received in Brainard's own private room, and the affairs of the penitent and sobbing boy were discussed over his head by his parent and his employer.

"You foolish child," said the elder Pratt to his son, in the self-conscious tone by which we address age through youth; "if you wanted anything, why didn't you ask me for it?"

This father, seriously handicapped as he was by his own temperament, was attempting to treat the matter as something rather slight and trivial. The pettiness of the amount involved, the perfect ease of restitution, the youth of the offender, the utter simplicity and primitiveness of his method—all these he touched upon with a feint of light-handed ease. Another might have blown an airy bubble like this, even in the face of Brainard's ominous and taciturn frown; but Pratt was not the man to do it. He soon left the upper air of informal jocularity for the firmer ground of argument and expostulation, and this ground, before he ended, was almost pressed by the knees of entreaty.

"It's plain enough," said Brainard, at length; "he took it, and he kept it."

Each one, from his own point of view, cast his eye on the culprit.

"But it can't be that you mean to ruin a boy's future in any such way as this?" snarled the boy's father with a rasping expostulation.

Brainard turned a look on him from under his overhanging brows.

"Um," he merely said, in a voice which might have meant anything.

But the affair presently came to adjustment—a treaty with several clauses. Brainard wished to use the boy in court; to dispose of the Vibert matter in the cursory fashion that he hoped to follow permitted scant margin for the plea of desertion, and he was depending on young Pratt for the recital of certain occurrences which, in a cumulative way, might have their bearings on the plea of cruelty. Pratt, Jr., was to testify in court, Pratt, Sr., was to reimburse the bank, and the boy's final dismissal from the Underground would then be timed in a way so disassociated from any particular cause as to excite no comment and to occasion no injury. But all this was scant and nominal payment for Brainard's clemency; a larger one followed.

Brainard owned a number of woe-begone tenements scattered here and there over that unattractive part of the West Side which is most affected by manufacturers of furniture. One of these tumble-down dwellings adjoined a large lot owned by Ingles—took out one corner, in fact, in such a way as to interfere seriously with its value for building purposes. Ingles, in treaty with a furniture firm for the putting up of a building, had made an offer for this corner. Brainard, informed as to the circumstances, had put a price on it that was excessive — exorbitant. Ingles had taken time for consideration; and at the very moment of Pratt's call a letter from him lay on Brainard's desk, to the effect that he was looking elsewhere; evidently, on principle, he was drawing off. Brainard had no use for the property, and it was hardly paying taxes. He wanted to sell it at his own figure, and he had expected to. Ingles's tactics nettled him; he solaced himself by a step that reached Ingles and Pratt at the same time. He sardonically raised his price a peg higher, and offered the property to Pratt with an intimation that refusal would not be entertained. He put his lot still further beyond the reach of Ingles's possible necessities, and he made it realize even more than Ingles had declined to pay. Pratt swallowed this mouthful with such grace as he could command; and with the celerity possible to a perfected system of land transfer when supplemented by the guarantee of a title company, Norval H. Pratt, in a day or two, became the owner, at an excessive price, of a piece of property for which he had no use, and for which, so far as he knew, no one else had any use either.

This transaction was at once noted by McDowell, whose study of the daily transfers as reported in the real-estate publications was minute, and whose attention had been fixed for some time on this particular piece of ground. He knew something of Ingles's intentions, through the people whom Ingles was endeavoring to accommodate, and he saw here the entering wedge that he had waited for so long. He had approached Brainard unsuccessfully; he now tried Pratt. Pratt, who figured himself justly enough as a lamb led to the shearing, made no effort to evade the role; he promptly made an agreement for the transfer of the Brainard lot to McDowell. He let it go at a decided sacrifice—he sold it at a possible shade under its actual value.

McDowell, whose eagerness had committed him to an out-and-out purchase, was now in a position to approach Ingles. He was willing to sell the ground for simply what it had cost him; his profits would come later, through that open door between 1262 and 1263. Ingles received him coldly. He had disposed, he said, of his holdings in that neighborhood, and was using the proceeds to build for his new tenants in another quarter. He bowed McDowell out with a faintly cynical contempt, and this enterprising person was left with an unpromising piece of ground on his hands to dispose of as best he might. He tried the new purchasers of Ingles's lot; his own was not necessary to their purposes.

McDowell was seriously embarrassed. This bit of ground was a trifle in itself—to Ingles or to Pratt it mattered little either way; but to McDowell, who was of a considerably smaller calibre, the thing came as a kind of last straw. In expectation of great activity in acres he had loaded himself down with outside property; everything of his own was invested in that way, everything that was his wife's, and something, to tell the truth, that was neither his nor his wife's. He was in up to his chin, and at this moment came Ogden, asking him in set terms for an accounting and a settlement.

McDowell met this demand with a promise of figures, and he renewed this promise several times. The intervals between gave opportunity for a slow insinuation of the truth—for a graduated confession that a considerable part of old Mr. Ogden's estate was tied up in the operations of his son-in-law. This confession was followed by his statement; but it was some time before the account opened at the Underground by George received any great enlargement through the agent of the administratrix.

"It's all right, though," McDowell said; "you don't need to worry, and there's no use in stirring things up. There's big money ahead, and you'll stand in."

But the statement was the ground, and a sufficient one, for a rupture. McDowell, in order to diminish his indebtedness to the estate, had charged it with various fees and percentages of his own, and with numerous items that properly concerned his individual and household expenses. He charged the estate with a new porch on the front of his own house, and with the full expense of railway travel which had been undertaken in great part for his own interests. He even made a hardy attempt to force the Brainard lot upon the indignant widow.

Mrs. Ogden immediately left his house, in spite of the good offices of her bewildered daughter. George himself, forecasting the future, beheld a long succession of wrangling days in the law-courts and in the offices of attorneys—days that threatened to surpass in worry, loss, expense, and nerve-wear anything that his family had experienced yet. He felt himself on the threshold of a struggle for which he was but scantily equipped, and in which he was certain to be seriously handicapped through consideration for Kittie.

Absorbed in these moody reflections, he was crossing the court of the Clifton on a Saturday afternoon when a pencil-tap on one of the great glass panes took his attention. The tap was sounded on the court frontage of Darrell & Bradley's branch, and George started from his revery to see the face of Bradley himself looking out at him over the rulers, mucilage bottles, and memorandum-books that formed symmetrical piles within.

Bradley hastened to throw open the narrow glass door adjoining the show-window, and motioned George in with a friendly and quizzical grimace.

"Let Jones walk," he said, crinkling up his eyes and laying his fat hand on Ogden's shoulder.

"He *is* walking," responded George, with a wan smile.

Bradley drew him in and closed the door.

"Well, let him walk in a different path, then. Let him come out to Hinsdale to-morrow and try the primrose path."

"Of dalliance?" asked George, with a doleful attempt to meet half-way the cheery facetiousness of the other.

"Well, I don't think a little dalliance would hurt him." Bradley made it seem quite absurd that a young fellow of twenty-five should have any real cares and annoyances. "All work and no play—you know."

"I'm afraid so," admitted George, with a pathos that the elder man found amusing.

Bradley stepped back to a snug office that was stowed away behind a tall piece of shelving piled with newly bound account-books, to pick up his hat. "I'm glad to have caught sight of you," he proceeded, with the friendliness of an elder brother; "I've just taken an hour or so to overhaul things here a little. If you're going north, I'll walk a block or two with you."

They passed out into the street and picked their way along through the splashing, slumping, and dripping that marks the spring break-up. They elbowed other pedestrians over miry flaggings, and they dodged the muddy spray that bumping trucks sent up from the street-car tracks at almost every crossing.

"My wife's wondering what has become of you," Bradley puffed out among many other things, as he tried to keep up with Ogden's supple and light-footed gait. "And Jessie, too. She's home to-morrow—just back from Evanston. You come out on the eleven fifty-five, and we'll have an early dinner, and that will leave enough of the afternoon to make things worth while. And we'll show you that spring is a little nearer at hand than you'd suspect in town. Your first spring here?"

"Yes."

"Pretty bad, ain't it?"

"Worse than Boston," said George, in a tone implying that nothing further could be added.

At the next corner Bradley paused, detaining him for a moment with a friendly hand.

"Sunday noon, then. You provide the dalliance and we'll see to the primroses. Care anything for 'em?"

"Oh, yes, indeed."

"Good thing; can't have chrysanthemums all the year round. Well, good-by. Jessie will drive down for you in the buggy."

"I'll be there," called Ogden, as they drifted apart in the thickening crowd.

He had reached the point where he felt it would be a relief to cut away from town and everything in it—the bustle, the uproar, the filth, the routine of the bank, the complications of the Brainards, the entanglements of the Ogdens. It was a simple thing to do—only so many miles of flimsy and shabby shanties and back views of sheds and stables; of grimy, cindered switch-yards, with the long flanks of freight-houses and interminable strings of loaded or empty cars; of dingy viaducts and groggy lamp-posts and dilapidated fences whose scanty remains called to remembrance lotions and tonics that had long passed their vogue; of groups of Sunday loungers before saloons, and gangs of unclassifiable foreigners picking up bits of coal along the tracks; of muddy crossings over roads whose bordering ditches were filled with flocks of geese; of wide prairies cut up by endless tracks, dotted with pools of water, and rustling with the dead grasses of last summer; then suburbs new and old—some in the fresh promise of sidewalks and trees and nothing else, others unkempt, shabby, gone to seed; then a high passage over a marshy plain, a range of low wooded hills, emancipation from the dubious body known as the Cook County Commissioners—and Hinsdale.

At the station Jessie Bradley sat drawn up in a buggy; she had her place in a small convention of phaetons, carryalls, and express-wagons. She tossed her head brightly and waved her whip.

"I could have walked as well as not," said Ogden, climbing in. "What's half a mile?"

"Three quarters—almost," she corrected. She gathered up the lines and secured the approved hold on the whip. "Unless *you* care to drive?" she suggested.

"Not particular," replied Ogden, leaning back easily. "Quite willing to be a passenger."

He took a look at her sidewise from behind. She wore a pert little flat-brimmed, flat-crowned hat, set straight on the top of her head; a stray lock of hair brushed across her ear in the breeze; she had a bunch of pale purple primroses at her throat.

"You may if you want to," she said, with a sudden turn in his direction. Her eyes snapped and sparkled.

"I'd as soon see you—unless you don't care to."

"Oh, as far as that goes! Just hold on tight, though. Get up, John!"

She drew a taut rein and flicked the horse over the ear. He was a mettlesome five-year-old, and he rushed into his best gait at once. "Here we go!" she cried, "Sunday or no Sunday. I hate to poke."

She rushed him through the outskirts of the town; she bumped over the cumbrous plank crossings, she grazed one or two of the wooden posts that held up oil-lamps, she charged a flock on its homeward way from church and cut it into two frightened and indignant halves. She was on her native heath; she felt it; she showed it.

George grasped the buggy-cover with his left hand and held his right in readiness to seize the reins. The buggy, with many a bump and sudden wrench, sped on over the stones and ruts and puddles and rough crossings of an indifferent country road, and presently it turned into a yard with a rasping graze on one of the two painted white posts that made the entrance way. On the side porch of the house stood the girl's parents. They were laughing.

Jessie jumped out briskly. She struck a masculine attitude on the carriage-block, her right hand resting on the stock of her whip, her left arm a-kimbo.

"I was to get yer through on time; them was my orders, and here ye are!"

George climbed out carefully.

"Poor Horace!" chuckled Bradley, coming down; "he's here all right, but is he able to give his lecture?"

Mrs. Bradley followed, to shake hands. She wore a black silk dress, and there was a bit of lace over her thin hair—an adornment which her consciousness seemed to put forth as a modish novelty. Her wrinkles all flowed together in a companionable smile.

"He may have lost his voice on the way," she joked, "but we hope he saved his appetite."

"They're both all right," said George, laughing in turn.

Bradley was at the horse's head. "The voice is there, anyway," he said in cautious acknowledgment. "And we'll see about the appetite as soon as you've got enough spare breath to say 'Amen' to our grace."

The Bradley house was a mere box of a building set in an acre lot. They had built for themselves, on finally breaking with the city, two years before; and they had accepted the gables and dormers and shingles and the brown and yellow paint that the modest suburban house of the period finds it so difficult to evade. They stood on high, rolling ground; there were half-hints of considerable vistas here and there, and they were surrounded by groves and copses through which, to-day, the first faint colors of the spring were hurtling. Bradley, after dinner, walked Ogden around the house—previous visits had been confined to the parlor. He dwelt on the swelling of the lilac buds, and he drew attention with an impartial interest to the first sproutings of his peonies and of his rhubarb. The back of the place was littered with the débris of a second green-house in an advanced stage of construction, and through this disorder he picked his way, along with his daughter and his guest, towards the door of the first.

"Hop in," said Bradley, lifting his own foot over the perpendicular threshold. The air within was but a few degrees warmer than the air without, yet closer. On either side stretched fragmental beds of young plants, with frequent breaks between. "It's late for prims, after all; and a good many of them are outside, anyway." He waved his hand over a few patches of color on the left; there were white, pink, cherry, pale purple, such as Jessie was wearing, and a few belated clumps of young and indeterminate green.

Ogden passed to and fro, with the oh's and ah's that accompany the exposition of any host's pet hobby, however partial and trifling the exhibit may be. He had done the same last autumn with the chrysanthemums.

Bradley took this tribute with the customary complacency, and presently drifted to one side for a word with his man about a small matter of glazing—he had quite an eye for broken panes. Ogden leaned against a damp ledge. Jessie had seated herself on one of the steps of a rude flower-stand; she brushed aside two or three small pots that had been left standing on it.

She showed an air of lassitude; it had been stealing over her all through dinner, and now it had completely overtaken her in the languid atmosphere of the flowers. Her slender arms hung limply, and she moved her back as if to find a comfortable rest for it. Here face, under the pallor of the painted glass, looked rather colorless and a little drawn, and a languorous apathy seemed to have taken the sparkle from her eyes.

She looked up at him as she dropped the petals of a primrose one by one. "You didn't care to drive, then?"

"Did you want me to? I'm sorry not to have understood. You drove down, and so I thought—Was it too much for you, both ways?"

"Oh, no. It only struck me that you might want to. You were not—that is, you understand horses?"

"Certainly; I drive on occasion." He

smiled serenely, not in the least disturbed by her perfectly obvious thought. "However, a wise man never goes out of his way to handle a strange horse—perhaps that isn't one of Solomon's proverbs, but it ought to be."

"You are awfully cautious." She rose undecidedly, and presently she sat down again with a little sigh.

"I have to be. That is my business—from half-past eight till four. Perhaps it's growing on me."

"I don't mean that. You were born cautious; you'd be cautious anyway."

"I'm a Down-easter, you know. Look before you leap. Perhaps I shall learn the off-hand Western ways in time. I'll try to. I'll make myself over."

"I wonder if you can," she said, half to herself. Then aloud:

"But I don't believe all Down-easters are as careful as you are. There must be lots of them who would have just laid the whip on that horse, and run over a boy or two, and knocked our gate-post to pieces, and come up to the door with a wheel just ready to break to flinders. Why couldn't you have done it? I shouldn't have minded it—I should have liked it first-rate." She spoke with a kind of lingering drawl, and there was a half-smile in her lack-lustre eye.

"Your father would have minded it, though, and so should I. Never begin to dance without arranging about the fiddler—good rule, don't you think?"

She threw a bare stem to the ground. "Oh, yes; but tiresome." She rose. "Close in here, isn't it? Let's go outside."

XIV

The sun that had given some warmth to the early hours of the afternoon was dimmed, later, by an overcasting of thin clouds, and the rest of the time was passed in-doors. George smoked a friendly cigar with Bradley in the dining-room, and after Mrs. Bradley had disappeared for a short nap he whiled away the remaining hours with Jessie in the parlor. They sat in two easy-chairs on opposite sides of the fireplace, in which a handful of coal was working against the last lingering chill of winter. The girl had partly recovered her earlier tone, and she chatted with him in a string of smart jocularities with the manner which sometimes assures a doubtful caller that he has not made a mistake in coming and that he has not remained too long after coming. But between these uptilted strata of facetiousness there came now and then a layer of greater seriousness, and in one of these intervals she trenched on the domestic affairs of the Brainards.

"Poor Mayme went

South the other day, didn't she? I hardly suppose you could call it a visit?" She looked at him soberly, with her eyebrows slightly raised.

George winced. "To visit her uncle's family," he answered. He half wondered why he reiterated her word and even emphasized it.

"Her sister was going to run down there with her."

"I heard so."

"You see Abbie occasionally?"

"Occasionally."

"I suppose she is at the bank a good deal?"

"Not often." He fixed his eye on the last flickerings of the coals and lapsed into silence. It was not so easy now as once before to discuss Abbie Brainard with Jessie Bradley.

Mrs. Bradley came in brisk and refreshed about half an hour before train-time. The young people were chatting amusedly enough on indifferent subjects, and she urged Ogden to stay to tea with the clinging insistency of the suburban housekeeper.

"You can go home by moonlight; I've arranged it all for you." She drew aside a window curtain and showed him a pale white disk in a bluish sky.

"It's full, you see. We just have cold meat and tea and biscuits—I don't want to keep you under false pretences."

The moon kept faith with his hostess;—lighting him to the station and following him in to town and keeping him in sight through a mile of noisy and glaring streets. From the car-window, now and then, as the train passed back through a string of scattered suburbs and crossed the flat reaches of prairie-land between he was conscious of her bland insipidity; and as he traversed the down-town business

144

district she raked the long parallels of the east-and-west streets with an undiscriminating indifference that a mind less preoccupied might have found irritating. It was all the same to that big, foolish face—town and country were one. It had its vacuous smile for trees and fields, and it had the same smile for the variant lights of the street-cars, for the clamorous cab-drivers around the depots, for the flaring jewelled guide-posts of the theatres, for the gaudy fronts of sample-rooms, for the cheap dishevelment of occasional strayed revellers, for the signs of chiropodists and the swinging shingles of justices of the peace, and for a certain meditative young man, whether he was traversing the rustic roads of Hinsdale or the sophisticated planks of the State Street Bridge. Ogden's thoughts flowed along with a quiet and grateful sense of the friendliness of the Bradleys, and with many a ripple, wave, and eddy to correspond with the changing moods of their daughter. He made a careful rehearsal of some of their bits of talk—why had she said this? what had she meant by that? why had she done the other? He dwelt on these matters with an absorbed speculation, and with a young man of Ogden's temperament speculation was but the first step on the way to love.

The spring trailed along slowly, with all its discomforts of latitude and locality, and then came the long, fresh evenings of early June, when domesticity brings out its rugs and druggets, and invites its friends and neighbors to sit with it on its front steps. The Brainards had these appendages to local housekeeping—lingering reminders of a quick growth from village to city. Theirs was a large rug made of two breadths of Brussels carpeting and surrounded on all four sides with a narrow border of pink and blue flowers on a moss-colored background. This rug covered the greater part of the long flight of lime-stone steps. In the beautiful coolness of these fresh June evenings Abbie frequently sat there on the topmost step, under the jig-saw lace-work of the balcony-like canopy over the front door, while her mother occupied a carpet camp-chair within the vestibule and languidly allowed the long twilight to overtake her neglected chess-board. They sat out, now, only after dark. Ogden called at intervals, and was not flattered that the poor girl brightened at his coming; it seemed as if she must brighten at the coming of almost anybody.

One evening he elected to tell off their long street on foot—the street whose ornamental lamp-posts and infrequent spindling elms had partly decided him in the selection of his first quarters. When within a few streets of the Brainard corner he passed a house (one of a long row) on whose front steps (as with its neighbors, right and left) were camped a large and merry party, whose exaggerated domesticity made it plain that they were all fellow-boarders. They occupied two rugs as well as two chairs and a foot-stool at the head of the steps. Through their light-minded hubbub came dominatingly a voice which Ogden recognized, and he threw up his head to meet the frank but overdone bow of Cornelia McNabb. Beside Cornelia sat a young man who bowed at the same time with a somewhat forced and conscious smile. It was Burton Brainard.

Cornelia had returned to the neighborhood of her early trials. She considered herself now on a distinctly fashionable street; she put "Washington Boulevard" on her cards, and thought her eight dollars a week was none too much. She had had a plate engraved and a hundred cards printed. She had not found it easy to dispose of many of them; sometimes she gave them in shops, when she was asked to what address the goods were to be sent.

"But just wait till I order my next plate!" she would say to herself.

She had left one of her cards with Mrs. Gore. The poor, good soul (come in from her baking) was quite taken aback. Then Cornelia, conscious of too stiff an application of the social code, kissed her on coming away and made herself more intelligible.

"Yes," Abbie was saying to Ogden, a few minutes later, "Cornelia is a pretty smart girl. Father has come to be quite taken with her."

He noticed that she said—Cornelia.

"She takes down some of his letters, now, too," she continued. "*I* never learned," she added, in a tone of slight self-reproach.

"Good Peter!" exclaimed Ogden, with a protesting admiration, "you can do almost everything else!"

She waved aside this ardent apology, and looked rather shyly through the rusty iron-work of the hand-rail. The syringas were in blossom; the asphalt path had stopped its afternoon's running and had solidified since sundown.

"I think he likes her because she isn't afraid of him. Neither are you," she added, in a low tone, as if on an after-thought. She did not look his way.

Ogden appreciated this appreciation of his behavior. He had always been prompt and respectful with Brainard, but he had never knuckled down.

"He gives her letters almost every day. She corrects his mistakes."

"And he corrects hers?"

"He says she doesn't make many. When she does she sticks it out. She talks back. That's where she's bright. It kind of irritates him, I think, to have his—his clerks—his employés seem afraid. It pleases him, though, when other business men are."

This piece of filial analysis fell softly and slowly on the thickening darkness. The lamp-lighter was zigzagging across the wide roadway with his kerosene torch, and the voices of talkative neighbors on the other side of the street were brought over by the breeze along with the fumes of burning oil.

Ogden was pleased with this touch of gilding that the daughter's devotion applied to the father's clay. Perhaps the old man was not hopelessly beyond the reach of idealization's hand, after all.

Besides the people on other steps around, many clattered by over the asphalt pavement, and others promenaded slowly along the sidewalk. These moved in couples towards the Park, whose scant clumps of citified foliage appeared a few hundred yards away under the light of a waning moon and a half-bemisted sprinkling of stars; many of them issued from basement doors.

Presently another couple came sauntering along, and they paused at the foot of the Brainard steps. They were Burt and Cornelia. Cornelia came up and found a place on the rug that suited her, and greeted Mrs. Brainard in a familiar and masterful manner, before which the good woman soon boxed up her chessmen and retired. Cornelia then turned on Ogden.-

"Stiff—or bashful?"

"H'm?"

"Why didn't you stop and say a word as you passed by?"

"Oh! Yes, bashful; too many people."

"Too bad about you!" She turned to Burton. He had seated himself on a lower step with his back to the others. His hat was on the back of his head and his chin was propped up by his knees and elbows. He was looking thoughtfully at the curbstone. "Come up and be sociable," she called.

Burt rose and ascended a step or two.

"Oh, how are you, Ogden?" he said rather absently. George felt that

148

he should have said more, and said it sooner and said it differently.

Cornelia passed a cushion down to Burt. "There; take that and be comfortable." She regarded him studiously. It was dark, but he was all there—the short, thick, yellow moustache, the virile chin lately shaved and powdered, the dense hair that rose in a level line from the top of his forehead. Cornelia would have seen all these things in darkness that was Egyptian. She felt her fingers working towards them.

Cornelia was dressed with a trim and subdued modishness. She had taken a good many cues from Mrs. Floyd, and she had not been above cultivating an intimacy with a girl who worked for the excessively dear and fashionable house that dressed Mrs. Ingles. Mrs. Floyd had had no need to teach Cornelia anything about grammar, but she had shown her, all unconsciously, the advantage of a regulated use of slang.

Her fingers, debarred by the cold conventions of society from any entanglement in the head of hair just before her, smoothed and patted the folds in her own skirt. She further relieved herself by a high, sniffling toss of the head and a long, deep respiration.

"Well, isn't this a great night!" she said, addressing the little party generally. "Isn't the air splendid! I declare, I could just ramble about till morning. And yet I suppose your mother"—to Abbie—"has checkmated herself and gone to bed. Dear me, if there wasn't any city, and no clatter-clatter on that machine! Seems as if I must just make a break for the country before long—just get up home and hop into my little boat and paddle all around that whole blessed lake!"

"Why don't you?" asked Ogden. "Can't you give yourself a vacation?" He spoke a little wistfully; there was none ahead for him—no Underground man ever had an outing during his first year.

"I don't see how. They say you

149

can't serve two masters. Well, I've got five— four too many. At least," she tacked on, as if a closer calculation would further increase the number of these superfluities. "Can I go all over the building and tell each one of them that my services are going to be demanded exclusively for several days by some other one of them? Or shall I be sick—just for a day, at first, and keep adding days, one at a time, until I've had a week? I don't know what to do."

"Drop the whole business," said Burt brusquely, without turning about.

"And leave all my poor people in the lurch?" she cried, as if her employers were her most poignant concern.

"They can get somebody else."

"Oh, yes!" cried Cornelia, with mock humility; "I'm nobody; I can be easily replaced." She cast her humility aside lightly. "I'll tell you what I would do, though, if I was up at Pewaukee this eve. I'd paddle down to Lakeside and back—by the light of that moon." She pointed down the street towards the park foliage. "The moon that gilds those fruit-tree tops—Shakespeare. And it would be a good deal brighter up there than it is in this smoky old place."

"Can you row?" asked Ogden.

"Can I? I guess. Pair of oars made to order; and I can feather with 'em, too. Speaking of Lakeside, I know who's going to be there the last of this month; that Miss Bradley—Mrs. Floyd's niece."

"Cousin," corrected George.

"Is it? Cousin, then. She's a lively girl; she and I would make a pair. Only she don't look very strong."

"I thought," said he, "that she was going to Ocon—Ocon—"

Cornelia gave an encouraging ha,

150

ha. "That's right! Take time and you'll get it. Now, then; Ocono—"

"Ocono—"

"Mowoc."

"Mowoc."

"Oconomowoc; easy enough when you have it. Accent on second syllable. The only trouble is when you write it; you never know where to stop. Well, so she *is* going to Oconomowoc, later—to stay through July. They're only twelve miles apart."

"You know Miss Bradley, then?" Abbie asked Ogden. "She was over here once or twice, to see—Mayme. She seemed like a real nice girl."

Ogden bowed assent. He found himself as unwilling to discuss Jessie Bradley with Abbie Brainard as he had been to discuss Abbie Brainard with Jessie Bradley. Whenever he debated them it was a silent debate, in which he himself took both sides.

"She's a high-stepper," volunteered Cornelia, filling in Ogden's silence. "Good deal of style, too. Yet they say her father isn't so extra well off. She's a great contriver, I expect. Well, gumption goes a long ways; it's wriggled *me* off my back a good many times." She turned to Burt. "Now then, young man, do you want to walk me along to the park? Haven't we roosted about long enough?"

"All right," said he, getting up promptly. He seemed to be smiling appreciatively at her pertness.

"Ta!" cried Cornelia, dabbing her hand to Ogden and Abbie; and off she went. "Perhaps you'll see us later—if you're good!"

A big, bulky figure came stamping along the walk, and reached the foot of the steps just as Burt and Cornelia started off.

"I guess they'll be good," a heavy voice

said. The voice was not greatly disguised by its assumption of unaccustomed jocularity, and George with a flush recognized it as Brainard's.

"Well, Abbie," he said, lumbering up the steps. And, "How are you, Ogden?" he said to George, as he passed on and seated himself with a loud grunt on his wife's chair.

George bit his lip; the old man had no business to misuse other people's pronouns in that way. Cornelia's "you" might have meant one person—if it meant more than one still it might have meant them separately; but Brainard's perverting "they" bracketed him and his companion in a fashion utterly unwarranted.

Brainard lingered a few moments above their heads. He made one or two clumsy attempts at facetiousness, and George surmised that this was his way of showing a friendliness. But his joking was much more painful than any hectoring could have been, and George was greatly relieved when he presently rose and retired unceremoniously into the house.

XV

After Brainard's withdrawal Abbie and Ogden sat for some time in silence. The moon sank; the clatter of hoofs on the asphalt sounded less frequently; some of the neighbors over the way had pulled in their rugs, and were now seen, by new-lighted gas-jets, at upper windows pulling down their shades. The breeze freshened; it rustled the lilacs and syringas in the side yard, and it swayed the stringy mass of wild cucumbers that had taken it upon themselves to hide the red hideousness of the barn.

Suddenly Ogden spoke.

"There! I knew I should forget it, and I have. I laid it on my bureau the last thing, too!"

"What?"

"Why—'A False Start.' You haven't wanted it, have you?"

"No; keep it if you like. I've read it."

She meant, "Keep it; please do. Keep it, for my sake."

"It's a pretty good book; didn't you think so?" he asked.

"Yes; I liked it ever so much. He married the right one, after all, didn't he?"

"Might have done it before," Ogden commented. "No earthly reason why not. Only you know how they spin these things out."

There was a sudden shutting down of windows over their heads. Ogden drew out his watch, and turned it so as to profit by the lamp-post on the corner. "Why, I'd no idea!" Burt and Cornelia had not returned from the park, or, if so, had passed on the other side of the street. "Good-night."

"It isn't late, is it?"

"Only for a North-sider."

"Good-night," she said, slowly, and sat alone on the steps until her father came down and called her in.

On the first of July Brainard summoned George into his own private room.

"We have about decided to have an assistant cashier here," he said. His voice was gruff, but his glance was a little sheepish. "Mr. Fairchild thinks it will be convenient about signatures and a good many other things. Burt's out a good deal and likely to be off all through August, and I don't like to have drafts signed in advance. You could make up the reports, too, and swear to 'em. Besides, it's elective—puts you in the Bankers' Almanac, for one thing. As to salary, I suppose we could stand an extra five hundred—or six."

He looked at George with some constraint, but his intention appeared to be friendly.

"We might expect you to go on helping with the

tellers' work on occasion—vacation-time, for instance. Now, about your own vacation—"

George bowed with an additional acknowledgment of the favor; he had expected to pass an unbroken summer in town.

"Thursday's the Fourth. Put five or six days with it, if you like—to get accustomed to the new deal."

He turned to his desk. "That's all right; talk to Fairchild." It seemed that anything beyond the merest word of thanks would be distasteful, and George withdrew.

He accepted his elevation and his vacation with unfeigned pleasure; he attributed his advance to the old man's softened mood occasioned by his son's engagement to Cornelia McNabb. Burt, a few mornings back, had told his father, plainly and promptly, that it was his intention to marry Cornelia—and soon. He had prepared himself for remonstrance—even for opposition, and he had braced himself to demonstrate to his father that he was going to have his own way. The old man, however, made no difficulties; Cornelia had certain qualities that he appreciated, and he knew that Burt had a strong and a strengthening will. Besides, a son-in-law was one thing, and a daughter-in-law another. A daughter's husband must come as an ally, offensive and defensive; he must contribute money, and if not money, then abilities. There must be abilities in actual exercise, or there must be the certain promise of their development in the pursuit of some such career as would be recognized and endorsed by business men of his own sort. That ten-dollar-a-week man—that anthem singer! His fist clenched and his eye glared at the very thought of him. But a son's wife could be moulded—if not moulded, then coerced. There was to be no breaking away from two such wills as his and Burt's. He liked vim; he recognized snap; he was prepared to welcome Cornelia as a vital force.

"Oconomowoc," murmured George to himself. He was

bending over his bureau drawer, sorting out his collars. The gas-flame reflected itself in the mirror and threw a doubled glare upon his face.

"Eh!" said Brower, sitting cross-legged on his trunk. He laid the book down across two of the top slats; it was "David Grieve"—he read everything.

They were still in the Rush Street house. Mrs. Ogden had a room on the floor below.

"Did I speak?" asked George.

"You said —Oconomowoc. Is that where you are going?"

"Queer name, isn't it? What's the place like?"

"If you've got a chance to go there, you go." The oracle spoke and retired into his book.

George went. The train made its rapid run up to Milwaukee, took its short stop, and turned westward on its way towards La Crosse. At Pewaukee there was the usual halt; it lengthened to an unusual halt. George paced the long platform impatiently; his mind had projected itself through Nagowicka and Nashotah and Okauchee to Oconomowoc, and his body was eager to follow.

"What's the trouble?" he asked the brakeman.

"St. Paul express late—passes us here."

The platform was swarming with passengers and townspeople. A figure rushed through the crowd and grasped George by the hand.

"So you're gallivanting, too? And I'll bet a nickel you've been aboard all the way up—parlor-car. Now, haven't you?" The voice sounded a trumpet-note of wide-flung triumph. It was Cornelia's.

Her cheeks blazed and her eyes burned with the

magnificence of conscious conquest. Her glory spread about her the same succession of flowing circles that a stone spreads over a pond. It seemed as if her expansiveness must crowd the train from its track and the station from its foundations.

"Ma," she called back into the crowd, "come here—do! I want you to meet Mr. Ogden. He's one of my most particular friends; but I guess you don't need to be told that—you've heard enough about him. Mr. Ogden, this is my mother, and she's about the best mother that ever lived."

Mrs. McNabb smiled bravely and took Ogden's slender palm in her large, capable grasp. She wore a sedate black bonnet; her gray hair was parted in the middle and fell right and left in two wide, crinkly folds.

"And I want pa to come, too; no dodging." An elderly man came forward reluctantly, in his loose, short trousers and his thick boots with broad, square toes; he seemed to find Ogden, in his modified tourist guise, a disconcerting object. He lifted up his shrewd but retiring eyes, placing one embarrassed hand on his grizzled chin whiskers and giving George the other; it was rough, and the nails were broken.

George shook hands with the old fellow—who went well enough with other features of the Wisconsin landscape: the shaggy tamarack swamps, the gashed sides of gravelly "hog-backs," the long stretches of disordered barbed-wire fences, the rusty reds of depots and storehouses, and the marshy ponds, edged by the ragged scantlings of gigantic ice-houses.

Cornelia did not perceive this harmony—or ignored it.

"Yes," she declared, "ma's the best ma, and pa ain't far behind. Now don't shy, pa; Mr. Ogden is more scary than you are. He'd been trying for near three months to ask me to go to the theatre with him, when along came Burt and plumped out and asked me inside of a week. Burt's enterprising; no mistake.''

The old people smiled at each other, half embarrassed by Cornelia's frankness.

"But we won't shut out George—oh, dear! I mean Mr. Ogden—altogether. Bear witness, both of you: I ask him to be one of my ushers.''

George stared. Was the girl meaning to be married in church after—everything? Then he bowed. "On Abbie's account—if at all,'' he thought.

"Going to Coonie for the Fourth, I suppose?'' Cornelia continued.

"Coonie?''

"Oh, well—'Con'm'woc, if you must have it all. Well, we're on the move, too. Good-by. But''—meaningly—"you'll find us all again in town pretty soon; and if pa and ma don't see the whole place from the tip-top of the Clifton, my name is McMudd. On a clear day, too—when you can tell where the smoke ends and the land begins. Good-by. Our house is on the right, a mile farther; watch out for it.''

Oconomowoc, from Ogden's point of view, appeared as one wide street running between two small lakes that were only a few hundred feet asunder. The business part of the street was built neatly and compactly of the cream-colored brick of Milwaukee, and the rest of it was a thickly shaded stretch bordered with a double string of summer cottages, which fronted on the street and backed on the water. In the midst of the cottages stood a big hotel of yellow brick; it was faced with a lofty row of seven immense white columns, and above the maples before it there rose a steep roof set with a series of dormer-windows. George was given a room which one of these dormers lighted, and presently stepped down the street to inquire at one of the cottages for Jessie Bradley. He soon stepped back again; she was not expected for two days yet. He thanked Brainard again for his full week, and threw himself into one of the chairs under the big colonnade.

The town was at the beginning of its annual patriotic flurry; after the Fourth it settles down, and the real season begins a week or two later. A good many young people were scurrying about, many of them in aquatic attire; those who did not carry rackets carried banjos. Nobody noticed him except the young wife of the proprietor. She stood in the doorway; her black eyebrows were contracted in a study of him. She wore her raven hair in a Japanesque fashion, but she corrected the plump dumpiness of the Japanese maiden by a tall and slender grace of her own. "He's all right," she said to herself, and sank down in a chair beside him.

"You poor, lonesome man," she began, with a graceful audacity that was her peculiar possession, "let me talk to you."

"Do," answered George, smilingly. He seemed to have known her a week.

"That is, if you're not just married or not just going to be. Are you?"

"N—no."

"We see so much of that sort of thing. May is dreadful; this year we had five couples in a week—it's so pleasant and quiet here then. The fifth was from Detroit; they stayed quite a while, and when they went away they thanked us all over. We hadn't done a thing for them—we simply left them alone and let them go about. But they were just chuck full of it—they'd have been in glory anywhere. What do you think of our columns?"

Two men could hardly have spanned their fluted shafts. George cast his eye up to their capitals, on a level with the third-story windows. "They're great."

"Aren't they? They've only been on two or three years. We call them the Seven Bridegrooms."

"The Seven Bridegrooms? Is each the gift of a happy man?"

"Not quite; one happy man gave them all. He was here a week; he gave us one every day. Think how happy he must have been."

She smiled at his inquiring glance.

"He wanted things his own way, and could afford it," she said. "His name was Ingles."

Ogden did some lounging up and down the street. He crossed a bridge where one lake fell into the other over a mill-dam, and found himself in another cluster of cottages. They stood on a bluff and looked down the three miles of the lower lake. Both shores were diversified by promontories and islands, and the red roofs of other cottages showed everywhere over the tufted foliage of the shores.

"How it balances—how it composes!" he said of the view, as he recrossed the bridge. "And how it's kept!" he said of the town, as he retraced his steps to the hotel. "Really"—with unconscious patronage—"it's the only thing West, so far, that has tone and finish."

He took a boat. The next day, the same. The town was full, but was lying back quietly for the excitement of the morrow; he had the water almost to himself.

Sloops and cat-boats were being rigged for a coming regatta. A scow for fireworks was being anchored two or three hundred yards from shore. He paddled about with a trolling-line. But the line was neglected. He had a good deal to think about; here was place and time to do it.

His future was assured. He could now marry. He wanted to marry. There was only the question—which?

He had surrendered his primitive theory that marriage was a matter which concerned only the two

160

principals. Kittie's marriage—who had come to be more deeply concerned in it than he?

He thought of Abbie Brainard, and he thought of her family—a divorced sister; a disreputable brother, whose future was to sound, perhaps, depths yet undreamed of; another brother, whose coming marriage was but conclusive evidence of the coarseness of the family grain.

And the father—his scandalous success; his tainted millions; his name a byword. Those bawlings in the streets; those disgraceful and degrading pictures; the stench of the whole scandal.

His oars dropped idly, and he sat with his eyes fixed on the bottom of the boat.

But the old man would die. Yes; and then would come the division of the spoil. If there had been so much trouble in a poor sixty or eighty thousand, how much more might there be in all these millions? If he had found such difficulty in getting restitution from McDowell—a restitution so incomplete as to be even yet largely in the future—what might there be to expect from other brothers-in-law and from other new relations that so much money would be sure to bring?

He ran his troubled eyes along the shore. A party of children were wading and splashing at the foot of a high, wooded point.

That money—those millions! It was the talk of the bank that Burt, on his wedding-day, was to have five hundred thousand dollars as an out-and-out gift. And if Burt, why not Abbie—in the proper degree? Those shameful, indecent millions—millions that it would be a disgrace to receive, to handle.

"Boat ahoy!" A sloop swept by. He dodged its bowsprit and was tossed by its wake. He threw out his oars to steady himself.

The husband of a rich

wife—another Valentine. My house—my furniture!

Then, he had meant to get on—in business, in society. Was he to marry a recluse?—a girl inexperienced in the ways of his world—perhaps incapable of adapting herself to them— surely careless of them.

Abbie was before him in her tender and steadfast serenity, in her stanch and genuine capability. He set his teeth, and took up his oars again, and rowed half a mile with a furious vigor. He stopped, panting and exhausted, in a clump of reeds off a sedgy shore, near a group of linden-trees. He had left Abbie behind.

An elderly couple were standing among the rushes. They regarded him with a friendly and companionable smile. They seemed to offer him the "middling lot" that the sage and poet have called the best and safest. "No hazardous and complicated relationships," they seemed to say; "no struggle over dead men's dollars, no swamping of self-respect in ill-got gains; only our daughter—"

George pressed his forehead confusedly and raised his eyes to get his bearings; the late afternoon sun dazzled him with its level beams. He saw a house set high among the trees; and on its porch, amidst a tangle of bittersweet, a girl was standing. He shaded his eyes; it was as if she waved a handkerchief at him. Presently she strolled to the brow of the bank.

"Glad to see you," she called; "We have just driven over."

It was Jessie Bradley.

XVI

Cornelia McNabb became Mrs. Burton Brainard during the first week in August. Neither of the pair was inclined to wait, and neither had such a circle of friends as to make a midsummer wedding less preferable than a later one.

The wedding took place in church—as Cornelia had intimated to Ogden. She was not disposed to let false delicacy clog the heels of success, and she had her way. They were married in the daytime, as a partial concession to the social inexperience of one father and the social indifference of the other. The young men of the bank were drawn on freely; Ogden served as an usher—as Cornelia had requested. Adrian Valentine supported Burt at the chancel-rail, and gave some friendly counsel as to details at both church and house.

Cornelia's circle of girl-friends yielded nothing suitable in the way of bridesmaids; but there was the groom's sister—and one maiden attendant was enough. Abbie therefore took this part—for the first time. She walked up the long aisle with a bashful modesty. She had a dozen opportunities to meet Ogden's eye, but her embarrassed shyness prevented her from once looking into his face.

Mary Brainard was still in exile, and her mother was confined to her room by one of her nervous attacks; but in one of the back pews, in the twilight under the gallery, a dark, meagre, and dissolute-looking young man had taken his post. And as Burt, with a proud and prosperous smile, led Cornelia down the aisle, tears of indignant rage started from the eyes of his banned and mistreated brother.

The Brainard marriage was celebrated in print, just as the Brainard divorce had been. Some of the cuts that had illustrated the one were also used to illustrate the other.

Mr. and Mrs. Burton Brainard went to California and were absent a month. On their return they took up their quarters in the Brainard house, while Burt considered the question of building. Cornelia had made up her own mind where this building should be done.

They returned to town in accordance with the mandate conveyed by certain cards that had been sent out, directed by the serviceable Abbie, during their absence. These cards announced that "Mr. and Mrs. Burton Tillinghast Brainard" would be "at home" on the "Thursdays in September."

Cornelia had gloated over these cards on their arrival from the stationer's.

"Mrs. Burton Tillinghast Brainard," she read, with a vigorous hitch of her shoulder. "H'm! now we're ready to knock out your Smiths and your Joneses." She tossed her head. "And then bring on your Floyds and your Ingleses!"

Before going away she had wrung Ogden's hand, and had committed her parents to him during the concluding days of their stay. Especially was he enjoined to take them up to the top of the Clifton on the very first clear day. A clear day came; he conducted them up to the roof-observatory and showed them the city, and they numbered the towers thereof.

The old people tiptoed gingerly around the parapet, while Ogden waved his hand over the prospect—the mouth of the river with its elevators and its sprawling miles of railway track; the weakish blue of the lake, with the coming and going of schooners and propellers, and the "cribs" that stood on the faint horizon—"that's where our water comes from," George explained; the tower of the water-works itself, and the dull and distant green of Lincoln Park; the towering bulk of other great sky-scrapers and the grimy spindling of a thousand surrounding chimneys; the lumber-laden brigs that were tugged slowly through the drawbridges, while long strings of drays and buggies and street-cars accumulated during the wait. "My! don't they look little!" cried Mrs. McNabb.

George smiled with all the gratified vanity of a native.

"And that," he said, pointing southward down the street, "is the Board of Trade."

"Where we was the other day," the old man reminded his wife. "And that gilt thing on the top of it is a ship, I swan. And wasn't they noisy, though. Well, now, Josephine, ain't it handsome?"

A simple soul found to admire the tower of the Board of Trade—let it be put on record.

George and McNabb had got on very well. The old countryman had felt rather frost-bitten on seeing George in full social regalia, but seeming to find him more human and approachable in a simple business suit, he had thawed out again. Mrs. McNabb had taken to him kindly from the start. Most women did, though he appeared never to have observed it. She joined with her husband in wreathing him in an atmosphere of simple friendliness.

other father concerned in the festivities had also thawed towards George, though it would be a mistake to attribute simplicity to any friendliness shown by the head of the Underground. At one stage of the proceedings Erastus M. Brainard had laid his hand on Ogden's shoulder, and the young man had asked himself with distressful circumspection what it meant. It might have been to his advantage if he had found an answer.

George's engagement to Jessie Bradley was now an accomplished fact; the nail was driven—only a formal announcement was required to clinch it. He had preferred to withhold this until his affairs with McDowell were more accurately adjusted. Freeze & Freeze had put on a pretty positive pressure, and an arrangement had been contrived that had some of the externals, at least, of an adjustment.

McDowell's affairs had not been taking a very favorable turn; some of his ventures had been too rank for even gullibility itself, and his hope of relations with Ingles was now completely at an end. Ingles, in fact, had signified to him that an accounting for of the St. Asaph funds was desired by himself and the other contributing members of the former committee, that a remittance in accordance therewith was looked for, and that his resignation of the financial guidance of the choir would receive prompt consideration.

This communication might have been made by Ingles personally, or it might have been sent by his office-boy, or it might even (as a physical possibility) have been pushed in under the crack of the door between them. As a matter of fact, it came through the mail. So formal a transmission of so formidable a communication was conclusive; McDowell felt at once that all possibility of personal relations between himself and Ingles was at an end—that door in the wall between them was as good as bricked up.

Kittie came around late one afternoon to see her mother. "Do you know, George," she said to her brother, "that Eugene is going to give up our pew at St. Asaph's? Can you imagine why?"

He had heard and read a good deal in his lifetime about the fine penetration of feminine intuition; he wondered why feminine intuition always failed when it came up for application to business matters. The pretty, high-held female heads that would droop in shame if they could come to learn the how and wherefore of their own costly bedeckings! Poor innocent Kittie—sitting there and twirling in unsuspecting surprise the sparkling novelties that encircled her fingers, and never caring or thinking about the means by which they had come to be there!

The principal instruments in McDowell's settlement with the Ogden estate were certain promissory notes and certain warranty deeds—warranty, after quit-claims had been refused; and Ogden found himself in possession of his brother-in-law's signature on several bits of paper which he hoped might realize their full value when the time came, and also of two or three largish tracts of suburban property in which the general public interest seemed rather diminishing than increasing. McDowell saved the best here, just as he had managed to secure the best of his father-in-law's estate for his wife. In the original division—fair, according to appraised values—his knowledge of tendencies of growth had put into his wife's third almost everything that was likely to show a quick increase in price. George took his notes and his lands, and the task of turning them into money; and he left to Kittie an unimpaired trust and confidence in her own husband.

The matter of a house shared his thoughts, along with the McDowell business—an October wedding, a week for a trip, and then the beginning of housekeeping on the first of November in a home of their own.

"You want to see

Mrs. Cass," Floyd had told him; "she fixed us up when we first came out here."

"Who is she?"

"A clever little woman who makes a sort of specialty of North-side houses. She has got desk-room somewhere upstairs—sixteenth or seventeenth. She married badly—her husband doesn't do anything. She began by renting friends' houses to other friends, and has kept on until she has worked up quite a business. In such a big town as this has got to be you need to go to a specialist for almost everything. You might take in the whole lot of those big house-renting agencies and never get satisfied."

The office of the Massachusetts Brass Company was as much a social exchange as ever. Jessie frequently came down with Mrs. Floyd and Ann and Claudia, and George would sometimes step up to see her for a few minutes during his noonings. Mrs. Floyd looked upon the meetings indulgently enough, but Ann seemed to hold against Ogden a deeply-seated grudge.

She had been considerably embarrassed in the matter of her special assessments, and she had as much feeling against George as against McDowell himself. Her efforts to fortify and to recoup herself had led her into other fields of business, and she was now spending a good part of every forenoon in the neighborhood of the Board of Trade. Thus far she had not been so successful as to lessen the grudge.

The particular institution in which Ann was interested bore some external resemblance to its great prototype across the street. It was smaller and, if possible, uglier; but it, too, had its quadrangular arcade, its big square skylight, its ladies' gallery. In this gallery Ann sat daily for several hours, along with other women of a like turn of mind, and kept an eye on the proceedings generally. After a few sessions she became accustomed to the mere externals of the place—the endless shuffle of feet on the grimy floor, the sharp yawps of raw and eager voices, the flinging aloft of excited arms, the little tangles of noise and passion that were instantly woven around every new-comer with an offer to buy or to sell. She looked over this choppy sea across to the promised land that was being portrayed on the opposite blackboard; the artist paced to and fro on a long, high, narrow platform, and worked in the uncertainty of a single drop-light. He frequently changed his mind, and his alterations usually had a deep and sometimes a discouraging effect upon Ann and her associates. Every now and then one would retire into the hallway and consult with her agent, and then there would be the rustle of greenbacks, and the agent would take the elevator down and presently be seen among the crowd of men on the floor. The agent was likely to be a gallant fellow, only too happy to be of service to a lady.

Ann was now a member of Floyd's household, in good and regular standing. She felt herself very much at home. What was her brother-in-law's was her sister's, and what was her sister's was hers. She was usually the first to unfold the morning paper; she pre-empted the bathroom with little regard to Walworth's established habits; and if the idea of some trifling delicacy occurred to her she would order it from the grocery, and after it had appeared on Walworth's table it appeared again in his bill. She did not stand on ceremony; she waived all stiff formality; cosily and frankly she was quite one of the family.

As such, she used Walworth's office quite freely, and in the same capacity she joined in the conferences which the Floyds were now beginning to hold with Atwater up under his great skylight in the roof. Atwater's little house for Claudia had given great satisfaction, and he was now about to do a larger one for Claudia's parents, who had begun to look upon their banishment to the West as a perpetual fact. Claudia's house had been delivered with its stairs, its windows, its red chimney, and its

169

chandeliers—which last were composed by a pushing young draughtsman who was as anxious to make interest with Atwater as Atwater had perhaps been to make interest with Floyd.

Atwater was accustomed to people who didn't know their own minds, to people who knew their own minds too well, to people who had too many minds to really have any mind at all, and to people who had so much money that they didn't need to have any mind. He was impeccably suave and unruffled, but he had the immense advantage of being able to impress the unduly brusque and capricious and exasperating among his clients with the fact that they were dealing with a gentleman and an artist. He also put a good deal of "presence" into the rendering and the collecting of his accounts; there was no more disputing his charges than his taste.

He took equally, with his urbane imperturbability, the anxious carpings of Mrs. Floyd and the easy joking of her husband. Ann he quietly ignored, and Walworth thanked him; for his sister-in-law's interest in the new house was becoming oppressively personal. As for Claudia, he always saw that she had, out of his sample cabinet, all the bits of tiling and scraps of marqueterie that she needed; and if she fancied a promenade among the boards and trestles of his drawing-room, her whim was gratified. Ogden and Jessie, who sometimes came too, he welcomed pleasantly—the guests of the present were the clients of the future. Ogden admired his beautiful manners and his whitened hair; one day he amusedly recalled Jessie's determination to make her husband's hair like it.

He looked at Atwater, who was explaining his preliminary sketches to the Floyds and was trying to fix the general bearings of hall, stairway, and closets; his hair looked whiter still under the diffused glare from the skylight.

George turned to Jessie, with his hand on his own head, so smooth and shining brown.

"This is the hair you are to whiten," he said, and he lifted his eyebrows in a smile.

"I never saw such a boy!" she murmured in a repressed ecstasy. "Do you remember *everything* I have said?" No one was looking, and she placed her own hand on his other temple.

"Wouldn't powder do?" he asked lightly.

"Only for girls."

"Couldn't it be bleached?"

"Not and get that color."

"Must I suffer, then?"—with his hand still on his brow.

"I'm afraid that's the only way." She lowered his hand in her own, and gave it a tender pressure on its descent.

"Must it be lingering, or something sharp and sudden?"

She pressed his hand again, and looked affectionately into his eyes. "Both, perhaps."

"Will it be fear or anxiety or shame?"

"Wait and see."

Atwater rolled up his sketches and threw them into a drawer. Then he went to his cabinet and took out a few small strips and squares of encaustic tiling in yellow and gray.

"And now I wonder if our little Colleen wouldn't like to take some of these home to play with." He turned courteously to Mrs. Floyd, while his hand reached out for a sheet of brown paper.

"They're not too—too heavy?" she asked, cautiously. "Nor too easily broken?"

The child opened wide her brown eyes, in one of

171

her sober little ecstasies. "Oh, plaze, mamma! Oh, lave me have them —do!"

Ogden turned to Jessie, mutely asking her to share his appreciation of this. But she did not seem especially amused. He remembered, then, that to himself he had frequently called her treatment of Claudia "uneven." Sometimes the child entertained her, sometimes she annoyed her. Jessie seemed to regard her—and he felt now and then that she so regarded children generally—as a doll to be played with until weariness came, and then to be carelessly thrust away.

"Oh, let her have 'em," said Ann, with an air of authority.

"Very good of you, I'm sure," said Floyd to Atwater.

"Not at all; I'm sampled to death. There, my child." He gave her a neat little package. "I'm sure they'll understand you when you get to Paris!"

XVII

George Ogden and Jessie Bradley were married during the third week in October. The wedding took place at St. Asaph's, with the participation of a small section of the choir, and the Floyds opened their house for the reception that followed. Walworth even gave George a small lunch at his club.

For some weeks previous Ogden had watched for the right opportunity to make a formal announcement of his plans to the head of the bank and to ask for a week's leave. For nearly a month, now, Brainard had not looked at him, had not spoken to him; and when he entered the old man's office to make his request Brainard still refrained from looking at him, and in speaking to him was as curt as possible.

"We need all our men right here; you must give up any idea of going off."

"Blow hot, blow cold," thought George, and asked Jessie what she preferred to do under the circumstances.

She had planned a long and rapid and lavish tour, and the tears of disappointment started to her eyes.

"Go anyway," she cried.

"Go? Do you know what he is?" And "Do you know what business is?" he almost added.

She lapsed into a sullen silence.

"We could arrange the wedding for a Saturday," he suggested, "and spend Sunday in Wisconsin."

This proposition stuck in her throat, but presently she gulped it down. "Only don't call it a wedding-trip," she said tartly. "Well," she went on, "we'll settle that. We must, because the cards have got to be started out pretty soon—all those people who have entertained me have got to be remembered. There's some in Providence, and in Detroit, and in St. Paul. And don't let me forget those Louisville people that took me to Old Point."

They spent their Sunday in Oconomowoc, along with the Seven Bridegrooms. The day was wet and gloomy, and most of the time they sat in-doors over a grate-fire. Mists dulled the blazing red of the maples, and a thick fall of leaves was churned into the mud before the house by the wheels of farm wagons returning home from church. Only at sunset did the clouds clear away, and the full moon rose over one lake while the sun sank below the other.

George recalled this many times in after-years.

They had taken a house in Walton Place for the year and a half from November first. The house had been vacant some little time, and the landlord made no account of an introductory fortnight.

Mrs. Bradley had come in from Hinsdale and had superintended most of the furnishing and fitting up. She saw the window-shades put into place and told the men where to set the refrigerator, and Jessie had looked on with the gay irresponsibility of a child who watches puppets being strung.

On their return from Wisconsin they found the house decorated almost throughout with chrysanthemums. The new green-house at Hinsdale had devoted the whole autumn to this specialty.

Jessie sank down into one of her big new easy-chairs. "Nothing to do but to be happy," she sighed, with a long and delicious expiration.

She had her days, but those dates were of course overridden by her intimates.

Among the first to call were the Floyds. Walworth came over with a pocketful of cigars—to christen the new wall-paper, he said.

"Have you got any closets?" was one of his questions.

"Plenty," replied George.

"Then I don't see but what you're all right—just as well off in a house that you rent as we are going to be in a house made to order. If ever I turn architect"—with a glance towards his wife—"I shall begin every house with a dozen closets and then pour in the various rooms around them. Four drawers in every one, and two rows of hooks. How stuff does accumulate!"

"Yes, the inside is rather nice," Jessie acknowledged; "but the outside might be improved. I have my own notion about the porch and the front door."

George turned to her, as if to ask what that notion might be.

Other friends followed—Brower among them.

He went about rather shyly, looking at the draperies and *grilles* and mirrors. In the semigloom of the dining-room he threw his arm over Ogden's shoulder and looked into his eye with a friendly and affectionate smile.

"I never expected you to do it," he said. "You have left me as lonesome as the deuce."

"Do it? Why not?"

"Because you're so careful; you always think things out—regular old Puritan sage."

"Oh, well," began George, with the air proper to a launching out into a broad and easy generalization, "aren't we New England Puritans the cream of the Anglo-Saxon race? And why does the Anglo-Saxon race rule the globe except because the individual Anglo-Saxon can rule himself?"

"Oh, I know," said Brower, discontentedly; "that's all right, up to a certain point."

Others came, among them the Valentines.

"And how do you like your new house?" asked Mrs. Valentine, effusively. She addressed Jessie exclusively; with her everything went in the female line. "We are new converts too, you know—just over from the West Side. We are very much pleased, aren't we, Adrian?"

Her husband gave his corroborative little bow. "We were being left rather aside, over there," he admitted. "And take the South Side, for that matter. Business is walking right over them, and the whole section is in a state of mild panic from the Courts to Oakwood Boulevard. Yes, we're safe and quiet, and settled to stay."

Still others came, among them Cornelia Tillinghast Brainard. She called frequently, she usually brought her husband with her, and she never failed to walk him all around the Ogdens' neighborhood. Her favorite time was Sunday afternoon; then she took him along the Lake Shore Drive and through all the adjacent streets, with the full benefit of daylight.

Cornelia now had command over a good seven hundred thousand dollars, and she was arming for the social fray. She meant to bang her shield against the shields of other amazons. The gladiator must come to the arena, and the centre of the arena seemed to be somewhere near the water-works tower. If Burton was going to put seventy or eighty thousand dollars into a house, the site of it must not be too far away from this point.

"I expect I shall cut a pretty wide swath," Cornelia acknowledged to herself.

Jessie had her receptions through November; her intimates appeared at these as well, and so did many of her more formal acquaintances.

On one of these occasions George, having left the bank early, after a light day, hurried home, dressed himself, and hastened down to the parlor. Its contracted space was beflowered and belighted, and quite a little throng of ladies were circulating and chatting there. Mrs. Floyd and Miss Wilde were among them; so were Mrs. Ogden and Kittie; so were Mrs. Valentine and Mrs. Atwater.

His wife hurried up to him; her cheeks were flushed and her large eyes burned brightly.

"If you had only been three minutes sooner! She has just gone. She was telling me why she hadn't been able to come to the wedding. I wanted you to meet her so much."

"Who is this?"

"Cecilia Ingles."

"There is such a person, then?"

"Why, George, what do you mean? Of course there is, and she was just as nice to me as she could be."

"Why shouldn't she have been? I see you call her Cecilia. Are you as intimate as that?"

"Everybody calls her Cecilia. See, Mrs. Atwater is trying to catch your eye."

A tall and rather stately woman of thirty-five was standing in the doorway; she seemed finished—in profile, figure, and carriage. "How well it's done," she said to him; "who is the presiding genius?"

"My wife's mother, I fancy." He turned and drew her attention to the rustling of Mrs. Bradley's black silk.

"Ah!" she said indifferently, and turned away.

He had been unable to apprehend the simple costliness of his questioner's dress, and he only half wondered how, in a dozen quiet words, she had conveyed the impression of an expert addressing a beginner; but he could not refrain from asking himself if there was a slight here on Mrs. Bradley. He looked at the old lady again. She was moving about with the greatest show of confidence and good-will. No thought of anything called "differences" had entered her head. She did not believe that anybody would want to slight her or that anybody could. She had come on the ground in the early days of simple friendliness, and perhaps she was too old to apprehend that anything different had developed in the meanwhile. She certainly seemed to need no defence, and George was assuredly in no position to offer any.

"Cecilia has gone off and left me," Mrs. Atwater resumed; "careless girl!" They were half-sisters, and Mrs. Atwater was several years the elder. The Atwaters and the Ingleses ran as a kind of four-in-hand. The rich sister had married a poor man, and the poor sister had married a rich man, and they all went along at the same pace. It was a somewhat rapid pace. "I'm going to see what Mrs. Floyd can do for me; I dare say she has a spare seat."

His wife caught at Mrs. Atwater and bade her adieu with effusion. Did Jessie regard it as a feat and a triumph to have secured her presence? So it seemed to Jessie's husband.

The last of these little receptions was disposed of, and the honeymoon drew to its close. Quiet succeeded this introductory flurry to married life, and George now took occasion to lay a steady hand upon the throbbings of the "pocket-nerve."

His apprehension of any suffering in this part of his financial anatomy was, indeed, largely anticipatory; it was not that the nerve had been roughly touched, but that it soon might be. He had no tendency towards a retrospective study of the journal-and-ledger aspects of his courtship. He had been spared the expense of the wedding-journey that Jessie had planned by the unaccountable veto of Brainard. And the remuneration of St. Asaph's choir and kindred matters had fallen to his wife's father to arrange. But, all the same, many small indications arose to make it worth while for him to remember that he was a young man on a moderate salary and that most of his available means were badly tied up.

He noticed that his wife was developing a disdain of the public conveyances; a carriage was sometimes required of afternoons, and invariably of evenings when dances or theatre-going might be the matter in hand. She was also cultivating her taste for flowers; she had employed them rather lavishly at her receptions (in conjunction with her mandolin-players), and her appreciation of them kept equal pace with the advancing coldness of the weather and their own advancing cost. She also betrayed a ravenous taste for the exasperating superfluities of house-furnishing, and his bills for things needful were attended by a train of little accounts for things quite worse than useless.

"Oh, well, we shall be fitted out pretty soon," he sighed; and he saw his studious face reflected from among the cluttered *bibelots* of his mantel-piece.

The point of completion as regarded the interior was finally reached, and his wife's intentions as to the exterior presently developed. She accompanied him out into the vestibule one morning, and stood at the head of the steps to bid him good-by.

"These doors are awfully shabby and old-fashioned," she declared. "Don't you suppose the landlord would put in new ones?"

"I'm quite sure he wouldn't. I wouldn't in his place."

"Well, we have taken this house for a year and a half, and are likely to take it again for a year or two longer. Why couldn't we fix things up ourselves? The entrance counts more, really, than anything else."

"That might be thought about."

"Yes, indeed. If Mary Munson is coming to see me, I want things as nice as they have everything."

Mary Munson was of the Louisville family that had entertained Jessie Bradley at Old Point Comfort. It presently transpired that she was under like obligations to many other acquaintances of her girlhood.

"I must pay them up," she explained. "Besides, I need company—all alone here during the day, and mamma away off there in the country."

The succession of Mary Munsons lasted, indeed, through into spring. Flowers, carriages, and matinee-tickets doubled up finely, and the hideous mien of the caterer was seen in connection with frequent lunches.

"I spoke to Mr. Atwater to-day about the front of the house," she said to him one evening towards the close of dinner. "Maggie didn't quite get around to pudding to-day," she went on, as the dessert came in, "so I sent out for this ice-cream. Take some of these lady-fingers with it."

"To Atwater?"

"Yes. Frances wanted me to go up with her and see the drawings for the front of their house. It's going to be lovely. He had some special little drawings for the outside doors, and things like that. He's got beautiful taste."

"I know he has."

"I asked him to design some doors for us."

"You did?"

"Yes. He said he had a new idea that he'd like to try."

"You must get your landlord to pass on that. He might not like the new idea."

"Think not?"

"He might object. It would all come on his hands in the end."

"We'd better go on with it, don't you think?"

"But don't let it be anything too unusual or too elaborate." Architects, he understood, generally charged a commission on the cost of the work; so much per cent.—five, he had heard. "We don't want to go in too deep."

They left the table and sauntered slowly into the parlor—the drawing-room, Jessie called it. The standing lamp sent out a broad glare from under its shade of crinkled yellow paper, and the floor of the room burned with a dull and unaccustomed red—the red of a handsome Turkish rug.

"Ah, what's this?" exclaimed George.

"I picked it up to-day," she said; "it was so pretty and just the thing for this room. Cecilia called it a great bargain—she knows all about rugs."

"Then you have been shopping with Mrs. Ingles?"

"Well, she was getting a few things. She said that sixty dollars was little enough for it."

"Sixty dollars! Did you pay for it?"

"I had it charged."

"Charged?"

"Yes; wasn't that right? Why, George, even poor mamma, away out there in Hinsdale, has her account at Field's."

XVIII

The drawings for the embellishment of the house on Walton Place were undertaken by Atwater, and their scope broadened under the artist's hands. George, at his wife's request, took the elevator one noon and went up to the roof to see them.

In Atwater's absence he was received by the head draughtsman. The scheme had widened, as such schemes will; there were suggestions for the porch and for new hand-rails. There was also a drawing for a cornice in harmony.

"Um," said George, thoughtfully. "This is all very handsome."

At about the same time that work on the Ogden house began, the work on the plans for the Floyd house received a check. This check was due to the first Western trip of Winthrop C. Floyd, treasurer of the Massachusetts Brass Company. He came on a general visit of inspection.

The morning after his arrival he sat in the office of the Chicago branch; he had come down with Mrs. Floyd and Claudia. His keen and quiet eye ran over the furnishings of the place.

He was a bachelor of forty; he was dressed simply but elegantly—he was completely *comme il faut,* except for his muddy shoes, which seemed to trouble him.

"Well, Walworth," he said, with the manner of an elder brother and of an official whose dictum had weight, "you are pretty well fixed up out here—better than the home office, in fact."

"Have to be," returned the other. "Down East everybody knows the company; you could do business in a coal-shed if you wanted to. Here it's different. People don't know us from a hole in the ground; they go by what they see."

"Do you use all these calls and things?"

The wall was set with electrical devices for calling boys from everywhere for everything.

"Sometimes. Anyway it looks as if we did, and that helps business."

Little Claudia came creeping up to his desk.

"When are you going to begin, papa? I've come down to see you do it."

"Do what, my dear?"

"Make money. You said you did it here. When are you going to begin?"

Winthrop swung his chair towards the window and looked out at the driving rain and at the crowds of vehicles and passengers in the filthy streets below.

"Yes," he said, under his breath; "when are you going to begin?" Then aloud, "What a beastly hole! Is there no government here?"

184

"Precious little for a million and a half of people, and precious bad what there is."

"A million and a half? Nonsense!"

"Why nonsense? There's the census, and there's the regular annual increase."

Winthrop favored his brother with a stare of frank curiosity. Walworth had spoken with some warmth; he seemed disposed to throw an undue ardor into his defence of his adopted home—a city where quality seemed to count for less than quantity, and where the "prominent" citizen made the "eminent" citizen a superfluity. Then, too, Winthrop coupled with the earnest lines in his brother's forehead a slightly dingy necktie under his brother's chin. He observed, moreover, in the polishing of the shoe which Walworth, for greater emphasis, was beating on the carpet, a neglect of the heel in favor of the toe. And there were several other indications of a growing carelessness in dress.

"Well, Walworth," he remarked, "you are getting acclimated, I guess."

"Not to this sort of thing. Yes, there's a million and a half of us here, and this little quarter of a square mile is probably the most crowded and the most active of any on the globe, and yet it isn't found worth while to keep it clean, or even decent, small as it is. On days like this you feel as if you just wanted to remove the inhabitants and annex the whole place to the Stockyards."

Mrs. Floyd paused in the adjustment of her bedraggled skirts and looked up fiercely.

"Why remove the inhabitants?" she inquired.

"Frances!" called her husband.

"Why, indeed?" asked Winthrop. "I never saw such a beastly rabble in my life."

"Nor I," she cried. All her

smouldering resentment against the town broke out with the appearance of a new Eastern ally.

"Except in Madrid or Naples." Winthrop had travelled in his younger days; he never made these European comparisons except under extreme provocation.

"Why are things so horrible in this country?" demanded Mrs. Floyd, plaintively.

"Because there's no standard of manners—no resident country gentry to provide it. Our own rank country folks have never had such a check, and this horrible rout of foreign peasantry has just escaped from it. What little culture we have in the country generally we find principally in a few large cities, and they have become so large that the small element that works for a bettering is completely swamped."

He looked almost pityingly on his brother. "This is no town for a gentleman," he felt obliged to acknowledge. "What an awful thing," he admitted further, "to have only one life to live, and to be obliged to live it in such a place as this!"

But pity was not an important factor in Winthrop's Western mission. The Chicago office was costing too much and earning too little. There was to be a general reduction and scaling-down; the most important part of Winthrop's baggage was the pruning-knife.

He remained a week. He used the knife pretty thoroughly. He snipped Atwater's plans for Walworth's house into very small pieces. He left Walworth in a great state of depression—a depression deeper than any he had felt since his failure in coffee and spices.

His last evening in Chicago he spent in Walworth's library. It was a sober little room, and Walworth was the soberest man in it. His wife made only an occasional emergence from her unquiet silence; she no longer looked on Winthrop as an ally. The Fairchilds were there, and the Ogdens dropped in during the course of the evening. Fairchild and Winthrop did most of the talking.

Winthrop's sensibilities had now lost their keenest edge; the weather had improved, and the general aspect of things was a little less disgusting. He listened to Fairchild with the cautious reserve of a maturity that was accustomed to meet elderly strangers. He acknowledged, too, that the city was a big fact, and perhaps a more complicated fact than he had imagined.

"You have seen the foundations," Fairchild said to him. The old gentleman lay back in his chair and spoke in a quiet and dispassionate tone. "It has taken fifty years to put them in, but the work is finally done and well done. And now we are beginning to build on these foundations. We might have put up our building first and then put in the underpinning afterwards. That is a common way, but ours will be found to have its advantages."

"I dare say," admitted Winthrop; "but you have made an awful muss doing it."

"Well," rejoined Fairchild, "you may look at the external aspect of things, which is distressing enough, I acknowledge, or you may consider the people themselves, who are perhaps the real essential."

"Winthrop finds them rather distressing too." It was Walworth who spoke; his voice came in a muffled tone from the darkest corner of the room.

"What have we done to him?" demanded Jessie Ogden, quickly. "Haven't we received him well?"

Winthrop had no ground for individual complaint, and he hastened to make this clear. Personally, he had been made a great deal of. He was rather a large figure at home, and he naturally grew larger still the farther he travelled West.

"I don't think it can be denied," pursued Fairchild, tranquilly, "that new-comers are pretty well received here, whether they come to stay or to pass on or to go back. All that a man has to do, in order to insure good treatment, is to put a certain valuation on himself. That done, the more he claims, the more he receives; we take him at his own figure. The more I think of it, the more I am astonished at so much humility among people who have accomplished such great results. Commercially, we feel our own footing; socially, we are rather abashed by the pretensions that any new arrival chooses to make. We are a little afraid of him, and, to tell the truth, we are a little afraid of each other."

"H'm," said Winthrop, rather grimly; "Boston goes farther than that. Some of our great lights are almost afraid of themselves."

"I've noticed," remarked Mrs. Floyd, "that there is a good deal of watching and waiting for cues—people of plain origin who are beginning to take upon themselves the forms of social organization." She spoke like a princess of the blood-royal.

"That is the point," said Fairchild. "Individually, we may be of a rather humble grade of atoms, but we are crystallizing into a compound that is going to exercise a tremendous force. To him that hath eyes this crystallization, this organization, is the great thing to note just now."

"I acknowledge to have seen the ferment of activity, as they call it," said Winthrop.

"You may have seen the boiling of the kettle," returned Fairchild, "but you have hardly seen the force that feeds the flame. The big buildings are all well enough, and the big crowds in the streets, and the reports of the banks and railways and the Board of Trade. But there is something, now, beyond and behind all that."

"Let me tell Winthrop," broke in Mrs. Floyd. "Since I can't take him to our club, I must bring the club to him. At our last meeting"—there was a sub-acid relish in all this—"it developed that the present intellectual situation in Chicago is precisely that of Florence in the days of the—the—"

"Medici," suggested Ogden.

"Yes, the Medici," said Ann Wilde, loudly. She looked at him with a sharp aversion; he seemed to be taking part in her sister's joke. "That's just exactly what my paper said; the Florence of the Medici after the dispersal of the Greek scholars from Constantinople by the Turks."

"Oh, murder!" said Walworth to himself; "what will Ann rig up next?"

"The Florentines of that day," pursued his sister-in-law, "didn't know so very much, perhaps, but they were bound to learn, and that was the main thing. And it's just so here."

"Quite right," said Fairchild; "we know what there is to learn, and we are determined to master it. Our Constantinoples are Berlin and London and the rest—yes, Boston, too; and all their learned exiles are flocking here to instruct us."

"And the books that are coming in!" cried Jessie Ogden. She was no great reader, and she spoke less as a student than as a Chicagoan—that is, she spoke more ardently than any student could have spoken. "Does the enemy know that four of the biggest buildings in this big city are built of books?"

"The new libraries," her husband explained—the ones that are going to make us the literary centre."

"Dear me," said Winthrop, "are you expecting that?"

"Oh, yes. And we expect to be the financial centre, and presently the political centre, too—Chicago, plus New York and Washington."

"And where is Boston?"

"A little behind," said Fairchild. "New York is the main-mast yet; Chicago ranks as foremast—at present; while Boston is—"

"The mizzen-mast," completed Ogden.

"And we Chicago folks stand at the bow," chimed in his wife, "and sniff the first freshness of the breeze."

"Yes," said Winthrop, in satirical assent; "the 'Windy City.'"

"Don't abuse our wind," cried Mrs. Floyd; "we should all die like flies without it."

"That's so," assented her husband. "The wind is our only scavenger."

"I see," said Winthrop. "If you can only be big you don't mind being dirty."

Then, half in amusement, half in amaze, he concentrated his attention on the banker. "Can it be that there are really any such expectations here as these?" He addressed Fairchild exclusively—the oldest and most sedate of the circle.

"Why not?" returned Fairchild. "Does it seem unreasonable that the State which produced the two greatest figures of the greatest epoch in our history, and which has done most within the last ten years to check alien excesses and un-American ideas, should also be the State to give the country the final blend of the American character and its ultimate metropolis?"

"And you personally—is this your own belief?"

Fairchild leaned back his fine old head on the

padded top of his chair and looked at his questioner with the kind of pity that has a faint tinge of weariness. His wife sat beside him silent, but with her hand on his, and when he answered she pressed it meaningly; for to the Chicagoan—even the middle-aged female Chicagoan—the name of the town, in its formal, ceremonial use, has a power that no other word in the language quite possesses. It is a shibboleth, as regards its pronunciation; it is a trumpet-call, as regards its effect. It has all the electrifying and unifying power of a college yell.

"Chicago is Chicago," he said. "It is the belief of all of us. It is inevitable; nothing can stop us now."

But Winthrop Floyd was glad to withdraw himself on the morrow from his temporary enlistment—or drafting —under the vociferous banner of the Western capital. He did all in his power, as well, to oppose its manifest destiny by transmitting to Walworth, immediately after his return to Boston, a full corporate confirmation of his own anathema against Walworth's office and house. The Chicago representative of the Massachusetts Brass Company was recommended to secure less expensive quarters at the earliest opportunity, and was directed to drop his architectural scheme forthwith.

Walworth at once adjusted matters with Atwater. The architect received his "reconsideration" with composure, but he was doubtless nettled to be balked in a work in which he had taken unusual personal interest, and he was also disappointed merely to be paid for his plans when he had looked for the fees that follow construction. These considerations may have had their influence on the account which he rendered a month later to the Ogdens —friends and relatives of the Floyds, and introduced, too, by them. This account was handed in much more promptly than is generally the case with an accredited client in other professions—the legal or the medical, let us say—and its final footing caused Ogden considerable consternation.

The account was mailed to the house instead of to the bank, and the stationery employed was such as to suggest a personal matter between gentlemen rather than a purely business matter between architect and client; and Ogden opened it under his wife's eyes to learn that design had cost him more than construction.

"Your drawings are more of an item than your porch itself," he said, rather faintly. "I shall have to step up there and see about it."

XIX

Late one afternoon Ogden drew down his desk-top, put on his street-coat, felt in his pocket to be sure that Atwater's tasteful memorandum was still there, and took the elevator up to the eighteenth floor. He had been as conscious of that memorandum all through the day as he would have been of a mustard-plaster. On taking it out and recreasing its immaculate folds he almost felt as if he were about to dispute a debt of honor.

Atwater was in, but he was completely taken up in radiating his careful affability upon some promising clients who wanted not only doors but the house that went with them. Ogden got no closer to him than to secure the attention of the clerk whose duty it was to mediate between the contractors and the plans they were to follow.

He was an alert, nervous young man, with a big shock of unruly hair and a pair of large, luminous eyes behind his hooked and shimmering spectacles. He ran his long, lean, inky fingers through his hair, and transferred his wide eyes from the memorandum to the man who had brought it in.

"No," he said presently; "it's all right—there's no mistake. Mr. Atwater took a good deal of interest in this work. He sketched out some of the drawings himself, to start with, and he even touched up a few of them to finish with."

"Touched up a few of them to finish with?" George repeated, inquiringly.

"Yes; he don't do that often. When he does, it makes a difference; it ought to."

The whole matter was coming to assume the aspect of a personal favor; it was a debt of honor, after all. The grocer, the upholsterer, and the rest of them might wait; it would give them time to learn the value of an elegant "presence" and the compelling force of personal acquaintance.

The doors, hung and paid for, swung open many times during the following winter and spring, to admit people whom, as his wife assured him, it was an advantage to know. He became conscious that she was actuated by motives quite different from his, and that she had a standard quite at variance from any that he himself would have set up. She strained for people that he would not have turned his hand for. Most of these had familiar names, and it sometimes seemed to him as if many of them had had their place in the social yearnings of Cornelia McNabb. Certainly, his wife's attitude was quite different from that of the Floyds, who had been disposed to pooh-pooh quietly almost everybody, and also from that of her own parents, who simply accepted the circle that chance and association had formed for them, and met everybody on the same dead level of good-will.

During Lent his wife arranged a small musicale; another Mary Munson had arrived—this time from Cincinnati. The names of the performers included only those of amateurs of the better sort—since she knew that good professional services were quite beyond her reach; yet chairs, awning, and refreshments called for the expense of outside supervision. The morning before it she put a slip of paper into his hands.

"You are going right past the *Tribune*. Won't you just leave this with them?"

It was an announcement of her musicale. It included a list of names—not those of the performers, but those of the listeners.

"All old friends—in print," her husband commented. "What do you care for these people? Why don't you ask the Fairchilds?—they're quiet, but they're nice; and they like music. Why don't you have your father and mother? I haven't seen either of them for a month."

His wife writhed delicately in protest. Her winter had increased her paleness. The blue veins were bluer in her temples; her large eyes looked larger yet, and there were faint circles under them.

"Well, Cecilia doesn't fancy Mrs. Fairchild very much, in the first place—"

George bit his lip. By the curious workings of chance he had never yet seen Cecilia Ingles, but he no longer joked about her non-actuality. She appeared to be looming up as the great power in his household.

"—and besides," she proceeded, "who would recognize their names if they saw them in print?"

George stood like a looker-on at a transformation-scene, before whose eyes the gauze veils are lifted one by one in slow succession.

"Oh, then," he said, and less in jest

than in earnest, "there is no use in enjoying ourselves unless we put it in the papers, and no use of putting it in the papers unless we can give a list of names, and no—"

"Now, George!" She flushed with vexation.

"—and no use of putting in a list of names unless they are names that will be generally recognized. Well, that *does* cut out the Fairchilds, and your poor mother, too. And mine." He looked at her narrowly.

"Now, George," she cried again, "how can you be so disagreeable? You know papa and mamma wouldn't care anything for this; nor your mother, either. And it isn't the only thing I'm ever going to have. I can ask her yet, though, if you want me to."

"Oh, fiddlesticks! Only don't lose your head. Here; give me that precious notice. Perhaps, before long, people who are after names will be just as anxious to get yours."

"You silly boy!" she cried, striking him lightly across the shoulder. But she was pleased and gratified by this, and she was not able to conceal it.

Following Lent there was the usual social aftermath. For Mrs. George Milward Ogden the major stress of the season was over, but she gave a few luncheons, and she went to a good many others. These little functions sent dozens of ladies tripping through the raw winds and the slushy streets of spring. The lake, weltering under the gray skies of March, dashed its vicious sprays high over the sea-wall, and sent its cruel blasts gashingly through the streets that ended on its confines. And at such signals asthma and bronchitis and pneumonia dug their clutching fingers into the throats and lungs of thousands of tender sufferers.

Jessie's supplementary doings were of too informal a nature to demand the entrance of outside help, but at the same time they were of a kind to lay the maximum strain upon the small and simply organized household which was all that her husband was as yet able to maintain.

About every so often the domestic tension overtook the breaking-point. An interregnum would follow, and then a change of dynasty. The blame for these economic hitches George was obliged to distribute with an even hand. He acknowledged frankly the mere muddishness of most of the peasant material that oozed in and out of his kitchen; but he was also obliged to recognize the utter tactlessness of his wife and the folly of her unguarded exhibitions of conscious superiority. She had never before been able to issue directions to two servants, and she had never acquired the practical experience necessary for the control of even one. She referred to her servants in their own hearing as servants; and this did not seem to her as inconsiderate from the point of humanity or unwise as a mere matter of policy.

The burden of this fell principally upon her husband. He was obliged now and then to temporize with an indignant cook to secure a dinner for the evening; on one occasion he employed all his finesse to effect without scandal the removal of a frantic chambermaid; and he became more familiarly known to the intelligence offices than he had ever expected to be. His wife was manifestly incapable of keeping a house, and he was committed to housekeeping for a year to come.

March passed and April came. One evening they sat together in their little parlor. The weather ouside was raw and rainy, and not all of its chill could be kept out by the grate-fire over which Jessie was cowering and shivering. She wore a fleecy wrap on which her thin fingers took a sinuous clutch, and she was nursing a cold whose sniffling discomfort seemed passing into an obstinate cough. She was running over the newspaper carelessly.

"I see Mayme Brainard's mother has

just died," she said presently. " 'On the eighth of April, at her residence'—and all that—'Abigail Brainard, aged fifty-six years.' Wasn't she any older than that? Well, I suppose not. No great change for her, is it?"

"What did she die of?"

"Oh, it was her lungs. It's a wonder that anybody lives through these springs. I can't think why we ever got so close to the lake as this. I don't feel sure getting through another winter here myself."

She leaned forward to stir the fire, and then lay back, coughing.

"I suppose they'll let Mayme come home, now—for the funeral, anyway. I wonder if she'll bring the baby; he swears he won't see it. Cornelia says it's a pretty little thing—Abbie was down there a month ago."

George stared at the fire thoughtfully, and reached mechanically for the poker.

"I don't know how they will feel, now, about staying in that house," she went on. "Cornelia wants to move the whole family over here, but Abbie won't listen to her. I don't know whether she likes her own part of town, but she seems to have taken a strong dislike to this. Anyway, she has never come near *me*, for all you helped them at her brother's wedding. Cornelia appears to think everything of her, though, and I guess she likes Cornelia quite a little. Funny isn't it, that those two— Goodness, George, don't knock the fire all to pieces. Here; let me have it."

She took the poker from him.

"Dear me, what a miserable flue!" She looked at him discontentedly, as she settled back wearily in her big chair. "And we've really got this house on our hands for a whole year more?" She seemed to feel in this one year the weight of eternity.

"That's what the lease says," he

responded, soberly. "What do you say?" his eyes seemed to ask.

She spoke her thoughts presently and at some length. She proposed giving up the house on the first of May. Was it a passing caprice or a serious desire? he wondered.

"Shall you take your porch and your doors with you?" he asked, with a sorry smile. "They cost enough to be worth considering."

"No," she answered, with the simple literalness that builds a stone wall in a moment. "We shouldn't need them in an apartment-house."

"That's the idea, is it?"

"Yes, it strikes me that that would be the best thing all around—an apartment-house, with a café or something. Lots of nice people live that way now. Look at Cecilia Ingles's cousin; she is invited everywhere, and she entertains just the same as if she was in her own house. It's too hard work for me to run things like this, and I've just got to get farther away from this miserable lake."

"There's all the furniture."

"We could use some of it."

"And store the rest?"

"Yes—or auction it."

"Small profit in either. What are you going to do with the lease? Store it, or auction it, or use it for furnishing?"

Her lip quivered sensitively. "Why, I supposed—"

"Yes, we *can* sublet the house—if anybody is found to take it. There was something of a wait before we took it. There might be another."

"There's that Mrs. Cass—"

"I don't know how much she could do in three weeks—a good many people are fixed by this time. Two weeks sooner would have made some difference. I couldn't very well afford to carry the house all through the summer. There's a bottom to our pocket-book, and we are getting to it faster than you think."

This was a figure of speech that called for no direct response. For—

"Well," she went on, "that's my idea: a flat, with our meals. This would give me my chance to get away for a part of the summer—I'm sure I need it."

"Away for a part of the summer?"

"Yes. Mary Munson was saying something about my going to the White Mountains with her in July. They would do me good. Though perhaps the sea-shore might be better; plenty of those Down-east people are indebted to me now."

Another of those gauze veils was lifting. Married life was but a prolongation of girlhood, with all its associations and peregrinations. Where did the husband come in?

They left the house on the first of May. George recognized by this time the essential slightness and incapacity of his wife, and renounced the possibility of a home in any but a modified sense. Part of their goods were sacrificed at auction, part were stored at a rate that would have provided a home for a working-man's family, a few pieces were utilized in filling up a partly furnished flat, and the deserted house remained vacant through the summer. It was not until October that its ornate front and its tasteful decorations caught the eye of the right man, and by October a complication of interests had made a vacant house the very least of Ogden's concerns.

The place came under the consideration of the

Floyds as soon as the intentions of the Ogdens became known. A decided change had come over Walworth's affairs; a less expensive house than his present one now seemed a great advantage. But his own lease ran for a year more; besides, his wife had too high an idea of their position and its dues to think of succeeding the young Ogdens in such a tenancy. The Floyds, as a matter of fact, were sinking to bed-rock—a foothold whose reality they had never tested yet; and there need be no wonder that the beginning of their downward course was marked by a slow reluctance. Walworth endeavored to make good the shortages occasioned through his brother's clippings by intrusting Ann with commissions on his behalf upon the Open Board—affairs in which she was no more successful for him than for herself; while his wife, for the first time, made some efforts in a society for which she had always had a shade of careless contempt.

The Ogdens established themselves anew in a large building where they had four or five small rooms, and where they could breakfast and dine with a few hundred persons of like requirements and like situation. George now began renewed efforts to turn to account the property for which he had received deeds from McDowell. His half-year of married life had put him in an awkward and straitened position, and the usual activity in real property that comes with the spring was something of which the utmost advantage must be taken.

He placed some of his outside acres with one or two good houses, but this entire side of business seemed pervaded by apathy.

"It's going to be an off-year," he was told. "Acres are down, and it looks as if they were going to stay so—for some time, anyway. We'll take this, though, and do what we can. You pay this year's taxes, of course?"

So much for the real estate.

McDowell's notes, which he had made to run for a longer term than pleased anybody but himself, showed the due and prompt endorsement of interest payments; and if there was anything else in the general situation to call for gratulation Ogden failed to discover it.

XX

Jessie Ogden's supposition with regard to Mary Brainard
was justified by events; the poor exile was allowed to come
back to town to attend her mother's funeral, and, thanks to
a providential escort, she was enabled to bring her child
with her. The two arrived under the charge of a distant
relative by marriage of the Centralia Brainards, who was
understood to be on the point of visiting the city anyway, for
the purpose of "buying goods." He was presented by the
name of Briggs.

He was a somewhat uncouth and slovenly
man of thirty-five—a fair specimen of the type evolved by
the small towns of southern Illinois. But he had a bright and
capable way with him, and it seemed likely enough that if he
were to transfer himself and his business to Chicago, as he
once spoke of doing, he might work himself up into pretty
fair shape. He was a widower.

He showed some fitting sense
of the solemnity of the occasion that had brought him to the

house; but it was fair to surmise from various tokens that his usual treatment of the subdued young mother was in the line of familiar kindness, which only genuine solicitude kept apart from semi-jocularity—a jocularity that had almost the effect of an understanding. He seemed to have about the same understanding with the baby; he had held it part of the time on the train, and he had shown a willingness to be useful in the same direction subsequently.

Brainard saw the child once. He looked at the boy's dark hair and eyes and vented a dreadful oath, and signified that while he and his mother were in the house the infant must be kept out of sight and out of sound.

Abbie Brainard made no effort towards further mediation between her father and her sister. The present status was endurable, and there was little to be gained by additional appeal to the irascible old man; it was irascibility rather than sorrow which now possessed him. Nothing irritated him more than an address to the deeper emotions, and the passing of his life-long partner was an address of this character. And this irascibility had risen to a pitch of fury on account of the unfortunate resemblance of Mary Vibert's child to its father.

Abbie was still leading her old life in her old way. She had her reading, her accounts, her church-work; but she went at these with less energy than she had shown a year ago. She had lost something in flesh and something in spirits, but nothing was slighted. She had no confidants and she made no moan.

"What *is* the matter with her?" Cornelia would now and then ask herself. "If she would only rip out and say something; but I never saw a girl who was so mum. I'll get her out of this place, though, if anybody can. She has got to come up there and live with me. I'll fetch that, if I have to pull her up by the roots."

And then, putting generalization in the place of any tangible particulars, "I believe she's just starving"—which was not altogether wrong.

Cornelia found no specific grounds for approaching her father-in-law about Abbie, but she had some words with him about Abbie's sister.

She went to him one evening in his den; it was the day after the funeral. The distant wailing of the baby's voice had caused him to shut the door of his little room with a profane slam.

"Mr. Briggs is right there in the parlor," she said to him boldly, "waiting for her to come down; I don't see that it's going to help things any to slam doors. If he don't mind the baby, I guess we don't have to."

He turned upon her fiercely and half rose from his chair. It seemed for a moment as if he was intending to put her out of the room.

But she stood her ground and stared him full in the face. She was the only one in the family who, when the real pinch came, could look him down. He fell back in his seat and fixed an uncertain eye upon the panels of the door.

"There's such a thing as sense at such places as this, if you'd only know it," she went on. She spoke out loudly; she knew that if she used a moderate voice her tones would tremble. "I should think we might hold in for the day or so that the man's here. He knows why she was sent off down there, and that's bad enough; but it's worse for him to bring her up here and have her treated bad right before his face. Why can't you speak to her at table? Why can't you have—"

"That will do, Cornelia." He beat on the arm of his chair with his doubled-up fist. "We won't have anything more of this sort of thing. That will do."

But

there was a kind of harsh grin on his face; he either admired her pluck or anticipated her point. She saw this and knew that she held him in her hand.

"No, it won't do, Cornelia—not yet. Why do you think he is here? Do you suppose a man goes travelling around the country with a woman and a three months' old baby for the fun of it? And he hasn't come up to 'buy goods'—don't you believe it. This is a great chance for Mayme, everything considered. He's a smart fellow, and you don't want to go and spoil it all. This is a thing that will take care of itself, if you'll only give it a show."

He stared at her—still rather forbiddingly. But she saw admiration appearing through indignation, and she judged that it was gaining the upper hand.

"Now," she said, with her own hand on the door-knob, "when you ask Mayme to-morrow morning if she would like another piece of steak, I want you to look at her; seems to me this is a time when a family should act *like* a family. And I guess it wouldn't hurt you much to put yourself out far enough to ask that man to smoke a cigar with you. You try. And I think this door had better stay the way I leave it."

She passed out, leaving the door open. And open it remained.

In such fashion as this came Mary Brainard to her mother's burial. But her younger brother came not, and no one knew where he was or what he might be doing.

Briggs left for Centralia on the following evening, his charges remaining behind, by an inconclusive arrangement that might terminate in almost any way. Cornelia, who attended his departure with a lively interest, noticed that Abbie, in her hat and cloak, was trying to take advantage of this same occurrence to steal out of the house. She followed her through the vestibule and overtook her half way down the steps.

"Abbie!" she called after her, "where are you going?"

"'Sh!" Abbie said, softly. "I'm just going out for a few minutes."

"Neighbors?"

"No, not exactly," the girl hesitated. "I'm just going a block or two."

"You don't want to be trotting around alone this time of night. Sha'n't I go with you?"

She placed her hand on Abbie's arm to draw her back while she put on her own things. She felt her companion tremble, and saw an expression of anxiety on her face which she took to mean embarrassment.

"No, Cornelia, I don't want you to go with me. I don't need you, I've got to go alone."

"Upon my word, I think you're acting mighty queer. I just believe, Abbie Brainard, that you are going out to meet somebody—you, of all people!"

Abbie started. "Supposing I am?" she stammered.

"Who is it?" asked Cornelia, peremptorily. Only an extremely eager interest would have made her take this tone with Abbie. "Well, I must say, I think your father is a little too bad. Why can't he see that girls have got to be girls? First it's Mayme and now it's—"

"Cornelia!" cried Abbie, with a violent blush and the trembling voice that foreshadows tears. "It's my brother! It's Marcus!"

"Marcus!" exclaimed Cornelia. "Then I *am* going, sure. Where are you to meet him—in the park?"

Abbie bowed assent.

"Well, then, you wait one second. I'll be right out again."

"Don't come. He won't speak to me if he sees anybody with me."

"I can stand around somewhere—I won't do any harm."

She was actuated as much by curiosity as by sympathy. She had never seen Marcus, but she remembered the "erring son" of her first play, and nothing more than one's first play has a fixed footing in one's association of ideas.

The park lay under the cold glare of the electric light, in the state of forbidding bareness that overtakes all such urban tracts during the earlier days of spring. Soggy footprints showed everywhere in the soaked brown turf that bordered the winding paths, and masses of dead leaves were matted together at the roots of the spindling shrubbery. The arc-lights threw a ghastly illumination on the flat white fronts of the houses that stood around in rows outside as well as on the stretches of theatrical posters which filled up the spaces between; and they flung deep shadows into the flimsy arbors and kiosks that started up here and there within. Abbie, with her companion, traversed a number of spongy, gravelled paths, and presently the figure of a man emerged from a summer-house and advanced to meet her. Cornelia turned off, and paused behind the thickened stalks of a bare bush.

"Marcus!" cried Abbie, as her brother moved towards her, "Marcus, why didn't you come? I waited at the door to let you in. Could anybody have made any trouble at such a time as that?"

He came up to her with a few unsteady steps. His eyes were blood-shot, and on his face, which seemed paler and thinner than ever under the white flood from the globe overhead, there was a long, half-healed scar. He looked at her in a dull, dazed way; perhaps he simply misapprehended these present words,

208

perhaps he was unable to fully comprehend any words at all.

"You could have gone in a carriage all alone with me," she went on, in pitiful reproach. "And you could have stayed in it—you needn't have seen anybody else at all. I wanted you so much. Mayme came; why couldn't you? Oh, Marcus, you were thought of; your name was almost the last one said."

She threw her head on his shoulder and burst into tears. He gave way a little, and then, with an effort, he mastered a steadier pose.

Her crape brushed his face; he felt it, rather than saw it.

"Is he dead?" Something like light came into his dull eye. The lamp above gave a sudden vast flicker, and the long scar on his face deepened and lengthened and came back to itself again. It was all like a sinister and cynical smile.

"Marcus! don't you know? Where have you been? Haven't you got any of my letters?"

He leaned against the silly rusticity of the summer-house, and looked at her with a dazed but inquiring eye.

"It's mother! It's mother!" the poor girl cried. "Why didn't you come?"

"Why, how is this?" asked Cornelia, stepping forward. "Hadn't he heard?"

"I mailed them to the same place. And the money—didn't you get that, either?"

He looked at her steadily and soberly, but his eyes had a heavy droop. "It's mother," he said at length; "it's mother that's dead." He sat down carefully on the steps of the summer-house. "And my name was the last. Always the last, Abbie. When was it?"

"Has he moved—do you suppose?" asked Cornelia. She regarded him long and steadily. She seemed about to recognize him—though voice was apparently counting for more than face.

"It was only day before yesterday," Abbie said. "I tried to see you, but it was so far and there was so much to do. But I sent you word."

"I haven't been there lately," he said slowly. "I couldn't have come day before yesterday," he added presently.

"Where have I seen him before?" thought Cornelia. And, "What is the matter with him?" she seemed to ask of Abbie.

"I couldn't come," he repeated. "I'm sorry," he added humbly. "I was—somewhere else."

"Have you been away all these three months? I haven't seen you since almost New Year's. Have you been away from the city all this time?"

"I have been somewhere—somewhere else," he repeated thickly. He rose tremblingly. "I suppose they'll have me there again, some time. Well, all right," he said, with resignation.

"What does he mean?" asked Abbie, turning appealingly to Cornelia.

Marcus followed his sister's eyes. He looked at Cornelia narrowly, his own eyes half closed. "Who is this?" he asked.

"It's Cornelia—Burt's wife."

"Burt's wife?" He held her with an enigmatical stare. "I have seen her," he said; "before."

"Where?" thought Cornelia. "Not possibly at—the theatre?"

"In church," he explained, with a slow gravity. "He isn't dead—Burt?"

"Dead?" cried Cornelia. "No, indeed."

"No, he isn't dead," Marcus repeated deliberately. His eyelids raised themselves. "He is married; he has half a million," he went on, with the same slowness. His eye lighted up with a malignant glare. "No, he isn't dead. But—"

He stretched himself aloft, and thrust out his arm, and staggered, and only half-saved himself.

"—but I will kill him," he added suddenly.

"Marcus!" his sister screamed; "are you mad?"

He lay slantingly against the corner of the summer-house. His arm caught at the crosspieces of the rustic carpentry, and he hung there panting. Presently a little stream of blood began to trickle across the palm of his hand—he had torn himself on a nail. He felt the warm fluid on his skin, and held up his hand to his own curious and impersonal inspection.

"Give me your handkerchief, Cornelia," Abbie implored pitifully. She folded her own and laid Cornelia's over it, and twisted it around his thumb and tied it over his wrist.

His fingers felt thin and claw-like, and there was a grime rubbed into their cracked and roughened skin—those girlish fingers (his mother's fingers) that had once held a pencil so delicately.

"I have seen her—before," he repeated. "Here." He jerked his hand out of his sister's hold and waved it over the circumscribed and shabby landscape. The light shimmered on the leaden surface of the pond behind them, and the wind rustled the stark weeds along it muddy edges. "I knew it was coming." Abbie caught his hand back. "Half a million; he never did anything for me. I will kill *him*," he muttered faintly.

Cornelia continued her inspection of him. "Abbie, just look at these clothes, will you? And he hasn't got any cuffs on, either."

"Marcus!" his sister called appealingly. Her raised voice indicated that, after all, she must acknowledge him as other than himself. "All that money I sent you—you need it. Go right away to-morrow to your old number and get it." She turned to Cornelia. "I haven't got any; have you? I forgot it, after all."

"Just this half-dollar," she answered. "Exactly what I paid," she said to herself, "to see him in this part once before." She recognized him now; she saw that she had been interested in the new actor because nobody else had seemed so; and she felt sure that his attempt on the stage had been the same brief failure that all of his other attempts must have been as well.

Marcus raised himself, and a sly smile came over his face. "Money?" he said. "Keep it. I don't want it. I can raise all I need. Vibert knew the ropes, and now I know them just as well myself. I can do business all right again. No money, Abbie; no." He thrust it back upon her. "He always said I wasn't *fit* for business; but I'll show him."

He braced himself and stepped out decidedly into the path. He turned in the direction of the exit. The other two insensibly took this direction as well, and fell to regulating their steps by his.

"You are a good sister, Abbie," he said, as they passed out. "You have been good to me. Good." He put his hand on hers; he had forgotten that it was bandaged. There was a soft stringency in the folds of the handkerchiefs, but she felt his grateful pulses underneath.

"Oh, Cornelia," moaned poor Abbie; "I must take him home—I must—I must! So near at hand—and the place where he belongs. I can't leave him to go wandering around like this."

Marcus laid his bandaged hand on his sister's shoulder. "No, Abbie." The earlier waves of a sodden stupor now seemed to be washing over him, and he looked on the two girls with a dull leer. "Not home. Better place than home. But some time—I will come home some time. He never treated me as well as he did Burt." His tones came thickly. "I will kill him," he murmured softly to himself in a drunken confidence.

He turned off, down a side street. Abbie stood watching him as he disappeared, to reappear in the light of frequent lamp-posts. Presently he turned a corner. Abbie clasped her hand tightly in her companion's and allowed herself to be led home.

"Another job for me," said Cornelia, thoughtfully.

XXI

The Ogdens, in their apartment, presented to their callers substantially the same aspect that they had offered in a complete house, save that the dining-room had been lopped off, along with the kitchen. They were a shade more compact and, if anything, a shade more luxurious.

Among the first of their callers here was the faithful Brower. As he lounged back in a familiar easy-chair he cast his eye around the drawing-room and the reception-hall; he recognized a number of things from the other house, and detected, too, a good many novel elegancies. In one corner of the room, in particular, there stood a delightful little tea-table; and he learned that the full paraphernalia of the delicate function known as "a tea" could be produced at a moment's notice.

On the purchase of this adjunct to polite living Jessie had brought all her insistence to bear. Life to her had now come merely to mean receiving and being received; and to receive at all she must receive correctly and elegantly.

214

"It's about all I feel equal to doing now—giving teas," she explained; "and that's all the more reason why I should do it properly. Now, Cecilia Ingles's table and china—"

"For Heaven's sake, Jessie, please to remember that you are not Mrs. Ingles and that I am not her husband. Can you expect me to compete with a man who has an income like his? Do you know what that building—that building alone—pays him a year?"

"Well, I only want things nice. I shall have to live quietly for a while—I don't feel as if I had any great strength; and I don't think I ought to be denied such a small thing as this."

Hence the charming little tea-table, the delicate and exquisite porcelain, and the beautifully burnished kettle; and hence, too, the cup for Brower, so that he might see how the whole thing went. But the hand that passed it to him was white and tremulous, and the graceful bit of lace over the wrist fluttered with a pitiful palpitation.

"I'm going to put another lump on your saucer; so sorry you have caught us without a lemon." She smiled at him as she spoke, and he could not but see that her lips had a bluish tinge. "So good of you to let me come in just as I was." She smoothed down the fall of lace along the front of her wrapper. "But I hardly felt equal to dressing this evening; besides, an old friend like you—"

The "old friend" went home and talked things over with his room-mate.

He lit the burners on both sides of his dressing-case mirror and slowly took off his coat. His room-mate was in his shirt-sleeves, too.

"I wonder if he is happy," said Brower, thoughtfully running his thumb-nail along the teeth of his tortoise-shell comb.

"He tried hard enough to be," answered his room-mate, running his thumb along the teeth of *his* comb.

Brower sighed and looked with frank but troubled eyes into his friend's face. "Too hard, perhaps."

The other returned his glance in kind. "I'm afraid so," he breathed.

"He figured it all out beforehand," said Brower. "We talked a good deal on the subject generally."

"That sort of thing doesn't always pay."

"We considered the rich girl and the poor girl," Brower went on. "But there's another kind of girl that we both failed to take account of."

"What kind is that?"

"The girl in very moderate circumstances who has spent all her time in going about among wealthy relatives and friends."

"The poor princess who makes the grand chain of other people's castles?"

"Yes," assented Brower; "the grand chain of other people's castles. It's demoralizing."

"Is he a disappointed man?"

"Yes; I'm certain of it. Disappointed, and worried half to death. I'm sorry for him. I'm afraid for him."

He sat down on the edge of the bed and began to unlace his shoes. His room-mate wore shoes of the same size and laced them in the same way.

"I wonder," said he, "if he really loved her?"

"'Sh!" said Brower.

"Wasn't there another one that he *did* love?"

"Not a word more!" cried Brower.

216

He undressed and got into bed. He took a book with him. It was "A Mistaken Marriage"—he read everything.

"What do you want to read for?" asked the other. "It's late."

"I read because I don't want to think." He opened at the mark and settled back on his pillow and started in.

"Where are you now?" demanded his double.

"Page 316; the castle's on fire."

"Do you want anything more about castles?"

"No."

"And haven't you had enough of fires?"

"Plenty."

"Well, then!"

Out went the gas, and sleep presently succeeded.

The Ogdens had other callers; among them was Frederick Pratt.

Frederick had left the Underground for the temple at the extreme end of the street, where he was engaged in an ardent study of puts and calls. The atmosphere of the Board of Trade is less sedate than that of the clearing-house association, and the new recruit had become still more volatile and giddy. He was skating on thinner ice and was putting more assurance into his movements.

Pratt, like Brower, made his own observations on the new status of the Ogdens; but unlike Brower, he did not keep his opinions and conjectures to himself. He gave the same currency to his reflections on this pair that he had given to those on the Viberts—and among others thus favored were the Floyds.

"What's the matter with George,

anyhow?" he asked Walworth one evening. They were sitting again in Floyd's library, and a light haze of tobacco-smoke prompted to elegiac revery. "He looks old. And he has come to be as poky as the deuce. He seemed last night as if he was worried half to death."

"I guess he is," answered Walworth. "He's anxious about his wife, for one thing."

"Well, she does look pretty bad, that's a fact. I don't believe she will live the year out. The first cold weather will carry her off."

"Don't say that!" exclaimed Mrs. Floyd. "She's delicate, and she has got to take care of herself. But to talk about dying—that's another thing."

"I'm not so sure." And Walworth shook his head gravely.

"But there's something more than that," said Freddy. "It's money. Gad! how they are fixed up! How can he stand it?"

"He can't," answered Walworth; "he's falling behind. And there is that house of his empty yet. I'd take it off his hands myself if it wasn't for being left in the same fix too. Wish I could help him; he hasn't said anything, though."

"He won't, either," replied Pratt. "He ain't that kind."

"Well, I don't see that we need trouble ourselves about help," Ann broke in. "He harmed me, anyway, a great deal more than he helped me—with that precious brother-in-law of his."

"I imagine he knows all about the brother-in-law, too, by this time," rejoined Walworth. "Haven't you got almost tired of twanging that string?"

He wondered if Ogden's brother-in-law were really as trying as his own sister-in-law.

Still other

218

callers favored the Ogdens. Among them was one that had not called at the other house—that had never before, indeed, called at any house whatever. About the first of August a little débutante appeared on the social scene and was "received" with all the care and flattering attention that the new apartment had at its disposal. She was a pale and fragile little bud, like many of the exotics with which her mother was fond of decorating her rooms; she had the same slender fingers that set these flowers around, and the same large blue eyes that studied their effect.

A nurse came, and she stayed long after the time when a mere nurse-maid should have taken her place. Curtains were pulled down and kept so; the doctor's carriage (and sometimes more than one) stood waiting before the big doorway of the "Westmoreland"; bottles big and little accumulated on tables and shelves; and cautious tiptoeing became the habit of the whole household; until, at the end of a month, mother and child were doing as well—and only as well—as could be expected. This was not well at all. But both were out of immediate danger, and presently both appeared to mend.

The nurse-maid now arrived, and the carriage and the cap. The languid young mother was capable of taking but a tepid interest in most things, but she rallied her powers to enforce the cap. Cecilia Ingles was her model here as in other matters, and the model was followed closely. Not every girl would wear a cap, but at last a capable one was found who was willing to. The lace cover of the perambulator and the white frills of its propeller were a frequent sight on the streets for a little time; then the necessity developed for the transfer of mother, child, and nurse, during a few weeks, to the convenient sanatorium provided by nature in southern Wisconsin.

The little party was back again in town at the opening of the fall season. Jessie employed her dwindling powers in a partial resumption of the duties which she felt that "society" demanded of her, and the child taxed the energies and resources of the maid, who received little real assistance from its mother. There were small gusts and starts of maternal affection now and then, but they would quickly run their brief course and baby would be carried out of the room. Ogden wondered, from a curiously impersonal outside standpoint, whether he was to attribute this to his wife's waning vitality or to an inherent incapacity for deep and genuine feeling.

But this matter soon passed beyond the confines of discussion. The day came when the nurse was dismissed, the carriage was put away, and Brower went with the stricken father to select a lot in the cemetery. It came that the two stood together one forenoon before a wide and polished mahogany counter, and bent their heads over a handsome plat that was neatly lettered and numbered, and was shaded in pleasant tints of blue and green. A man stood on the other side of the counter and tapped the drawing here and there with the reversed end of a fat pen-holder.

"This is a good section," he said; he was pausing over a green oval which was intersected by four or five fine black lines. "You are right on a leading drive-way"—carrying the pen-holder along between the waving of two other and wider lines that ran parallel—"and just over here is the lake"—with his little finger on a tangled and shapeless patch of blue.

"That small lot could be made to do," said Brower, softly.

"This is the most fashionable part of the whole place," the man went on, with an indifferent loudness. "See here." He took down a large warped photograph from its place on a dusty shelf behind him, and gave it a dexterous wipe with his elbow. "This monument here is just across the drive-way, and it cost twenty thousand dollars. Put up this summer by Arthur J. Ingles—I guess you've heard of *him*."

220

"Good God!" groaned Ogden. "Have I got to compete with that man even in the graveyard?"

The next afternoon a sombre little procession took its way limits-ward to a tract outside, which was tenderly enclosed by great stretches of barbed wire, and was neighbored by the noise and glare of several stone-cutting yards. This little train traversed the raw and ragged edges of the town, and trailed across the succeeding reach of open prairie-land, over which led a long, straight, sandy road, dotted here and there with houses of refreshment for the occupants of mourning-coaches and for their drivers. There was the raw chill in the air which the north sometimes sends down into our early October days. The poor mother sobbed and coughed and shivered in her corner of the carriage; she returned to her home ill and exhausted, and entered it never to leave it alive.

It costs when a baby comes, it costs when a baby goes, it costs when a wife lies sick and dying, and Ogden now confessed himself almost driven to the wall.

"I know, George," his wife said, "that everything has been a great expense; but I'm sure papa would help us if you only spoke to him."

"What!" he cried, harshly.

She started, and presently was all a-tremble. Then she fell back weakly and coughed long and violently. "Oh, George, how could you?" she gasped.

"Forgive me, my poor child," he said, and took her hand. "But I could never do anything like that—never."

The next day he took the McDowell notes and spent what time he could spare among the brokers. They passed commendingly on the prompt payment of the interest as shown by the endorsements; but McDowell was pretty well known, and it

221

was intimated that endorsements of another sort would be needed to make negotiation possible.

Then he got out the abstract of one of the McDowell tracts—the only one that he personally and individually had any right to use. "You've got considerably more than a pocketful there," the door-keeper of the Clifton Deposit Vaults said to him as he passed out. He left the abstract with a firm of mortgage brokers for examination. In the course of a week they advised him that a release had been overlooked—an instrument which must show of record before a loan could be effected on the property.

The tract had been put through a good many paces, and some of McDowell's work had been too hurried to be careful. The man to give the necessary release was a professional tax-buyer. He lived on the mistakes and misfortunes of other people—their sins of omission and commission; and such an act from such a man would cost something. It might be ten dollars, or fifty, or five hundred.

He waited in this harpy's outer office, while another caller, a woman, claimed attention in the inner one. It was Ann Wilde; he recognized her and she recognized him. She threw a scowling glance upon him, and her harsh and vindictive tone fell on his ears for several succeeding minutes. She knew his necessities; could she be making them known to another?

It seemed so when his turn came. The release would be given only on payment of a sum that, in his present circumstances, was simply impossible.

He seemed now to have exhausted all expedients—all legitimate ones. A bitter recollection of that Sunday drive in the country came over him; he had indeed given a free rein to his wife, and just how close he was to graze against ruin only the future could show. He spent a miserable, sleepless night, and at daybreak he had decided to tax the bank for his

222

own necessities—relying upon the present maturing of his notes to set himself right within a month or two. Do not inquire as to his precise method—there are many ways to take: the actual appropriation of currency, the abstraction of securities, the over-issue of certificates of stock, and so on and on. He chose the method which seemed liable to the lightest misconstruction and allowable of the promptest reparation. He avoided seeing himself in the aspect of a criminal by pleading his own cruel needs and by believing in his ability to make a prompt and complete restitution. Perhaps neither of these two reasons could have stood alone, but they leaned together and held each other up—a precarious poise that was not long to endure.

XXII

It endured, in fact, scarcely a fortnight. It lapsed at the close of a dull October day—a day that was within one of the first anniversary of his marriage. Let the means by which he was detected be asked no more than the means through which he transgressed. The delicate mechanism of a bank's accounts responds sensitively to the slightest and most ingenious variation; and it may be, too, that some one in this particular bank was watching for the slip and was waiting for the chance to expose and punish it.

The smoky dusk of the short afternoon was falling outside, while within, under the illumination made by a single electric light, a mother, in the same room where one of Brainard's daughters had plead for the other, was now pleading with him for her son.

No taint had ever fallen before on any of her family or connections. She was crushed and dazed at the thought that anything like this had happened, could have happened, had had the slightest need of happening. And she was dumfounded that all explanation fell upon heedless ears, and that all offers of restitution encountered such stubborn, brutish, and determined opposition.

"We have lands," she cried, with the tears coursing down her anxious face. "We can make this good, twice and three times over. What more can you want?"

But Brainard *did* want something more. He wanted the ruin of her son.

"A bank can't deal in real estate," he said doggedly.

He sent a malevolent glance across the table on whose far edge Ogden's bowed head was resting. Beside Ogden stood Fairchild; there was a look of sympathetic distress upon his kindly face.

"It is true," he said, in a low and quiet tone, "that it is not allowable for us to make a loan upon real property; but it would not be amiss for us to take it in payment of this—this—"

"Theft!" cried Brainard loudly. Ogden winced and shuddered; his mother sank into a chair with a low moan.

"Look here, Fairchild," the old man went on, holding up his forefinger with an offensively masterful effect of caution, "it will pay you to go pretty slow just about here. This"—he wagged his head contemptuously towards the bowed head of the culprit —"was *your* man. You took his letters; you put him in here. Just stop and think of that!"

Fairchild bit his lip.

"And the other man, before him, was yours. Don't forget that, either." His face showed a cruel and malignant grin.

Fairchild flushed, and lowered his eyes to the floor in silence. Ogden half raised his head to look at him; what could these words mean? He looked at his mother, too; she was lying back with her face in her hands.

The young man's own face was mapped with the lines of a worry that goads one on to desperation, and it was painted with the blended hue that comes from shame and anxiety and fear and the exhausting struggles carried on through long and sleepless nights. It was hard to face these other faces; it was hard to face even the light of day, thick and dulling though it might be. His head drooped again to the friendly dusk of the table-top before him.

"By Heaven," Brainard went on, "not another man comes into this bank except under a guarantee; and he'll pay the premium for it if he don't stay more than a week. You might think, in a small bank like this, that some kind of eye could be kept on things; but is seems not. It's pick and steal, all the time; first one, then another. No sooner is young Pratt rooted out than this fellow comes up. One steady string of flea-bites—I can't stand it; I won't stand it. Do you think I am going to have Shayne and Cutter and all the rest of 'em go around and tell how Brainard's always got somebody else's hand in his pants pocket and never finds it out? Not very much. I do find it out and I'm going to punish it. You needn't ask me to hold off—it's no use. There's a law for this, and that law is going to take its course."

His white hair stood up in a stiff shock over his forehead, and the gray gristle sprouting on his lip moved up and down forbiddingly as the lip itself worked over the broken row of his teeth. The red veins in his nose showed more redly yet, and his fists were clenched at the ends of his down-hung arms with the straightened tension of an inexorable will.

"My poor boy! My poor boy!" his mother cried. She came over to him and bowed her head on his.

Fairchild looked at Brainard—a look that called for all his

self-control and fortitude. "This is too hard," he said. "There was provocation for him, and there are means to make everything good."

"See here, Fairchild," cried the enraged old man, "you have got to keep out of this, if you want to stay friends with me. We've pulled together a good while, but we shall pull apart after five seconds more of this. That young man there has fooled along with us a little too far. He has had his fun, and now he shall pay for it. He shall; by God, I say he shall!"

His voice rose to a harsh and strident cry, and his great fist fell with a ponderous thud on the table before him.

A second later another hand was heard—on the other side of the door. It was faint, but it was audible. It had been preparing for five long and hesitating minutes. To the heart that guided this hand the five seemed five-and-twenty.

Fairchild moved swiftly towards the door and laid his hand upon the knob to prevent any intrusion.

The knock was repeated. He opened the door to a narrow crack. Then he opened it wider.

Abbie Brainard stood on the threshold.

She stepped in swiftly and softly. She shut the door behind her quickly and then leaned her back against its shining panels.

Her face was pale; her bosom was heaving; but her gray eyes gave out the strong and steady light of courage and resolution.

Ogden saw her. He locked his jaws, and took a firm hold on the two arms of his chair, and raised himself and stood erect before her. Had not she herself, on this very spot, once done the same for him? However it might be, or might have been, with others, here, at least, was one who should not see him humbled.

There was no salutation of any kind on either side. She saw him, but seemed to be looking beyond him rather than at him; and in his eyes she stood there with the remote inaccessibility of some distant snow-peak.

Her father turned towards her.

"Abbie! You here? What do you want? What do you mean by coming in like this? Go out again!"

She looked at him with a cool and quiet inflexibility. But her voice was low and trembling as she said,

"I shall stay."

"You can't; you mustn't. You don't want to mix up in this business—you don't understand."

He laid one hand on her arm, and with the other he reached out towards the door-knob.

She withdrew her arm from the hold of his fingers.

"I understand," she said, immovably.

He drew back. "You do? Well, stay then, if you will, and understand better. Learn what kind of a man he really is."

He thrust out his arm towards Ogden, with a cruel and contemptuous smile.

"He came here with letters," he began. "We gave him a chance. Nobody really knew what he was—"

Ogden stood there straight before him. He ground his teeth together to keep his face composed; behind him his nails dug into the palms of his hands, as he held himself back from springing forward and fastening them around the throat of Abbie Brainard's father. There was a ringing in his ears, and through it there sounded faintly the fine tones of Fairchild, speaking to Mary Brainard:

"Nobody really knows who he is, or who his people are, or where he is from . . . a town full to overflowing with single young men . . . from everywhere. They are taken on faith. Most of them are all right, no doubt; but others—"

He was now one of the "others"; his "people," whom no one had known, were to be known now, after years of probity, as the relatives of a—

"Nobody really knew who he was," Brainard repeated; "but he was taken right in and given a good place. Hasn't he ever wondered why? Is it so easy to go into a new town, and get a good job in a bank the very first thing? Wasn't there any other men to jump at the chance of a position half as good—ain't the city full of 'em? Wasn't there any of 'em in the bank itself who was waiting for the place themselves— and had a right to it, too? Why was there a vacant place to fill, anyhow? Because, a week before, another man had done just what this man has done. He was your man, Fairchild, too. And why did this one here come stepping in ahead of all the old ones? You fixed it, Fairchild; you liked his looks and his talk, you said. Another bad guess for you."

Fairchild studied the carpet with abashed eyes, as were he himself the culprit.

"Yes," Brainard continued, "he was put in a good place and he was pushed right along. Hasn't he ever guessed why? Does a new man come into an office like this, and get as far along inside of a year as he has, without there being any reason for it? I'll tell him the reason for it. I did it because my girl here—"

"Father!" cried Abbie, with face aflame. "No! No!"

"You say you understand," he said, turning towards her. "Now, let *him* understand, too. I advanced him to this position," he went on shamelessly, "because my girl here asked me to."

229

"No, father! No!" the
poor child cried. She threw her shamefaced head on Mrs.
Ogden's bosom. She had never seen her before, but under
such circumstances the only place for a woman's face was
on another woman's breast.

"Yes, you did, too—ask me," he
went on, with increased hardihood. "Or just the same as
asked—I knew what you meant, well enough. And I said to
myself I'd do it. One girl went wrong," he continued, with a
choking in his throat, "and I wanted to do what I could to—I
wanted Abbie to do different; I wasn't going to have her
carried off by another infernal scoundrel."

Ogden flushed
and paled and sank down into his chair. His head dropped
into his hands; there was no possibility of his holding it up
before anything like this.

"And so I helped him on. I said, 'If I
do the right thing by him, he will do the right thing by—her;
he will act like a man.' I *did* do the right thing by him—and
what then? He had been hanging around all the spring—taking walks and sitting out in front and borrowing books. But
the moment I put him on his legs what did he do?"

He was
addressing the young man's mother now, whose tear-
stained face showed over Abbie's black hat, and whose poor
old hand was laid tenderly on Abbie's shoulder. It was plain
to every one now that the question was not one of money.
Ogden saw clearly enough at last why he had suffered wreck
when so many others had ridden the waves. Pratt had
filched and had escaped. McDowell had plundered right
and left and had never been brought down. Brainard himself
had piled up a scandalous fortune and yet had contrived to
evade the law. But none of them had come athwart the
mortified rage of a father—a father who had humbled his
inborn savageness and pride for a daughter's sake and had
humbled himself in vain.

Ogden glanced across towards

Abbie. She rested on his mother's shoulder as once, almost, and in this very room, she had rested on his. He knew why she had come; he recognized her devotion and her bravery. She had overlooked his pitiful palterings; she had forgiven the final slight to which they had led; she had imperilled her modesty and mortified her self-love by coming here that she might save him from her father's vengeance.

Her father looked at her now and took a softer tone.

"She's the best girl there ever was in the world," he declared, with a choking voice and a moistened glimmer in his eyes; "and the smartest—she knows how to do everything; she's the only real comfort I've ever had. She would be a credit to any man, I don't care who. And what does he pass her over for? For another," he went on, with a recrudescence of his insane and primitive jealousy, "who can't care for her house, who couldn't be a mother to his child, who has ruined him by her extravagance—"

"Stop!" cried Ogden. He rose and approached Brainard. There was a threatening glitter in his eyes, and convulsive twitches played among his fingers.

"Yes, stop, for Heaven's sake," said Fairchild, laying an expostulatory hand on the old man's arm. "Stop," he murmured again; "his wife is dying."

Abbie rushed between Ogden and her father. "George! George!" she cried. "Don't! Be patient!"

"What if his wife *is* dying?" called out the infuriated old wretch. "Is that any reason for lying down when he has slighted my daughter and robbed me?"

"For shame, father! For shame!" She hid her face in her hands, and her tears gushed through them.

Ogden paused, stung and quivering. His hands dropped; his fingers relaxed. His

231

wife was dying! Nobody had told him that before, and he had never dared to tell it to himself. But it was true, and he knew it.

Abbie rose again and confronted her father. The tears were still in her eyes and a wide blush suffused her cheeks.

"Father, you shall not punish him. He may have done wrong, but there was reason for it. And any wrong he *has* done can be set right."

Ogden's eyes were bedimmed, but through the moisture he seemed to see again the sight that closed the evening of his one-day wedding journey towards the north; again he stood on the bridge, and the sun set over one lake while the moon rose over the other. Only now, with Abbie Brainard's blushes before his body's eye and his wife's pale face before his mind's eye, a confusion came alike over his thought and his vision; it was now the sun rising on him at the moment that the pallid moon was going down. He looked at her and she looked at him, and in the eyes of both there was read the confession of a great mistake. Then her eyes drooped for shame and his for disloyalty, and neither one was able to look into the other's face again.

"Do you defend *him?*" her father cried. "Can you forgive *her?* I can't do either. No quarter; don't ask it, Abbie. He has chosen his course—he is responsible for his acts. And he shall answer for them, as any other man must who crosses me."

He flung open the door and passed out. Fairchild stood anxiously over the chair in which Abbie lay back panting for breath. Ogden pressed her hand and turned towards his mother.

"Come, let us go," he said, and the two passed out into the great vestibule of the Clifton. He signalled the elevator.

"Wait for me here, mother—five

minutes;" he spoke in a voice which she hardly recognized as his. "Twelfth," she heard him say to the boy inside.

"Twelfth!" she gasped. "Twelfth? It's Eugene!"

She tried to stop him; her fingers merely caught in the grille-work that shut off the empty shaft.

Why do we go mad? Why do we kill ourselves? Why is there more insanity and more self-murder to-day than ever before? It is because, under existing conditions, the relief that comes from action is so largely shut off. How has humanity contrived to endure so well the countless ills of countless ages? Because society has been, in general, loose-knit, so that each unit in it has had room for some individual play. What so increases and intensifies the agonies of to-day? The fact that society has a closer and denser texture than ever before; its fine-spun meshes bind us and strangle us. Indignation ferments without vent; injury awaits with a wearing impatience the slow and formal infliction of a corporate punishment; self-consciousness paralyzes the quick and free action that is the surest and sometimes the only relief.

McDowell was in his office alone. A single light was burning in the room, and nothing remained but the drawing down of a desk-top and the quenching of the light before locking the door from the outside and calling the day's work over. He looked up as Ogden entered.

"Oh, it's you. I haven't seen you for some time past." He used the dubious intonation that marks a half-smothered enmity.

"Yes, it's I. And you won't see me for some time to come. You see me this once."

He stood with his hand on the back of a chair. He made no motion to seat himself, but he was unmistakably planted there to remain. McDowell therefore resumed his own accustomed chair beside his desk.

"Well, what is it?" he asked.

He scrutinized Ogden with an undisguised curiosity. The young man's voice sounded strange in his ears; his face had an expression which made it almost the face of an acquaintance now first met.

"I have come to square with you," began Ogden, slowly. He passed an unconscious hand along the varnished back of the chair; it was a chair in yellow oak, whose frame was light but strong, and whose seat was of cane.

"We *are* square," said McDowell, curtly. "You have your deeds for that ground—all put into the settlement at a fair value. I have paid your interest as it came due, and shall go on doing so. The principal the same. I'm all right; what is it *you* want? Try the courts, if you think you can reach me."

"I shall reach you."

"I wonder how?"

Ogden lifted his hand from the chair to his forehead, across which he passed it once or twice. McDowell gave him an amused smile.

"You have robbed me," Ogden said; "you have disgraced me; you have brought me to the edge of ruin. You took advantage of my trust, my inexperience, my strangeness to the city. You have stripped us all, and you have used my sister for a shield. You knew we would stand everything for her, and we *have* stood everything. You have acted like a sneak and a coward."

McDowell's eyes dropped to his desk. But no flush mounted to his face; that would have been a physical and a moral impossibility. He looked up again after a moment.

"You will reach me? I wonder how?"

234

Ogden, for
the first time in his life, passed completely out of himself.
There fell away from him all the fetters that shackle the
super-civilized man who is habitually conscious of his
civilization.

"Like this."

He seized the chair, raised it over
McDowell's head, and went out, leaving the man crushed
and bleeding on the floor.

XXIII

Brainard, after leaving the office of the bank, had also taken the elevator, and before Ogden had reached McDowell's floor his chief stood at the door of Freeze & Freeze; the firm did some legal business for him now and then, under his own general designation of "odd jobs." But their door was locked, as it usually was at that hour; and the old man descended again, took the street-car, and went home to tea.

"I've got him, all the same," he muttered to himself. "He can have a little leeway if he wants, but it won't carry him very far off—as things are now."

He stamped and fumed through the parlor floor for the quarter of an hour during which he attended the preparation of tea in the basement dining-room. He sat down with Burt and Cornelia and his younger daughter; Abbie had shut herself up in her room, and had sent down word that she was too ill to appear.

The
table was set with the plated ware of twenty years ago,
hideous in varied quirks and chasings. Just within the door
of the room stood a baby's high-chair; and Brainard, in
passing to his place, contrived to put a vicious foot heavily
on one of its sprawling wicker legs.

He went through the
meal with a great grinding of molars and a loud smacking of
lips. He said nothing; he handled his knife and fork and his
goblet with a heavy-handed clatter, while his eyes stared
fixedly at the table-cloth. The others watched him in
silence; his teeth were grinding something other than food,
and the smacking of his lips indicated a relish beyond that
for any mere eating and drinking.

After his second cup of tea
he arose and pushed back his chair, and planted his feet
with a ponderous stamp on the space over which the chair
had stood.

"Burt," he said, as he moved towards the door,
"you can step down the street when you get through, and
tell Albert Freeze to come up here. I shall be in my
room."

He commanded the attendance of his attorneys as
lightly as he commanded that of his clerks. The Freezes
happened to be youngish men, but it would have been the
same with older ones.

He withdrew to his den. He
rearranged the coke-balls that he had had spread on the top
of his grate fire, and then he began to rummage among the
disordered papers on his desk.

A book was lying among
them—a thin volume, with the place marked by a
paper-cutter.

"I wish Abbie wouldn't leave her things
around everywhere," he said, grumblingly.

He tossed the

237

book across to a table. The paper-cutter fell out of it, but landed by its side, where it balanced on one corner of the table-top. It was a cumbrous implement, somewhat after the fashion of a dagger, and it was smeared over with something that produced the effect of green bronze.

He went to the window and looked out before pulling down its shade; the window opened, after the manner of a door, on the side porch. A misty rain was falling—slight, but deadly chill, and through it there appeared the discolored flank of the stable, draped with the autumnal stringiness of its wild cucumber vines.

The door of the room opened with a swift and sudden quiet, and a young man stepped in. His shoulders were covered with a thousand shimmering rain-globules, and his breath gave out a strong reek of brandy. It was Marcus.

"I want to see Mr. Brainard," he had said, at the outer door, to the strange servant-girl, and he had pushed straight by her without further word.

He stood there pale and tremulous; his eyes glittered like two knife-points.

"I'm out again," he said. "I've got another chance, and I don't mean to lose this one."

His father turned on him with a fierce frown—a frown full of malevolent intention.

"It's you, is it?" He was silent for a moment. "Well, you can stay. I've been thinking about you, lately. I can 'tend to two as well as one."

"You've been thinking about me lately, have you?" Marcus repeated. He spoke with a hardihood that came from draughts of brandy more than once indulged in. "You had better have thought of me before."

"I'm thinking to just as much purpose," his father declared grimly. "I haven't been altogether in the

238

dark," he went on, "about your goings and your doings. I know what you've been living on, and how you got it, and who put you up to it all. I know how you have been figuring on my dying and preying on me before my dying; but I'm alive yet, and the next time you see that singing Canadian scoundrel you can tell him so. And I know all about your latest tactics, too. Do you see that?"

A pass-book was lying on his desk, and between its covers there was a packet of checks, bound by a rubber strap. He drew out the top check and extended it towards his son; he used his clumsy thumb and forefinger to keep a strong hold on one end of the paper—the end that bore the signature.

"You've seen it before, too, unless I'm mistaken," he went on, with a glance in which indignation was overlaid by a cruel sense of power and a cruel determination to use it. "You didn't expect it to get around to me quite so quick, did you?"

"I see it, yes," said the young man. "And I've seen it before. What of it?" He spoke like one who had nerved himself to this—and to more.

"What of it?" cried his father, in a sudden fit of rage. "There's this of it! Do you think I'm going to stand being stripped by a thieving scamp like you? Do you think I'm going to be bled drop by drop by a couple of infernal scoundrels? Oh, that whining about your drawing, and your not being allowed to go on with it! You can handle a pen all right enough! You can draw checks for me, and you can draw yourself to Joliet! That's the best place, all around, for both of us."

"I shouldn't mind meeting you there," said Marcus, with a contemptuous sneer. "*There* would be a 'couple,' sure enough—the only one *I* know anything about."

"Where is that wretch?" cried Brainard, seizing the youth by the arm. "You know; you do, too—you see him

239

every day! Tell me where I can find him! He must be followed up. Let me get him, too, and put him where he belongs!''

"Keep off!" called his son; keep off, you fool! I haven't seen him for a year, and I don't want to see him for another. It's you I want to see; you and Burt—brother Burt.''

His eyes glittered with a sharpened anger, and his dilated nostrils quivered with the indignation that the thought of his elder brother always aroused.

"I want to see the vice-president of the Underground National. I want to see the bridegroom who got half a million on his wedding-day. And I want him to see me. I want him to have a look at the poor devil who has been knocking around from pillar to post for the last two years, who has hidden in dives, and who has been dragged through the slums, and who has been driven from the variety stage, and has served his time more than once. Let him feel the difference; let me help him to feel it!''

"Your own blame!" cried his father. "You had the same chances and threw them all away. And you'll serve another term now—a longer one."

"I guess not," said Marcus. He looked about the room with a sharp and wary eye. It might have been thought that he sought at once both means of offence and means of escape.

There was a rap on the door; Burt's voice was heard outside.

"Here's Mr. Freeze, father. I suppose he can come right in."

Marcus reared his head suddenly.

"It's Burt!" he trumpeted. "He's here! he's here!" He sprang towards the threshold and clamped his long fingers about his brother's throat. Burt's head struck with force against the wide jamb; he half fell, and his legs and arms writhed in company with his brother's.

"Get them apart, Freeze! Get them apart!" cried Brainard, with a loud roar. "Am I going to see Burt strangled before my very eyes?"

Marcus released his grip and staggered back into the room. He reared himself pantingly against the table. His face was deadly pale, and the perspiration was starting out in beads beneath the dark, disordered locks that lay on his forehead. The screaming of women's voices was heard in the corridor outside, and the light hastening of women's feet.

"Three to one!" panted Marcus. "It's a plot! it's a trap! I know you, Freeze. I see through all of you. But three ain't enough. You can't do it; no!"

Abbie Brainard came rushing through the hall. She reached the threshold and paused there to see her brother catch up her paper-cutter from the table, plunge it into her father's neck, and break through the window, and to hear his nimble feet clatter escape down the stairs of the side porch.

Brainard fell heavily against the marble slabs of the fire-place. Blood soaked his high, old-fashioned collar and trickled down the plaits of his shirt-front. He lay there stunned and bleeding, and lifeless—as it seemed.

His huge bulk was gotten laboriously to bed—half dragged, half lifted. He lay there for a fortnight, between life and death.

The doctor came, and with the chill gray of the first dawn came the nurse. It was to be a hand-to-hand struggle, and all the forces were engaged at once. The nurse spent the first half-hour of uncertain daylight in bringing order out of the chaos that had established its instant sway in the old man's room on the evening before. She raised or lowered the shades, adjusted the transom, quieted the fire, and arranged her bottles and bandages. She wore the dull uniform of a public institution; and she was accustomed to carry this uniform at a moment's notice into strange places and among strange people. She accepted her assignment blindly, and took up its details afterwards.

She seemed of a rather rugged, stolid build, but her eyes were eloquent with a haunting sorrow. It was as if time had redraped her figure with the flesh that sorrow and suffering had once stripped from it, but had been powerless to reclothe her spirit in its pristine hope and cheerfulness.

She stood at the window, endeavoring to get her bearings in the early light of the dim morning. The lilacs and syringas in the yard showed the crinkled brownness of latest autumn. A boy was crossing and recrossing the street to put out its lamps; and in the second-story window of the stable the flickering of a single gas-jet was helping the coachman and hostler to make up his own bed.

Behind her she heard the heavy grunting breath of the sick man. Presently another sound mingled with it—a creeping and rustling sound that made its little track along the hall and across the threshold of the half-open door. She turned; a baby was on the floor beside her—a beautiful boy with dusky, liquid eyes, and the beginnings of a poll of dark and curly hair. An inquiring pain plucked at her heart and set its signal in her eyes; she saw a resemblance that it was impossible to overlook. She cast a hungry and timorous glance about her, and presently, with a great yearning and a steadying resolve, Jane Doane was kissing Russell Vibert's child.

For this privilege she was indebted, in a sense, to Erastus Brainard. She had never been indebted to him for anything else.

The old man lay in a kind of stupor; his head had been seriously injured by his fall, and blood-poisoning of the most virulent type pointed

242

to his inevitable end. He had occasional moments of recurring consciousness, and at such times he attempted, with the help of Abbie and of Freeze, to bring his affairs into order, and to dispose of his belongings by will.

The Ogden affair, meanwhile, stood still. No formal steps had been taken, and the young man had Fairchild's assurance that an accommodation was sure to be brought about.

The situation became known to the Bradleys—in its general outlines, at least. They caught at the end and ignored the means, as would have been done in by anybody else in their position. They considered that their friendliness towards Ogden had been misplaced and that their confidence had been betrayed. They preserved appearances with him through their daughter's final illness; and by a great effort they even produced an effect of a common suffering and a common sympathy at the funeral. But after that they never saw him again. The difficulty with the bank did not become public, but they considered themselves, all the same, no less disgraced than deceived.

The desperate illness of Brainard dragged itself along, meanwhile, and the house was saturated with gloom. Abbie assisted actively in the nursing; she watched in alternation with the first nurse and with the succeeding one. Cornelia was given an opportunity to put her hand to the household helm. As she said to herself, she was soon to manage a house of her own, and she might as well be brushing up her knowledge.

"And she has got to go with me," Cornelia said to herself for the twentieth time; "she can't live here after—*this*."

Cornelia had fought out many a fight during her year in this grisly old house; but she saw now that her intended campaign on behalf of Marcus was an impossibility, and that all the forces might as well be withdrawn from the field.

Nobody had seen the youth since that fatal night; nobody, that is, who had cared to make the fact known. Neither did anybody know where he was keeping himself, save the sister on whose night-watches he had once or twice stolen by way of the window through which he had made his escape from his brother and Freeze.

He came again—for a third and last time. It was one o'clock in the morning when she heard his light touch on the window. She hastened to him with her mouth set for a terrified whisper.

"Yes, I know it's dangerous, Abbie; I know I promised not to come again. But I can't help it—I've got to hear. How is—how are things going on to-night? Is there any improvement over yesterday?" He locked his fingers in a convulsive strain. "I thought they had laid a trap for me," he said chokingly. "Just tell me yourself how it is, and after this you can send me word, as you have before. I won't come again, I promise you."

She threw herself on his breast and burst into an agony of tears. "No, you never will," she sobbed; "he is dying. There is no hope; he won't live till morning."

The young man trembled like an aspen; tears rolled out of his dark and hollow eyes. He tried to speak, but no word came. Then he clasped his sister in his arms and withdrew as he had entered.

The night, laden with anxiety and fear, dragged out its weary length. In the early morning the house resounded with a great cry. The dying man, in a brief moment of consciousness, half raised himself and heard the sound and the tidings thus conveyed. The word was passed from man-servant to maid-servant, and came to their master through the voice of a Swedish girl whose mind was capable of dealing with emotions only in the most primitive way, and whose imperfect command of English made her communication come with a horrible and harrowing directness. One second before Erastus Brainard fell back dead he knew that his son had hanged himself; the last picture that rose before his fleeting vision was that of his boy pendulous from the rafters of the stable, his slight body swinging to and fro and his tongue protruding uglily from the purple-black of his face.

XXIV

The months passed by, and autumn came around once
more.

Ogden's first year as a widower was lived with his
mother; he used the same time to establish himself in the
real-estate business, whose ins and outs he had now
mastered in the bitter school of experience. He had left the
Clifton altogether, and had established himself in another
street and a different neighborhood. Every stone of the great
pile seemed to have raised its tongue against him, and to
have driven him out with the loud and insulting hubbub of
its angry clamor. He had no wish ever to see again the room
in which he had first met his wife, the room in which he had
wrestled with his brother-in-law, the room in which
disgrace had forced him to bow his head. Bradley lay in wait
for him in the court, Jane Doane dogged him through the
long corridors, Marcus Brainard rose up as a pallid spectre
within the entrance-way. He left the building for once and
for all. The placards that he placed on vacant tenements and

246

the signs that he caused to be reared on open corners in the suburbs directed inquirers to a street and number quite different from any near his old neighborhood.

Within this year Cornelia Tillinghast Brainard had moved into her new house and had moved out again. For three poor months she occupied her French Renaissance château on the Lake Shore Drive, and then she gave it up forever. In vain her anxious plannings of chambers and stairways, her long waitings for the slow finishing of the carved oaks and walnuts of her vast interiors; in vain (for the present, at least) her lofty aims in the direction of social distinction. For Burt with his father was one man, and Burt without his father was another. He had relied upon the elder's advice more than he had realized, and he had felt the steadying and restraining power of his father's hand to a greater degree than he would have been willing to acknowledge. When he came to act for himself and by himself the difference soon became apparent. He operated in a variety of directions; he was confident and daring and ambitious, and one day he risked all and lost all.

His failure swept away everything of his and nearly everything of his sister's. Abbie had come into the new house along with Burt and Cornelia—no great urging had now been required to induce her to abandon the house on the West Side. She led the same retired and quiet life in the one quarter that she had led in the other, save that she never felt otherwise than utterly strange and forlorn. And as she had placed herself in her brother's house, so she put a great part of her share in her father's estate into her brother's hands when ruin came and every available resource was required. She had never used much money; she may not have realized the gravity of her sacrifice. Perhaps, too, she had hoped to rest her disappointed soul on something that money could not buy.

To Cornelia the failure came as a sudden and awful blow. Considering the brief time at her disposal, she had made a distinct impression on society. A great many people of consequence came to her house and invited her to theirs. They laughed at her freedoms and familiarities; they enjoyed her picturesque and untrammelled phraseology. Some of the more insatiable invited her twice. She encountered but one decided check; this was from Mrs. Floyd.

The ship of the Floyd household, now navigating regardless of its customary dependence on the distant admiral of the whole Floyd fleet, was tossing in shallow yet stormy waters; there were not lacking indications that it was occasionally grazing bottom, and there was a notion abroad that it might presently beach or founder. Mrs. Floyd therefore manned the helm with more than her customary caution. For one thing, she set the ship's chronometer by local time. That is to say, her own watch, which had now been giving the time of Boston for the last three years (and she had become very expert in the deducting of the hour and some minutes of difference) came to be set by the hour of Chicago. For another thing, she must think twice before speaking every strange craft—such a one, for example, as that propelled by the Brainards. She did think twice, and concluded to remain silent.

"Huh!" said Cornelia; "all because I worked in her husband's office, and she met me there! Thank goodness, I wasn't allowed to have my wish and work for Ingles, too! I'll fetch things around, though—you see if I don't; and I'll capture Cecilia Ingles yet!"

Abbie, along with many other persons and things, became a mere piece of driftwood in the general wreck of her brother's fortunes. She swirled and eddied about for some time through a succession of boarding-houses, and after a while she found refuge in the latest home that her sister had made. She found her new brother-in-law a good-humored and well-disposed fellow. Briggs had established his family in the old neighborhood on the West Side, and readily admitted Abbie; he made no more objection to his sister-in-law than he had made to his sister-in-law's nephew.

Ogden saw nothing of them, heard nothing of them. He merely went around in a quiet way among a few old friends, and he dropped in at frequent intervals on the faithful Brower. Brower was sometimes at home and sometimes away; the fire-fiend still kept him on the move. One late September evening, after an interval of a month or more, Ogden repaired again to the house which had once been their common home, and found Brower just back from Minnesota.

He was seated on his trunk, the rigors of whose cover he had softened by the doubled folds of a striped travelling-wrap. He had his brier-wood pipe in his mouth and a book in his hand. It was a paper-bound volume; the back cover was missing, and there was exposed to view the fine, close tabulation of the books composing a well-known "library."

"Well, my dear fellow," cried Brower, rising and grasping his hand, "how are you? Say, I believe you're looking better. Here; put yourself in the light where I can have more of a chance at you."

George stood immovable, and Brower jerked out the elbowed gas-jet, so as to make the light fall upon his visitor's face. It fell on his visitor's head, too, and the whole brown head was sprinkled with silver.

Ogden put his two palms on his temples and spread out his hands until the finger-tips met over the part in his hair.

"There are more," he said, with a smile of quiet sadness; "don't count them again."

"I won't," said Brower. He drew away his eyes, but threw his arm over the other's shoulder.

"I've had quite a trip, this time," he went on, in

the tone which we employ when contriving a light diversion. "Been away out into Dakota—Bismarck, Mandan, Yankton, Sioux Falls. I was at the Falls one Sunday."

"Is that any great place to spend Sunday?"

"Lots of folks go there to spend a few Sundays—twelve or fourteen Sundays, and the week-days between. On the evening of *my* Sunday I went to church."

"I've known you to go to church on Sunday evenings before. Service any different from any other?"

"It was a song service. Don't you suppose the poor creatures waiting along out there in Sioux Falls have got to have their little consolations? Ain't music the great consoler?"

"They were consoled, then?"

"Oh, yes, indeed; the principal consoler had been there himself. He sang tenor."

"Better tenor than the average?"

"Good deal better. The most touching, pathetic tones I ever heard. He sang the 'Angel's Serenade,' with another man playing the violin. It was affecting. One poor lady near me, with a sort of Eastern look about her, just caught up the child in the pew by her side and burst right out crying. I was all broke up, myself."

"That's a good song," declared Ogden. "I always like to hear it."

"You've heard it before, then? At St. Asaph's, perhaps?"

"At St. Asaph's; yes."

"Well," said Brower, "the man you heard sing it at St. Asaph's was the man I heard sing it at Sioux Falls."

"Vibert!"

"Vibert."

George dropped his eyes; he had no wish to pursue the theme further. "What have you there?" he asked. He indicated the book that Brower had left lying on top of the trunk.

"Oh, nothing special. It's just one of those cheap novels. I was merely running it through to see if he really did marry the right one in the end. Might have done it in the first place as well as not." He passed the book to Ogden wrong side up. "I guess it's yours, by rights—one you left behind when you moved out."

Ogden turned the book over and read the title. It was—"A False Start."

He started. He blushed. "Yes, perhaps it is," he stammered. He held it awkwardly in his hand for a moment. Brower watched him curiously, yet sympathetically. "Yes," Ogden repeated, in a bold, firm voice, "it *is* mine." He put it in his inside pocket and buttoned his coat.

"Oh, come," cried Brower, trying to throw a veil of jocularity over his earnestness, "that isn't fair! I've got to finish it. I've got to know whether he did or didn't. Anyway, let me see the end."

"There is no end," said Ogden, soberly. "Or if there is, it has come."

"Then I can only guess." Brower looked at him, with a studious anxiety in his brown eyes. "He made a mistake, sure enough, but I think he sets it right. Yes, I think he sets it right."

Ogden's eyes sought the floor.

"No; he abides by it."

"He *can* set it right," said Brower, gravely; "and if he can he ought."

"Not now; not after—everything. Let bad enough alone."

251

"Make bad enough better," cried Brower. "Is he the only one to be considered? Upon my word," he went on, with a nervous attempt at lightness, "we are getting these great truths down finer and finer. A couple of years ago we agreed that marriage concerned but two people; now we are finding that it concerns only one. The question simply is—which one?"

"The one who would be most exposed to injury," said Ogden, with a distant mournfulness in his face and voice.

"There are different kinds of injury; there is the injury of commission, and there is the injury of omission. Sometimes the last is harder—on a woman. Why not let the victim choose her own particular woe? Why not be generous enough to give her an opportunity?"

"Not now," groaned Ogden. "You don't know. Not after all—that's happened."

"Well, then," continued Brower, with kindly perseverance, "out goes generosity. Now bring in selfishness and give *that* a chance. What is our hero going to do? Must there be more sorrow for him, more suffering, more self-punishment, and everlasting dissatisfaction generally? What is he made of? Can he stand it? If so, how long? And if he does, why should he?"

"Brower, Brower!" Ogden cried; "not another word if you care for me—if you care anything at all for me!" He crossed his arms on the table and bowed his head upon them.

Brower passed his hand softly over this head and said no more. He was a patient husbandman; he would sow the good seed and wait for the harvest.

Ogden took the book home with him. He fluttered its leaves a few times; then he sat down on the edge of his bed and read the title-page for an hour. The next night he read it some more and dreamed about it. The next night he was reading it still, and he lay awake thinking of it until daylight.

On the following evening he took the old, familiar way to the West Side.

He found Abbie Brainard at home alone. Mary and her husband had gone out, and the baby had been put to bed.

Abbie was sitting in the half-gloom of one small lamp; the parlor was a little room, and a rather cheap and ugly one. But the lamp, thanks to its beflowered shade, was discreet and reticent in the disclosure of unprepossessing detail; besides, twenty lamps would not have had power to divert his thoughts from the channel through which they were now coursing.

On his entrance she started up to light the gas. She looked pale and worn, and older than he would have believed possible. But he looked older, too, and felt much older than he looked. The light beat down upon his silvered hair, and heightened the glance of pitying surprise that shone from her eyes.

In this increased illumination he saw that fortune had left her, as well as her youth and beauty, as well as the father whose life he had felt to make their union impossible, and whose memory might still keep it so. But she herself, in her own essence, was before him—the same courage, the same resolution, the same tenderness and fidelity. And in him she saw the only man she had ever seen, or had ever cared to see.

To her, he came as a messenger of pity to heal the wounds that knavery and scandal and violence had hacked upon her quivering heart. A messenger of pity, yes; but could he, by any possible chance, find her worthy of the pity that was akin to love?

To him, she appeared as the victim of his own faint-heartedness and faithlessness. After all that he had done to wring her heart, could he venture upon the crowning indignity of offering her his tarnished name?

To her, he stood there as a tower of refuge—a tower from whose summit the swathing fogs might be cleared away by the warm breath of trust and confidence, and whose smirched walls—if smirched indeed they were—might be purified by the tears of love and the fingers of forgetfulness.

To himself, he lay before her as a heap of crumbling and smoke-stained ruin. Every stone cried out for the cleansing power of pity and for the firm and friendly hand that was to rear them all again to their pristine use and comeliness.

The clock had struck eight as he entered; it was striking eleven as he rose to go.

"Not yet," she said, softly. She pressed him back into the depths of his great easy-chair, and, leaning upon its rounded and padded arm, she looked down upon him.

"You take me, then, as I am?" he asked her, soberly.

"How else do you take *me*?"

He raised his hand to his head. "There will be more of them," he said. "They tell me I shall be white at forty."

"How many of them are mine?"

He pressed her hand.

"Not one, not one! Or, no," he continued, with a stronger pressure, "they are all yours—do with them as you please."

He felt something warm drop on his head and trickle down his temples.

"Yes, that is the best thing to do," he said. "To think," he added, with a tender seriousness, "that you might have saved me from them—from every one!"

254

They were married within a month, and they began their married life in the same house in which he had begun his Western life as a bachelor. Mrs. Gore's kindliness still survived, after the hard rubs of three years of city life, and she spread her sympathetic interest over her new couple with an unstinted hand.

Their wedding involved no social celebration, unless we note their participation in one of a series of great public functions that sometimes mark the early winter. This took place in a vast hall that was luminous in ivory and gold. They sat before a vast curved frame brilliant with a myriad points of light, and listened to the united endeavors of many voices and instruments to please the four thousand people about them. Ogden and his wife had taken places in the balcony. They had toned down existence to a a quiet gray; they recognized the middlingness of their lot. Cornelia and her husband, unknown to the Ogdens, had seats on the floor beneath.

One box in the two long, parallel rows remained vacant during the first and second acts. As the prelude to the third act began among the violins the box was claimed. A party of four entered.

"There she is," said Cornelia to herself, in her place on the main floor. "Just you wait. Burt's smart and I'm careful, and we shall catch up to you yet!"

"Who are those people?" asked Abbie, turning towards her husband. "Who is the gentleman with gray hair?" She was beginning to admire her husband's own.

The two ladies of the party had seated themselves; the two gentlemen were busy with their own and their companions' wraps in the back of the box.

"That is Mr. Atwater, the architect. The lady in yellow is his wife. The tall, brownish man, just handing the glass, is Mr. Ingles; he owns the—the Clifton."

"And the other lady?" his wife continued. She indicated a radiant, magnificent young creature, splendid, like all her mates, with the new and eager splendor of a long-awaited opportunity. This newcomer had nodded smilingly to many people on entering —to her neighbors on either side, to a large dinner-party that filled three boxes across the house. She seemed pleased to have so many persons to bow to so publicly; and everybody whom she favored seemed equally glad of an opportunity to return her attention.

Ogden looked at her and turned his eyes away.

"I—I have never seen her before," he said. "I don't know who she is," he appeared to imply.

But he knew perfectly well who she was. He knew that she was Cecilia Ingles, and his heart was constricted by the sight of her. It is for such a woman that one man builds a Clifton and that a hundred others are martyred in it.

THE END

Rinehart Editions